07A

CONFLUENCE

CONFLUENCE

A Novel

Mary Elizabeth Gillilan

Independent Writers Studio Press

iws
PRESS

CONFLUENCE

Confluence is a work of fiction. All of this novel's characters,
names, incidents, organizations, and dialogue are either
products of the author's imagination or are used fictitiously.

ISBN: 978-1-7341878-4-7 (pbk)
ISBN: 978-1-7341878-5-4 (ebk)

The front cover art features a painting of Yeshe Tsogyal from the
Sunapati Thangka Painting School—traditionalartofnepal.com

Independent Writers Studio Press

PRESS

For Andrea and Samantha

What you think, you become. What you feel, you attract.
What you imagine, you create.
—Buddha

CONTENTS

Acknowledgments

Thanks again for the cover art by the Sunapati Thangka Painting School. It features Yeshe Tsogyal, an eighth-century Buddhist scholar and healer. Yeshe transcribed Guru Rinpoche's teachings, leaving them as treasures across the Tibetan plateau. Obstacles and dangers beset Yeshe Tsogyal, but she set her remarkable eyes on spiritual liberation and achieved it. Life takes us on mad adventures, and Yeshe Tsogyal is good company.

Thank you to my dear writer friend, Susan Chase-Foster, for all the consults throughout the process of bringing this story to life. Thank you, Norman Green, for your insights and hand-delivered help whenever I called. Thank you, Deborah Bruner and Lisa Ahmari, for reading the early drafts. The Independent Writers Studio writers' groups motivate and challenge me; thank you for your support. Most of all, thank you to my children for your constant and consistent unconditional love. And, of course, thank you to my dog, Betty Bananas.

· 2014 ·

Chapter 1 One Flight Up

A spray of dust lit the air. The attic steps angled upwards into graying light. If I was ever going to move out of this house, I had to get rid of the ton of stuff Mother coveted and kept up those skinny stairs. I contemplated how to navigate them. Mother had died two years before and I hadn't been in her attic art studio since I was about twenty—forty-five years ago.

Dust motes sailed in sunlight. Mild cerebral palsy affected my body's right side. My right arm tended to curl up, and my foot's short tendons caused cramps. Scoliosis, stenosis, osteoporosis, osteoarthritis, and my mother's favorite word, spondylolisthesis, were all related to my back. Vertigo created illusions that stair builders could never imagine.

The word "spondylolisthesis" danced through my head: it's a condition that causes the last vertebra in the spine to stick outwards. Mother liked how the syllables moved over her tongue. She made a light business of what she perceived were heavy burdens for me. She raised me inside her bubbled fantasies. Murals on my bedroom wall took me to places where mushrooms became houses. Princely fathers flew in clouds. My mother never talked about my father. An enigmatic smile would wash across her lineless face, and she might shrug, but her eyes sparkled.

Odd to say, I believed the house mourned her. We all did, even my dog. As I studied the steps, quiet consumed me. At times, Mother's perennial optimism annoyed me. As a little girl, I came home with a story about being chased in the schoolyard by a bully. "He'll be kissed by karma someday," Mother laughed as she bandaged my knee. I didn't know what karma was or why it pleased her that this kid would get anything. After college graduation as an English teacher, I remained unemployed. School district superintendents and principals passed over my application once they observed my weak hand. I was turned down from one job because the superintendent of the small school district in Silver Bar, south of us, said the position called on a candidate who could be an assistant coach for the girls' basketball team. Mother opened a bottle of champagne and said, "Let's drink to unemployment!" A free spirit, my mother was. I missed her madly, that moment, at the bottom of the attic stairs.

Penni-P was at my side. Miss P was a cross between a Chinese crested "naked" dog and a long-haired Chihuahua. Personally, her lower overbite and long Fu Manchu delighted me. I trimmed the beard in proportion to her ears that feathered out and up. What a pair we were. I felt displaced in my life and rescued by Penni-P. Her black eyes and tense small body anticipated any direction I might take. Right then, she was on high alert. Her tail wagged. She waited for me to make the first move.

I might have been great friends with Emily Dickinson in the nineteenth century. I hadn't bound my hair in an Emily-fashioned slicked-back bun, but I had managed to grow out a ponytail, and at sixty-five, my hair hadn't grayed. I hadn't worn all black as Emily had the first part of her life or all white as she had the last part of her life; I settled on sweats and loose long blouses, three of them in gray. Comfort clothes. Like the Belle of Amherst, my reclusion created mental space for the poet-writer to breathe in our La Conner, Washington house.

My dearest friends had been my dearest friends for ages. I belonged to a book club my friend Carol Andrews organized. It met monthly at dinner time in a Greek restaurant down on Mills Street. I always managed to think of an excuse not to go, and I felt relief about not attending each time. Carol fostered dogs for the alternative dog shelter folks and showed and sold houses through her realty company. She exuded charm with a smile and the ability to string words together faster than anyone I knew. I adopted Penni-P through Carol. She called me a natural dog person.

My other great friend lived next door to me, or he used to. Jack Reynolds and I grew up together. He moved here when I was in third grade. After a life as a travel agent, Jack retired semi-permanently to the Island of Corfu. Greece—Jack, the Romantic, still sought the love of his life. Blue skies and ouzo on his balcony. Jack appeared to be content. His mother, Avery, still lived in La Conner at an assisted living facility called Trout Creek. Avery and I shared movie nights and occasional meals. Jack came home three times a year—Christmas, Easter, and birthdays in October. Avery and I were Libras, and Jack was a Virgo, and as a Virgo, Jack liked order: A rented maisonette in Corfu Town, three trips home a year, and an undisturbed house next to mine. Carol encouraged him to rent it or create an air bed and breakfast she would manage. Jack deferred. A cleaning service dusted out his large Tudor twice a month, and I tended his houseplants. The system had worked for almost three years.

I loved the photos Jack shared of goats and winding paths on the ancient rocks of Greece. Jack encouraged me to travel after Mother died. I had no intention. Patrick Dennis once said the mark of a good writer is his ability to develop a believable story/lie in less than five minutes. On that basis, I had the makings of an excellent writer. I could come up with innumerable reasons not to travel, usually centered around Penni-P. I honestly did not want to leave her. She'd been through hell before her rescue, and she thought I was the alpha and the omega. I breathed in that love. The year I had back surgery was such a relief. No one asked me to go anywhere.

Jack accepted my reclusiveness, and I looked past his attachment to stuff. His wanderlust brought home stories. He changed light bulbs and batteries in the smoke detectors when he was here. After my laminectomy, he came home for a few days and enlisted his cleaning service to care for my house. Before Mother died, he came back, brought her roses, and for me, a tray of miniature roses for the garden.

Cheers, Jack! The attic door was open; dust began to settle. It had been Carol's idea to clean out the attic as a first down-sizing attempt. Carol insisted that I consider a one-level townhouse. "You can't afford a fall!" she said over soup and sandwiches in my kitchen five days ago, resonating with effortless grace and original artiness, much like my mother's. That day, Carol wrapped her curly graying hair in a fringed Turkish scarf. She smelled like gardenia, and her copper and silver bracelets masked her ever-present watch on her right hand. She pointed her ringed index finger at me. "This house is too much."

"I need to take care of Jack's house, too," I said.

Carol rolled her eyes. "You need to get rid of the junk in the attic."

"That's Mother's art studio," I said. "Don't call it junk. And I can't do the stairs. It can wait. I don't think Mother would want me up there."

"She'd be the first one to call in the disposal truck. She was a good Buddhist. You should have a talk with your soul about that. And get it cleaned out—attic," she laughed, "not your soul. Your soul is pretty solid. But come on—this huge house is too much for you. It's too much for me."

We split a piece of chocolate cake from our local co-op. "You're right, probably right," I remembered saying. "I'll take a look." I was temporarily out of excuses.

"Just have Jack's cleaners do it. You don't have to go up. They can bring anything worth saving to you down here. You don't have to go up there."

But I did. I had to climb those stairs. I peered at my eight-pound companion and said, "Penni-P, let's give it a go."

Penni-P raced ahead on her tall skinny legs. Afraid of losing my balance by going up by foot, I sat on the bottom rung, wide enough to comfortably position myself, facing forward and pushed myself upwards. Penni-P, at the top of the stairs, barked encouragement. I moved upward, rung by rung, until I reached the top, then crab-crawled sideways from the stairwell. My head felt light as I stood to appraise the room: two easels and palettes with dried paint, tubes of oils in a box by one, and a can of brushes. The emptiness of the attic gave me chills. The faint smell of turpentine lingered.

I used to play under the north dormer as a child. Mother's pile of old pillows and blankets was still there. By the wall was a Shayder Brothers Samsonite suitcase. I remembered Mother saying that the valise took her to Narnia before I was born. I recalled the brand name and smiled; this was something to save. I must have been five at the time: Mother at her easel and lemonade we shared.

Half-finished canvases fell into Carol's junk category. Penni-P sneezed at the dust we stirred up. I didn't think the attic wanted to be disturbed. I ached with loneliness and admitted it was time to call the cleaners. I hauled the suitcase to the edge of the stairway and sat behind it. "Come 'ere, Penni-P."

Penni-P hopped onto my lap. I hugged her close, and with a good shove from my feet, the suitcase shot downstairs and burst open on the landing. Penni-P's ears went back, and she shook.

"Honey, it's OK," I said. "We had to get that old thing out of the way before we go down." I held her securely as I began the return journey downstairs, facing forward step by step on my behind.

All the contents of the suitcase spread across the floor. Penni-P decided to stage herself on the bed in my room, just left of the stairs. She could see me from her vantage point, and the bed was her safety zone. She was not budging.

An old photo album with a mirrored half-moon on its cover lay to one side, and near it were two books as old, by the first appearance, as the album. I lugged the books downstairs into the kitchen and opened the window to an invigorating punch of the air. I was going to need that.

Chapter 2 The Passport Stone

THE FIRST BOOK TOLD the story of a woman named Madeline Caron-Martin, who must have traveled to Tibet; I translated that much from the French title: *Voyage au Tibet par une aventurière.* I thumbed through faded gold-edged pages. Photos in the book center had linen sheets protecting them. I carefully lifted one to see a young woman peering quietly at the camera. She was dressed in a heavy coat outside, near the Potala. In other photos, the woman appeared with Buddhist monks. My mother's keepsake, perhaps. Why would she have hidden these books? I grew up on her stories about Tibet. *Journal d'une yeshe* was the title of the lesser damaged volume, and it also had photos. The same woman appeared in monk/nun garb. I wondered who the mystery lady was and wished any of my college French might show up. All I knew about her was her name: Madeline. Tucked inside the end cover, I discovered a fat envelope in my mother's distinctive handwriting with my name on it. "Holy God," I murmured, "what is this?" Inside was a letter: "Darling Maya," it began:

> Hello from the other side of the urn, honey. I hope you are sitting down.
>
> Sell this house!
>
> I left an old map and a family tree that shows your father's side of the family. The books belonged to your grandmother. Oh, and the sunstone. DO NOT LOSE IT. It's a passport to where you were born. Tibet, darling. At a special place.
>
> Follow the map; you'll need Jack and the sunstone.
>
> Your father might be alive. If he is—find him.

Jack promised he'd give you the suitcase and books—if you're finding them on your own—kick him in the butt.

Seriously, sell the house. Find your father. It's time.

Gate gate paragate parasamgate Bodhi svaha—It exists.

I love you eternally,

Your Mother

Two enclosures fell out: a hand-drawn map of the Himalayas with a circle drawn around a border area between India and Tibet. In the circle's center, she printed in capital letters: S-A-N-G-A-M. She hand-wrote the genealogical diagram of my father's family. Mother wrote at the bottom of the page: "Ask for Yeshe Maya—Yeshe Shabdkosh. Her, too."

Never had Mother mentioned my father by name. "Your papa cannot live in two worlds at the same time—just know he loves you forever and ever." I grew up believing my papa lived in the land where Santa Claus resided, and when my mother explained that she was Santa, I rethought where my papa might live. I guessed on top of a rainbow and was satisfied with my conjuring through the years. Mother often stopped my questions with a generous smile or shrug and nothing more. Mother kept her secrets close. Jack called it "the mysterious veil"—Jack and Mother loved one another, and he liked that she had mysteries.

This is how you wanted me to find out about my father? Anger mixed with exasperation. Mother didn't have to answer any questions, and she stuck me with the contents of a suitcase. I was surprised at how angry I still was for her dying, for sucking the life out of this house and out of me. An inner voice counseled I could have taken a DNA test and found relatives if that had been my goal. But it was never my interest. My interest was to protect the fantasy of the flying prince on a cloud that Mother had painted in a mural on my bedroom wall when I was a child. And now, well, look at this, I thought.

A paper with my heritage shown in square boxes tagged with names I had never known: my father's name, Tenzin Neil Caron-Martin, right across from my mother, Olivia Eden Moore. My grandmother and grandfather's names, too. Then I paused and took a giant breath. My grandmother was the woman pictured in the books? Madeline Caron-Martin. Not some friend Mother had known in her Bohemian days, but a blood relative of mine. I looked at her picture again, at the nose. Then I rushed into the bathroom and studied my nose. We had the same noses. "Holy shit," I said to my mirrored image.

At Mother's instigation, since I was a kid, I had read about Tibet and the Dalai Lama and the sacred mountain, Kailash, reputed to be the center of the universe. And my real, honest-to-God grandmother had been there!

I needed to talk to Jack. What time was it in Greece? Ten hours difference; it was still early enough. I called him on video chat.

"Hi, Sunshine!" Slouched on his couch, the double doors leading to his balcony were opened. He yawned. "Beautiful night here; there was a regatta earlier, sailboats still coming in. Can you see them?" He rose from the sofa and turned the phone towards the harbor. Indeed, boats with sails in a lit field of sea languidly were coming into berth.

My mind was not on the sights of Corfu Town. "Jack," I said, "I found a letter and some books in an old suitcase of Mother's in the attic. It involves you. Do you know anything about it?"

He shook his head and paused. "Wait," he said. "She told me a story about Shangri-La or Shambhala. I think she corrected me when I called it Shangri-La. It was on my last visit before she passed. She said a suitcase in the attic explained everything. She talked about a secret kingdom or something." He closed his eyes and opened them. "I thought you were there, too. But you might have gone to the store. Olivia was high on marijuana and morphine, and I thought it was a fantasy like so many she told us. Yeah—" he said after a momentary reflection. "I scouted out the attic before I left, but there wasn't anything there. Just junk."

"It isn't junk! Mother painted up there. And, yeah, there were books and a family tree that documents where my father lived or lives. The map is of northern India near what looks to be Tibet. She talked about a sunstone that was important—"

"Coming from your mother—Maya, your mom ladled out magic to us as kids; we grew up on it."

"I think it's legit, Jack, and she told me to kick you in the butt if I found the suitcase instead of you. She wants you to take me to this place on the map."

"Who's on the family tree?" Jack's tone was more serious.

"People I've never heard of. One of them is a woman, apparently my grandmother, Madeline Caron-Martin. She traveled to Tibet in the 1920s and trips to India and Nepal in the 1930s. There's a whole book about her in French! And I have her fucking nose."

"What?" Jack sounded confused.

"Never mind."

"Well, if you find any magic beans," Jack said.

With Penni-P at my heels, I walked upstairs as Jack spoke. "That stone might be in the suitcase." I aimed my phone at the opened Samsonite case on the landing. A dusty rock was by the open railings of the stairwell. "Found it." I picked the stone up and wiped it off on my jeans. The honey-hued stone sparkled. "I'm going to wash it off." I put the phone on the bathroom counter and held it under a stream of water. Red shimmers showed from sunlight through the bathroom window. "What does a sunstone look like, Jack? Can you look it up?" I focused the camera on the rock.

In a moment, Jack said, "You have an extraordinary example of one. What did the letter say? Can you photograph it on your cell and send it to me? The family tree, too. And the map. I'll call you back after I get it. We can talk." He shook his head. "God, I thought your mom was hallucinating."

I laughed. "Apparently, not. Don't be too hard on yourself." And we hung up.

Penni-P ran with abandon in the backyard. She sniffed dandelions and buttercups. I followed her around, then leashed her, and we went for a walk around the block. Jack called as we entered the house.

"What troubles me most is that Olivia couldn't remember where she put the suitcase in the house. She thought it was the attic. I promised her. I mean, on an oath like she made us do as kids, that I would find your father. What is killing me right now is what she said in reply."

"What'd she say?"

"She said she would die in peace, then." Jack paused. "I said that she could always trust me, and she gave me that smile, and she answered. 'You're supposed to find it.'"

"It's nearly one; that makes it afternoon, right? I think I'll have a glass of wine," I said. "Then do some research."

"That sounds like a marvelous plan," Jack said.

"Don't worry about this, Jack. She loved you like a son. She had manipulative powers and was not afraid to use them, so be easy on yourself. We'll figure out what we can figure out. All the major players are probably dead, but I think we need to keep this between us—I'm not telling Carol. Or anyone. The vibe of the thing."

Jack said, "Agreed, Sunshine. Love you."

CHAPTER 3 PANDORA'S SUITCASE

I SAT IN THE BRIGHT KITCHEN light and paged through the books. Old photos of my grandmother appeared on the high plains of Tibet. Several images showed a hotel where I supposed she had once stayed in India. I chose the most vivid picture of her and moved my finger across it. Had she touched this book? Had it belonged to her? I used a flashlight and a magnifying glass to enlarge and brighten the image. Tenzin, her son, and my father, his photo should be here, too. I held my breath for a moment, then turned my attention to the photo album with the cracked half-moon on a bed of velvet fabric on the cover. These had to be photos of my family. My father might be in here, maybe, Mother, too.

There she was: My mother in a wide silk scarf knotted at the top of her head, her undisciplined silky mane refusing confinement and a smile that lit her face. In another photograph, she wore loose linen pants and an open-necked silk shirt with a striped tie. She was beautiful. I cried as I saw her pictured with an elegant, tall young man whose arms were firmly around her. There he was, Tenzin Neil: "Hello! I'm Maya. Did you ever wonder about me?" He looked like a handsome kid.

At that point, I was traipsing back and forth between my computer in the bay window and the kitchen table where the books rested. With a cappuccino in hand, I began searches first for "Sangam," the name inside the circle on Mother's map. Penni-P rested her head on my right arm as Google sent the name of a river called Sangamon and a restaurant in Toronto. I asked for "Himalayas Sangam." A resort called Sangam called itself "a piece of paradise." Not what I was searching for. I googled "Sangam kingdoms Himalayas." I came across the history of the Tamil people, and in a chronology, I found the Sangam age, three hundred to two hundred BCE, known for its literature. I categorized this as a dead-end. I kept at the keyboard until the dog began to squirm. She started patting my left hand, Penni-P's signal that she was hungry. I stretched—yawned, and followed her to the kitchen. I filled Penni-P's dish, had a bite of yogurt from the large container in the fridge, and poured myself a chilled chardonnay. I needed to take a serious break.

In the early afternoon of the next day, Jack called me on video chat. I watched the moonlight reflect into the Ionian Sea. "Have you made any headway in the books?" he asked.

"The books are in French," I said. "I looked at the pictures in the album, mostly. There are some photos in the other. You'll love the ones of Mother. She was stunning."

"That's nice," Jack said, a hint of excitement in his voice.

"Did you find out something?" I quizzed.

"I made a major hit," Jack said, "major!"

"Well, spill." I propped the phone against a yellow bowl on the counter to continue fixing Penni-P's midday meal.

"'Yeshe' is an active sect of nuns," Jack informed me.

I furrowed my brow. "I don't understand."

"At the bottom of the genealogy chart, your mother named two nuns: Yeshe Maya and Yeshe Shabdkosh. I started searching 'Yeshe,' which led me to Yeshe Tsogyal; she was the founder of the sect of nuns in the eighth century. Thirteen hundred years later, your grandmother, Madeline, became one; her nun's name was Yeshe Shabdkosh, and I found a reference to the books you have."

"Wow, that's big news!" I said.

"The biggest news is about Yeshe Maya."

"Bigger than my grandmother, the French lady who wrote this book, traveling to Tibet, solo, in the 1920s?" Penni-P pawed my ankle. I placed her dish on the floor, and she gulped its content down, tail wagging furiously.

Jack continued, "A name came up in one of the hits on Yeshe Maya: Matipokhara—it's a hospital in Nepal, and I just had a long video chat with its director. She is wonderful!"

"What'd she say?"

"Yeshe Maya (*your* Yeshe Maya) was the hospital's founder. The director hadn't known her—this is going to blow you away—but she knows where she retired."

Penni-P yipped at the back door, and I let her outside to pee. "Is she still alive?"

"Yes—on Chamberlain Island."

Rain began falling, and Penni P dashed to the yard and quickly to the door. "Is that close to you?"

"No, honey. Chamberlain Island is close to you. She lives in a nunnery less than two hundred miles from La Conner—one of the Gulf coast islands."

"Wow." I slumped into my kitchen chair. "In Canada?"

"Stay seated. There's more," Jack said. "According to Natalie, Yeshe Maya may have delivered you."

"What?" I said incredulously, "she'd have to be a thousand years old."

"Natalie told me that Yeshe Maya delivered a Caucasian child in the late forties. I asked her about this place called 'Sangam,' and she laughed. She told me she could only refer me to some dude in Sangla in India. He's retired and owns an inn there. She said I'd have to talk to him in person."

"Where's Sangla?"

"Close to the Chinese border." Jack held the phone up for me to see the look on his face. All serious. Steady blue eyes with that Paul Newman vibe straight at me. "I'll go to India if you go to the nunnery and meet this woman."

"Jack, Jack, I can't do that. Who would take care of Penni-P? I don't drive on the freeway. I don't even know where the ferry leaves. It's summer—crawling with tourists. Long ferry lines and waits at the border." My blood pressure rose with each excuse. "Where would I stay when I got there?" My voice wound down.

"Are you done?" Jack shook his head. "Natalie, the doctor I talked to in Matipokhara, will make introductions to the man in Sangla. Natalie welcomed me to visit the hospital—they encourage that—I think—for fundraising. She was just the most delightful human being. Curious and engaged."

"You sound smitten."

"I am, and I think she was, too. She's Irish. Lilting voice. Redheaded. I'm going to take her up on the invitation."

"Good for her," I said. "And you, I guess." I was jealous. Who can pick up and leave like Jack could? "You are fortunate to be footloose."

"I am willing to open myself up to new people and things while you sit at your computer alone. I worry about you. A road trip to Canada is a wonderful possibility for you, Maya. I wish you could see it. Within your grasp—you could meet the woman who has a connection to your mother. You were named after her, for God's sake. In computers, there is always a walk-around for problem-solving. Always a means if you want it badly enough. But right now? You? And all you can offer is excuse after excuse to do nothing."

"The people in my life, you, being one of them, are people enough." Had he forgotten who was watering his houseplants? "Introversion is not a fatal disease; it is a choice," I blurted.

"Honey, I love you. I'm going to this hospital and meet Dr. Natalie St. Ans (isn't that a lovely name?). I'm keeping the itinerary open. Maybe go to Sangla and check out the innkeeper. See what he knows. I'll come home to La Conner with stories. Meanwhile, promise you'll investigate the nunnery on Chamberlain. OK?"

"Maybe I could write? OK, Jack. I love you, too. And I hope this Natalie lady sweeps you off your feet. I really do."

Every time I sat at my computer, I pictured Jack conjuring me, a lonely old woman, at the keyboard, plugging away. The mental image made me restless, so I took Penni-P on numerous walks, however the Samsonite suitcase remained by the attic door; I had no plans to open it again. Pandora's suitcase. There might be a poem in that.

· 2015 ·

Chapter 4 Emily Would Understand

"Emily Dickinson was an enlightened poet, and she never left home." I wrote in Jack's Christmas card. "I would, if I could," I continued, then signed my name. Jack hadn't come home for our birthdays and texted in early November that he would be absent during the holidays. I believed Jack had turned a page away from our friendship, and that hurt me deeply.

After he made his initial trip to Nepal, I heard from him less often. I figured he was angry with me for not being adventurous enough, a feeling dictated by some random standard I had recently conjured. I compared poorly to a French grandmother who meditated in Tibetan caves.

He sent me pictures of the hospital in Matipokhara and photos of Natalie and him. Jack beamed with his arm hooked over Natalie's lanky frame. She wore old sneakers; funny how you notice small details. Her teeth appeared slightly crooked, but her smile was as wide as the Asian continent. So was his. The hospital put me on their email list of donors. Jack sent a photo of Yeshe Maya. Her graying mass of hair parted in the middle, touched her shoulders. Ageless, smooth skin characterized her face. Her eyes peered through the camera lens as if she saw something beyond the ordinary. Divine Mother came to mind. I saved and printed her photo and taped it on my computer. It was a candid photo. She was in a garden. She was older, but how old, I couldn't tell.

Jack followed through on a trip to Sangla, and after going to India, I heard even less from him. Jack said that text or video chat was not the place to discuss anything related to the Samsonite suitcase, and not to mention anything to my book group, especially Carol, who had a blog, Instagram, Twitter, and Facebook accounts. He insisted I not say anything to his mother, either.

Avery was pleased that Jack was happy wherever he was. She enjoyed her budding friendship with Natalie, who, she claimed, reminded her of my mother.

After months of indecision, I wrote to Yeshe Maya, explaining who I was and where I lived. I included a copy of Mother's letter. And I mailed it at the same time I sent Jack's Christmas present a few days after Thanksgiving.

Then in January, Penni-P stopped eating. She had a category four heart murmur and occasionally coughed, but she had grown lethargic. The vet increased her heart medicine, and we returned home. I held my small dog as I scrolled through YouTube, perusing videos of Sangla inns, and found La Maison Fortune, the inn owned by the man who knew my father. "How weird is that?" I said to Penni-P, who only cared that I held her.

Cold late winter rain brought snowflakes, and the world became a vision of calming white when I checked the mailbox on my wide porch. One of five envelopes had first-class postage from Canada. I wrapped a woolen shawl around my high-buttoned shirt and sat at my table. A resealable bag of M&Ms was open. I'd been revising some older poems into a chapbook earlier, and M&M's were part of my writer's process. As I wrote, I often stopped to think about word choice. I paced as I made considerations. A few pieces of candy encouraged my deliberation and gave me an end destination.

I grabbed candy for bravery as I opened the envelope. In precise, neat printing, I was invited, along with a companion, to a statue dedication at the nunnery on Chamberlain Island. The statue was of Yeshe Tsogyal. The gathering was a joint celebration with a Buddhist meditation center on Vancouver Island, which had recently installed a statue of Guru Rinpoche. There was a spiritual connection between Guru Rinpoche and Yeshe Tsogyal; both were eighth-century Buddhist masters. He had been her teacher; she had been a healer. "You are cordially invited to join us on 14 March 2015 and to have a private audience with Yeshe Maya, our abbess. A return response is kindly requested."

I walked to my computer and back to the kitchen. I had informed Jack, albeit to curry favor for courage, about sending the letter to Yeshe Maya. I questioned if I should ask him to take me to the statue dedication for the audience with Yeshe Maya. The more I thought about it, the more I wanted to go. Carol would take care of Penni-P for the weekend, and my passport wasn't outdated yet. Jack hadn't been to La Conner for such a long time, and this was a big deal for me. I kicked myself for my inability to get to the nunnery on my own, but my twenty-year-old Honda and me, a nervous driver, were not a fit combination. Besides, Jack had been part of this from the beginning. I decided to text him the letter and see where it went from there.

"Jack!" I texted. "Read the letter I got from the nunnery— I pasted below. You want to go camping? They say there's a campground. And you could meet Yeshe Maya, too."

An hour later, Jack replied: "Yes, and yes. We need to have a long talk. Have booked a flight. Home for short of a week but will be in LC for Christmas this year. Tell Mom. I am in Sangla presently. I'm proud of you. You figured out how to get there."

I wondered what he had found out. He was proud of me, not mad at all. I was going to a Buddhist nunnery and meeting the midwife who brought me into the world. She knew my parents. She could tell me about Sangam and my father. I assumed he was dead, long dead, I reasoned. Jack emailed his itinerary. He would be home from March twelve until March nineteen, six weeks from today.

Chapter 5 Homecoming

I SCHEDULED AN EXTRA VISIT from the cleaners for Jack's house, watered his plants, and turned the heat to sixty-nine degrees the day Jack arrived. Everything I wanted to share with him at my place was organized and sat in my living room straight across from the bay window, which overlooked our properties. Penni-P preened with particular pride in her adorable new pink sweater.

I knew Jack was home because the lights were on upstairs. When I took Penni-P out for her morning yard run-about, I saw the van Jack rented for our island trip. After a flight that took him into Seattle in the early hours, I imagined he would be asleep. Rain fell, and puffy clouds marked the horizon. I had hoped for an early spring. Winter camping and me—I shivered at the prospect. There was no getting out of the excursion. Jack had invested time, money, and plane fare to accompany me. I wondered (as I always wondered) if I could go on a simple camping trip? If I saw myself fully participating, I would be excited, too. I had to act engaged for Jack's sake, as if camping was a natural thing to do, no matter what I truly felt.

"Hey, Sunshine, give this old man a hug," Jack shouted as he let himself in my back door. Penni-P ran, gaily barking from the bay window where I sat at the computer to the kitchen. I hadn't heard Jack come in.

I jumped to my feet. "Oh, it's so good to see you." His hug felt like home.

Jack appeared taller to me, dressed in jeans and a heather gray wool sweater. He was trimmer, his thick hair shaggier and combed back. He smelled like Ivory soap. Jack's good looks were more evident now than I had noticed before in tortoiseshell glasses emphasizing his even, square jaw.

"Thank you for getting the house ready for me," Jack said. "Do you happen to have a coffee handy?"

While the coffee brewed, we began to catch up. We moved to the living room, where I had laid out all the artifacts on the table in front of the sage-colored sofa. I brought in some pastries, too. Jack paged through the books and admired the photos of my mother and father. He then put the stone in the center of his hand and stared at it.

Penni-P demanded I hold her. As I sat by Jack, she wiggled her tail and nestled into my arm. I waited for him to react and tell me what he had learned. Finally, I burst, "So does Sangam exist? Is it real? Do you know anything about my father?"

"Yes. In English, Sangam means confluence. Imagine that you have crossed a major river called the Sutlej, entered a deep cave, and then come across an underground river and, at that juncture or close to it, enter a force field. Yes, Sangam exists."

"Like a vortex?" I asked.

Jack smiled. "Yes, like a vortex. As your mother said, you cross the Saraswati River to enter a mysterious Himalayan valley." He held the sunstone to light beaming through the bay window. "You can see red glitter in the sunlight like regular sunstones, but it sparks purple in the moonlight. This stone is only found on the far shore of the Saraswati: Sangam. It identifies you by the stone. Like a passport."

"You mean it identifies my mother?"

"No, I mean you. You were born there."

"Like she said in the letter." I lifted my cup and put it down. "And my father?"

"Your father is still alive."

"How do you know all this?"

"The innkeeper in Sangla is a frequent traveler, but he needs the stone and the letter to make absolute identification. And Yeshe Maya's confirmation."

"Have you been there?"

"I'm working on it."

"Well, of course, of course, you can take the sunstone and the letter, map, and the photos if that helps, but Jack, I could never go there. You know that's impossible. I've looked at the geography of the area. Sangla is way the hell remote. With my back and CP and, you know, my issues, I couldn't do a trip like that."

Jack touched the end of my nose with his index finger. "I am not surprised by your reaction, and I agree with you. Are you surprised?"

"I'm relieved. I could write him a nice letter, my father, I mean." I put Penni-P down on the shiny fir floors. She jumped back up onto the sofa and into Jack's lap.

"I missed you, too, little lady," Jack cooed at the dog. He turned toward me. "You couldn't cross the Saraswati unless you truly believed in the far shore, even with help from the river goddess. But Ravi could deliver a letter to your father."

"Ravi?"

"Ravi Jones. He's the innkeeper and a doctor, too. And he knows your dad, well."

I felt relief and defeat. I stared at my hands. "What do you mean, river goddess?"

"The Goddess Saraswati." Jack poured more coffee from the carafe. "She's reputed to be the cave's guardian. Yeshe Tsogyal is said to have manifested from the goddess."

"Well, this all sounds like something out of Mother's playbook, and if we didn't have the stone, I'd dismiss it." My cheeks pinkened. "Why do you think I don't 'truly believe in the far shore,' anyway?"

"You can't get to this place unless you're willing to put aside everything you think you know about your capabilities."

"So!" I said with a sigh, "Sangam does not allow people with disabilities to go there? Maybe that's why Mother left with me."

"Then why would she tell you to go find your father?"

"I can't answer that any more than I can imagine me trekking in the Himalayas or me, outside the body I was born in."

My defensive tone slid over Jack. "But you will write your father a letter?"

"Yes. I'll work on a letter for you to give Dr. Jones. Jesus, I have such a jumble of feelings. If I had another body, I'd go in a minute."

"When you get beyond your body, maybe you'll go." Jack handed Penni-P to me. He walked over to the gear I had stretched out by the fireplace wall. "We're all set to go camping—you've done your usual great job!" Jack said. "Let's do that for now."

"For the trip, I have a sleeping bag and a jacket that promises to keep me warm in minus thirty-two degrees. I have Hershey bars and marshmallows and graham crackers, too!"

Jack joined me on the couch and peered around the room. "You have taken care of snacks; I'll take care of dinner and breakfast. This is going to be fun. If the skies are clear, we might see the northern lights!" Jack stood. "We have to be in Bellingham for the ferry at half-past ten. I'll be over a little after nine—I know we're dropping off her ladyship at Carol's for the weekend."

"She knows I'm going, and she's not happy about it." I scooped Penni-P into my arms. "Isn't her sweater cute?"

"She's a teacup of perfection," Jack said. "I'm jet-lagged but promised Mom I'd have dinner with her at Trout Creek, so I'll see you both in the morning." He pecked me on the cheek and left through the back door; I watched him dash through the hedge to his house.

Before going to bed, I stepped into the yard. The night was cold, and Penni-P barked from inside the house. Jack's lights were on. He wasn't his usual self. Maybe the change I witnessed was jet lag, or perhaps the new woman? He dismissed my invitation to meet with Dr. Jones or this Natalie person before I had a chance to offer an excuse. Maybe he had heard too many excuses from me? Who were Dr. Jones and Natalie St. Ans, and what hold did they have over Jack? As for a trip to India and China? OK, he knew I'd say no. He said I had to believe in the far shore to get there. I didn't have the body to trek in the Himalayas, mystical realm or not, and I had Penni-P; she needed me. And who would take care of Jack's place or visit his mother? And why was I making excuses to myself?

Jack's lights went out; I opened the garden door, and Penni-P raced into the yard, peed, and retreated. I didn't sleep well. I worried about the camping trip, how Penni-P might do without me, and the state of my enlightenment.

Chapter 6 Go! Father!

Jack and I packed the Nissan van rental, and then I held Penni-P as we motored off to Carol's early the next day. She greeted us at her door, dressed in an Asian-inspired caftan. I had a grocery sack containing Penni-P's sweaters, halter, leash, treats, six small cans of dog food, and her heart meds. Carol checked the bag and rolled her eyes. "She's only going to be here overnight!"

"Let's just say I'm prepared." I handed Penni-P to Carol, and all Penni-P's perkiness dwindled. She faded. Jack honked from the van and waved to Carol, but my eyes were on my little dog, who, I felt, was sure that I was giving her back to Carol—forever.

"Mama will be home tomorrow, honey." I kissed the dog.

"She'll be playing with Freda and Kahlo in ten minutes," Carol said.

Her Chihuahuas barked excitedly from the kitchen where Carol had sequestered them. "Don't you dare cry!" Carol pointed to the van. "Have a great time at this temple thing—go—give my love to Jack." She waved and shut the door before I turned away.

"God, I hope she'll be OK." I buckled my seatbelt, and Jack backed out of Carol's driveway. "We've never been apart; in the five years I've had her."

"She'll be great and probably five pounds fatter." Jack laughed. "Hey, you're on an adventure, lady. Natalie said that Yeshe Maya is enlightened with a capital 'E,' and you'll be meeting her. She knows your father."

"Just how old is my father?" I asked. "I was doing the math last night. Mother died at ninety. Do you know how old he is? And Yeshe Maya has to be ancient."

"Ravi said your father is in his mid-eighties but looks younger; Yeshe Maya is over one-hundred."

"So we're like youngsters?" I mused. I pushed my fingers into my forehead and wished I could see the day as it was and not with all its complicated layers. "What if she tells me to go see my father? I don't want to disappoint her. Is it OK to lie?" I sighed and shook my head. "I suppose that's not a good idea." I studied a mural of tulip fields on the side of a thrift store. "Maybe I could explain about my bad balance and back problems?" I checked the stop sign at the intersection. "That sounds pretty stupid," I answered myself.

"You want a coffee before we hit the highway?" Jack interrupted my monologue of doubts as they ping-ponged in my brain.

I had to snap out of my lethargy. "Yes, to coffee. Tell me about Natalie," I said with forced gaiety. Jack hadn't come thousands of miles to hear my long-winded whine.

He pulled into CoffeeNow! After receiving our mochas, we were on our way. La Conner was soon the town behind us. Jack told me about the Matipokhara hospital and Natalie. She spoke several languages, had once dallied with becoming a nun, and was prettier than her pictures indicated. He split his time between the hospital and the inn at Sangla. Ravi Jones owned La Maison Fortune, and he was curious about me and wanted to see the original letter and map Madeline had drawn along with the stone. Both Ravi and Natalie said I needed to meet Yeshe Maya, "Oh, and by the way," Jack added, "she's blind."

"Blind?" I looked over at Jack as he parked the car on the ferry at the Bellingham Bay dock. "How can she confirm who I am if she's blind?"

"I'm just telling you what Ravi told me." Jack unsnapped his seatbelt. "I presume she can hear. Let's go upstairs. I understand they have free food."

We watched the Salish Sea hoping to view a whale breach, but no such occurrence happened. I did enjoy the forested islands popping up and bobbing away. Gulls scrolled through the sky. The boat slowed as it was about to deliver us to Chamberlain Island. "Oh, Canada," sang in my mind.

We watched the ferry leave Chamberlain Island as the only ones off the boat.

"Welcome to Canada," the customs agent returned our passports. Jack pulled our vehicle over to set Google Maps, then exited the ferry terminal.

"Well, that was pretty easy," I said.

Jack slid an Eva Cassidy CD into the player and leaned back with one hand on the wheel.

While Eva sang "Time After Time," I checked out the outskirts of an unincorporated town called Amber. A shuttered white motel in need of fresh paint stood alone, ghostlike. Closer to town, a little market with baskets of produce on the sidewalk, and no one in sight, caught my attention. A box of books with a sign propped at a crooked angle stated Free Library and marked the entry to a mom-and-pop store. I snapped a photo with my phone. Meantime, the computer voice directed Jack onto a graveled road. Its steep incline made me nervous. I closed my eyes.

At a pullout, Jack stopped the van. "Look at the view!" he said. "There's our ferry going north."

"Vancouver Island's not far away?" I cautiously opened my eyes to a windswept view of the Inside Passage—whitecaps on a bobbling deep blue sea with distant islands covered in mist.

"About twenty minutes." Jack opened his car door. "You want to take a photo? Great view."

"It's just too steep for me." I folded my arms across my chest. "You go ahead. I'm fine."

"We live on a hill above La Conner, not much different than here," Jack replied. He shrugged. "I'll be a minute." As he stood and squatted and stretched his body, taking photos, I wished I could open my door and feel free enough to join him. The mere thought made me dizzy.

When he started the Nissan, Jack rubbed his hands together and backed slowly onto the road. I averted my eyes from the seascape below as we wound our way to the temple where, in the middle of March, we would attend the statue dedication of an eighth-century female Buddhist spiritual master called Yeshe Tsogyal. I would meet Yeshe Maya, the abbess who brought me into the world long ago.

Jack and I set up camp on the temple grounds—mostly, Jack set up camp, and I watched. The temple itself had a pagoda-like roof and a covered garden in front of the structure. Koi luxuriated under lily pads on the still waters of a natural pond. The air smelled of cedar and sea. I breathed it in as we carried kindling to our campsite. Jack went to the van to get his wool hat. While absent, one of the nuns hosting the event called me to see if we had arrived and where we were camped and told me that a messenger would be on his way over—the end of the call. I barely said more than hello.

The messenger was a monk. Along with his maroon robes, he wore rain boots. He shook both my hands inside his and bent his lanky figure over to touch forehead to forehead. He smiled at me and told us that Yeshe Maya was not well enough to meet us that afternoon, reserving her strength for the next day's ceremony. She hoped to meet me then.

"Gosh, Jack, what if we miss the ferry tomorrow?" I said as soon as the kind man left.

"We'll work it out—stay over if we need to," Jack pulled his cap over his ears.

Good enough, I thought: I worried about Penni-P, but if we missed the ferry, I would text Carol. It would be fine. I had just met a Tibetan monk, and tomorrow I was to meet Yeshe Maya.

Jack brought out his air pump and filled a mattress for me and one for him. We would sleep outside in our sweats and use the restrooms on the temple grounds. Thank God he had a tent, and I had long underwear. Other campers arrived, mainly from Vancouver Island, and joined us for dinner. After veggie hot dogs and iced tea, we ended the evening making s'mores. I ate four.

As I pulled on an additional sweatshirt and slipped back into my coat, a graying couple wearing matching khaki shorts made a beeline to Jack. "You're Jack Reynolds, right? We were in Sangla?" The man spoke while the woman zipped her jacket.

"Getting a little nippy," she said to me.

"Well, it is nighttime." I tucked my hands into my pockets.

She smiled and cocked her head toward me. "Do you follow Motu?"

"I'm sorry, I don't know who that is?" I muttered and pivoted to Jack.

"Motu Amul. He's a highly influential yogi in India and well known here, as well." Jack hugged my shoulder.

"We regard him lovingly," Mrs. Khaki Shorts said, "Amul is held in the highest esteem by everyone he encounters.

"He stayed at the inn," Jack said. "I met him."

Mrs. Khaki Shorts raised an eyebrow. "Motu's a mystic yogi with an *amazing* foundation. Our group stayed at La Maison Fortune; life-changing meditations. Invent possibility—one of his sayings. He led a group of us to a remote cave where dakinis meditated. You could feel their vibe."

"Well, isn't that something?" I responded. "Imagine encountering Jack here. Isn't it funny how small the world is?"

"Oh," Mrs. Khaki Shorts said. She pointed her finger at me. "Well, you missed out by not going to Sangla. You really should! Look Amul up on YouTube. He's the real deal." She turned her attention to Jack. "Do you remember us?"

"I thought you looked familiar," Jack said.

"Do you follow him?" Mrs. Khaki Shorts said. "Inspiring!"

"I'm a new kid on the block," Jack answered. "His Kawasaki Ninja impressed me for sure."

"What's that?" I asked.

"A motorcycle," Jack shrugged. "Amul favors expensive—"

Mrs. Khaki Shorts did not give Jack time to finish. " Motu believes that good things come with strong beliefs. Beautiful things are attracted to Motu and he collects them. Goodness rains on him. He has many motorcycles and why not? He's a giver. He takes groups out to meditate in some of the holiest places in India and Nepal. We've signed up for the Kailash tour for next summer."

"He takes you into China, then?"

"You can see Kailash from Nepal. You stay at the ashram and get a plane ride partway to Nepal, then some hikes with catered dinners. Watch the videos—the beauty of what he creates is astounding. And he gives so much to charity."

Jack gave me a slight shrug. "That's his gig." He threw a stick on our campfire that sparked in flame. Jack's laugh sounded forced. "He's quite convincing."

Mr. Khaki Shorts said, "Amul talks to the mountains." His voice swelled with reverence.

Mrs. Khaki Shorts continued, "We enjoyed the inn; La Maison Fortune is a lovely destination. I think you were behind the desk when we arrived."

"Yeah, I took over for a few days," Jack answered. "Where do you folks live?"

"Seattle," the couple answered in unison. "We came in our camper van; we parked behind the temple."

"A long drive, but you should be snug this evening," Jack said.

Mr. Khaki Shorts checked his watch with the fluorescent dial. "Almost ten; we best get set up for the night."

They both produced flashlights and disappeared into the night.

"So, who's this guru guy?" I threw another stick in the fire. "You didn't seem too impressed."

"Amul—like our friends said, check him out on YouTube; he's all about money and exploitation," Jack said. "That Kailash sighting tour lasts twelve days, costs sixty thousand dollars each, and you go in a group."

"So he can afford the bike?" I shook my head. "That's a ton of money the guru makes."

"That pays for the watches, the jewelry, the Rolls, and the helicopter. At Maison, he rented what is comparable to a penthouse suite above the main lobby of the inn. He had his private cleaning crew, volunteers from his ashram, clean it to the holy man's standards. By the way, his nickname, Motu, means 'sweetly chubby.'" Jack laughed.

"Is this cave he took them to close—"

"In the same vicinity." Jack nodded at a passerby who stopped and asked us to join others at a campfire not far from us. The camper helped Jack douse our fire and we walked back with the man.

Seven of us gathered. The campfire crackled with another small log, and night birds called from tall cedars while a young woman strummed on a guitar. I wanted this moment to satisfy a yearning opening up inside me. Did I need to go to India? Why couldn't a night at a Buddhist temple with the promise of tomorrow's meeting with Yeshe Maya be enough adventure? My mind drifted to my father's home, high in the Himalayas. The couple we talked to were my age, gone to India, and were going again. Why not me? A quiet inner voice began to whisper.

Intermittent rain and cloud-covered skies hid the northern lights. A breakfast of eggs and toast was interrupted by a sudden downpour in the morning. We quickly cleaned up our campsite, and Jack and I got our camping gear back into the van in time for the sun to show itself briefly. The monk in the Jeep reappeared.

The monk looked ready for unwrapping with a transparent vinyl raincoat covering most of his head and robe. He stood with a booted foot on the bumper of his vehicle. Through a bullhorn, the monk announced the cancellation of the ceremony. Yeshe Maya was ill. Twenty of us stood around in quiet uncertainty. Murmurings of "That's too bad" . . . "Can we offer prayers" . . . filtered through the sweet morning air. My heart sank.

The monk motioned me over for a private word; our invitation to visit Yeshe Maya remained open.

"Yeshe Maya wants to meet me. You too," I said to Jack after the monk left. I didn't question anything. A thread of excitement lit a fuse, and I hustled to get ready. I brushed my hair into a ponytail and washed my face in cold water in the outdoor restroom, shivering until I zipped myself into my coat. Jack slid the passenger door open, and with my hand on his shoulder, I pulled myself into the front seat and immediately felt something give in my back. There were two water bottles in the cup holders that Jack, the ever-efficient traveler, had placed. Pain zigzagged down a nerve from the lower spine to my knee. I fished through my bag for pain meds and took half a Vicodin with a gulp of water.

Jack looked at me, "You need to get off that shit."

Tired from a sleepless night and on edge because of the conversation ahead with Yeshe Maya, I snapped at Jack. "I have five blown discs— osteoporosis, osteoarthritis, scoliosis, cerebral palsy, and God knows what. The only relief I get is half of a pain pill that I strictly regulate. It isn't 'shit' to me." My voice rose. "And by the way, I hurt my back getting into this marvelous machine." I crossed my arms tight to my chest and stared straight ahead. I felt sorry for myself. There's no India for the likes of me. No caves, no Sangam, whatever it was: No meeting my father. No one, not Jack, not any so-called normal person, understood how difficult it was for me to act like I could walk without tripping or falling, cut my meat, open a sealed box, style my hair, lift a heavy pot off the stove, and on the list went. Everything able-bodied people did easily; I had to deconstruct and reconstruct for a person with an ability to use one hand without the benefit of good balance and coordination. I fought with myself about leaving my house to go on this trip to Canada because I could not turn down the chance to meet Yeshe Maya and learn about my father, and I sure as hell didn't need Jack warning me about opioid addiction.

I felt safe with my dog in my red house, with the door shut and the lights on. No one was around to judge me or advise better daily living methods. And yet. Yes, I wanted to go to India with all my heart. Sitting in the Nissan, I was fiercely disappointed at the cards dealt me. I could not see myself on an airplane or dealing with strange customs and steep stairs in a faraway place. I couldn't carry a backpack. I resented that locked door.

"I'm sorry you're hurting, honey." The van door shut on Jack's side.

"I didn't mean to yell, Jack. I'm overwhelmed and so grateful for you putting up with me." I peered at my soot-stained jeans. "I should be dressed better to meet her."

"You look pretty," he said with a smile. "Remember, she's blind."

"Well, I've got that going for me." We both laughed. My attention turned toward a line of blue-black clouds on the horizon. The tips of the tall firs bent in a sudden wind. "Was that lightning?" A crack of thunder answered my question.

Rain drummed on the Nissan roof as Jack eased the van onto a narrow gravel road with potholes. I closed my eyes because the lane went straight upwards, and I opened them when Jack shut off the engine. We had arrived at Yeshe Maya's home, which was also home to all the nun-residents.

"Stay there. I'll get your door." He jogged around the vehicle to the passenger side. We walked bent low to ward off the rain and wind. Arm-in-arm, we mounted the metal stairs of the cedar-sided lodge. "You ready?"

"Yeah," I said.

Two nuns greeted us and led us to a darkened, mirrorless room where a small Tibetan woman lay in a bed with a lace coverlet over a pastel blue blanket. One of the nuns motioned me to Yeshe Maya's bedside. Her hair fanned out from her soft face; her eyes were closed. One of the nuns spoke to her in low tones. The nun squinted towards me and said, "She wishes to hold your hand. She says the right hand." The attending nuns backed away.

Yeshe Maya's palm was open, and her fingers pressed gently around mine. She smiled. I bent my ear to her lips. Her mouth opened and, in the weakest voice, uttered one word. "Go."

Startled, I didn't understand. Did the abbess mean for me to leave? "Father." Another whispered word.

She squeezed my hand. The gesture felt like a blessing, but at that moment, everything changed. Eons fell away. Words I did not know in a language I could not speak swelled in mountains, swarmed in bees, melted in honey, and hung like a moon of a thousand lost lovers. The pulsating presence of the small woman's hand shocked such thoughts into being and shocked me into the present as it intersected with the past and strode to the future too almighty bright to see—I felt India. I opened my fingers against the grip of Yeshe Maya's hand. Her fingers clung to mine as if to say, Listen. And that is when lightning struck a tree, and the lights went out. The tree fell with such strength that one of the nuns screamed.

Yeshe Maya let go—her life force left. Gone.

The sunstone, tucked inside my jeans pocket, warmed against my leg. I checked it as we left the room. And it had turned violet. My hand warmed as I held the sunstone, then the stone's honey color returned.

A busy scene unfolded around us: Jack and I sat in an anteroom while Yeshe Maya's doctor formally pronounced her death. Three nuns arrived and prepared Yeshe Maya's room for the ritual that would come next.

When we returned to the abbess's bed, a maroon silk robe with gold panels draped her body. Folded blankets and pillows set upon the floor provided seating for nuns, monks, and mourners. Lama Chokra Rinpoche, the abbot of the nearby Buddhist center on Vancouver Island, led the meditation and mantras.

Jack whispered that the words we repeated were called the Heruka Mantra and said after someone died. I witnessed Jack recite these prayers in Sanskrit. He had been doing his homework.

I kept my head bowed and hands folded in front of me, my legs numbed after an hour spent on the floor. As I became acquainted with the rhythm of the words, my voice joined the others. At one point, I glanced up at Yeshe's silk-covered body, and I believed her head turned towards me. A hallucination? Shortly after that, the abbot stood and said, "Yeshe Maya's meditation is finished."

No siren or mortuary attendants—that would wait.

A monk with a long face and deep-set eyes told me that Yeshe Maya had predicted her death the evening before. He said she had smiled, drunk her rose hips tea, and asked that her cremains be placed inside the statue to Yeshe Tsogyal. Everyone accepted this story as the normal thing a person might say the night before she died.

Not long after, Jack and I attended another vigil at the temple. This service took the place of the statue's dedication. Again, Lama Chokra

Rinpoche led us. We chanted and sang. In the background, someone drummed. Rain alternated with sunlight; seagulls soared through torn clouds when the temple doors opened.

"Such a surprise, her death," Jack started up the Nissan.

"Not for her." I told Jack what the long-faced monk had said to me about Yeshe Maya predicting her moment of death the day before. I turned my face towards his. "Jack, I saw things! The lights went out, then the big bang when the tree fell. And it was like the world sucked itself in and held its breath. Then let go. Right when she died. Coincidence? I don't think so."

"I don't think so either," Jack said.

I stared at the temple as it faded into the background. "Did you learn the mantras from Natalie?"

"More from Ravi than Natalie. I have books Ravi lent me, and I started attending a community group in Sangla led by a guy who looks like Hemingway."

"Oh my God, it sounds wonderful," I said. "Can I ask you something?"

"You can ask me anything." The little town of Amber reappeared. "Let's stop for a minute to talk." He pulled the van over by the mom-and-pop. It was closed.

"You're really over the moon in love, aren't you?"

"I've, ah—" Jack drank from his water bottle. "Yeah." He patted my hand. "I am that." He took a breath and laughed. "I wish you could see her. Meet Natalie. The hospital. Sangla. The Himalayas truly are spirit guides. And the caves Ravi took me to. As big as a high school auditorium."

I shook my head and began to cry. "She told me to go."

"Who told you?"

"Yeshe Maya told me right before she died. She said two words, and I swear, only I could hear her. She said 'go' and 'father.'"

"Wow."

"Yes, but I can't; I just can't manage it." I began to cry. "But I really want to."

In a quiet voice and with his eyes focused on me, Jack said, "You'd have help; every step of the way—if you ever thought you could do it—I'd help you figure it out."

"I can't. I'm trapped inside here." I hugged my arms around my body.

He handed me a tissue. "You've taken a huge step today. Let the idea play in your mind. You've been given a sign, yes?"

I nodded my head and wiped my nose. "Something else."

"I'm listening," Jack said.

"I brought the sunstone." I reached inside my pocket and held it up. "It warmed up in my pocket when she died and turned purple. I saw it. Then it faded."

"She was a living Buddha, you know."

"I have chills," I said, "if only Mother could have been here." I touched Jack's hand. "Would you do something before we go? Can you write out the mantra for me? Put it in my journal, OK? Tell me what it means." My bag rested on my foot. I reached inside, grabbed my journal, and handed it to Jack. "I have a pen."

"It's called The Heart Sūtra; the mantra is the last lines." Jack wrote it out in his looping, delicate letters: "*Gate, gate, paragate, parasamgate Bodhi svaha.*" Underneath, he wrote the English translation: "Gone, gone, gone, beyond, gone utterly beyond, Buddha celebrate!"

The day Jack left La Conner, he surprised me with a bouquet of daisies. "I will see you at Christmas," he said. "My mom loves your visits—thanks for that. Flowers are from her. Keep your heart open."

I had an additional backpack for Jack containing the books, the stone, the letter from my mother, and a letter I had just finished composing that morning.

> Dear Father,
>
> I send you love and greetings from La Conner, Washington. My mother died a few years ago, but I know she adored you. I hope you are well.
>
> I have enclosed some photos of my mother and a few of me. I miss her very much.
>
> A lifetime has happened between us. Impossible travel separates us, but I will always be your daughter.
>
> Signed with Affection,
>
> Maya Margarita

I said goodbye at his open van window and turned toward the house. Jack tooted the horn, and I turned back toward the vehicle. "Remember, Christmas drinks at Haliday's are on me!"

Chapter 7 The Great Empty

"I know, he's gone, darlin'." My pert little dog adjusted herself at the bay window desk in my lap. "But Jack will be back at Christmas."

I stared over at Jack's house while I made a computer search with my father's name: Tenzin Neil Caron-Martin. A teenager interested in cameras showed up on Facebook. No record of my father. I googled my grandmother's name, and a book list appeared: her books were no longer in print.

Jack's first destination would be Sangla. If I had been braver, I would have had Carol take care of Penni-P, bought a ticket, and gone with him. I shook my head to stay centered in the life I lived alone. I certainly had Penni-P; according to her, we were all we needed. She taught me that. I didn't need this far shore place I wasn't sure existed or a father, a real Johny-come-lately. I spent that afternoon on YouTube watching motorbikes go from Sangla on the Himachal Road to Chitkul, the last village in India. Next stop China. The road was less than an alley's width and serrated with deep twists and turns. Vistas of the Baspa River below and the Kinnaur-Kalish Mountain Range highlighted the ride. I tried to see myself hanging onto Jack from the back of a motorbike and blanched. A travel writer said vomiting was common at the high point of the pass over fourteen thousand feet. If I tried going, I would have to accept my death in high places; make peace with that. My father lived in a valley between heaven and earth amid snowy peaks.

I shrugged at Penni-P and got her leash. I wasn't going anywhere except around the block with my dog. Limitation accepted, I counseled, but I was curious and restless in ways I hadn't been before.

My searches had become daily rituals. I thought maybe I'd write a story about it. Every day the thought coursed through my brain. I researched how disabled people travel, and there was nothing of note to find. "Enough of this," I said to my pup and switched off the computer. Clear off. Not in sleep mode, but off.

"Time for you to eat." I moved Penni-P to the floor. Nighttime lights twinkled from Morris Street below the bluff. According to his last text, Jack had said he'd been in Sangla for several weeks and traveled to Chitkul and another village called Tashigang by motorbike. I asked him if he had vomited. He sent a puke-faced green emoji back but did not comment further. I looked at the setting sun in the western sky; it would be morning in India. "Aw, to have a morning in India," I said to Penni-P as I prepared her dinner.

She perked her head to the left.

"Oh, don't worry. I'm never leaving you."

She pushed her dish around with her nose, drank a little water, and then disappeared. I found her in my closet by my shoes. "Oh, baby," what's the matter?" I picked her up and asked her to eat a little. She ate some food that I offered with a teaspoon. She loved to eat, but not that night nor the next day.

The vet told me that she needed a boost in her heart and pain medications and that I needed to monitor her water intake. He emphasized the latter. She was twelve with a bad ticker. "Be prepared," the vet said, "she can go fast."

I watched Penni-P's sparse black hair dull to muddy brown in the weeks ahead. Her belly became distended, and she coughed and vomited periodically. We had our good days, and she slept on my chest each night. She continued to bark at the neighbor on the corner. I didn't like the old bald man with the skinny mustache any more than Penni-P. He asked why Penni-P was so badly behaved on our last walk around the block.

I stared the man down. "She has great manners and impeccable taste!" I picked up Penni-P. I walked off, our heads held high; Penni-P growled under her breath.

Not long after, a bad spell put us back at the vet's office. He increased the dosage of her diuretic, and we returned home. She refused to eat. She drank a little water from a teaspoon I offered, but she became weaker as the day wore on. I carried her outside to pee, and she could not stand up. Inside I put her on my best towel that I laid out for her on the couch and watched something on Netflix. Television was merely noise as my mind spun. My dog was dying. I sat with her just like the nuns had sat with Yeshe Maya.

Penni-P would not allow me to give her any more medication, and she turned her head away from me and shut her eyes when I offered her anything. Now and then, her back leg twitched. Nighttime fell, and all I could think to do was pat her, yet, I knew. I had to do something. She was ready to die, but she needed my help. After midnight, the emergency vet in Anacortes encouraged me to bring her in. My dog was suffering.

As I drove to the all-night vet, twenty-one miles away, I prayed every prayer I knew with Penni-P on the front passenger seat. Some truckers were out at one a.m. on Highway 20, but I drove my old Honda at a steady fifty and continued to pray for my little dog. I felt at fault for not extending her life with better care and guilty that I had allowed her to suffer. Yeshe Maya—I pictured her holding my precious dog wrapped in my best towel. I whispered lines from The Heart Sūtra along with *Om mani padme hum*. I prayed to Mary for intercession. Hail Mary. Was anyone listening?

The vet, who greeted me, was the essence of kindness. Penni-P hung onto consciousness, to her small life, for as long as she could. She didn't want to say goodbye to me, nor I to her. The vet told me I was doing the right thing. She injected my darling dog, who died in my arms.

The great empty came upon me as I drove back to La Conner.

I texted Jack from my computer chair. My phone rang ten minutes after, and I wept when I heard Jack's calming voice. "I am so sorry, honey," he said. "You gave her the best life possible."

"She did the same for me." I sucked in a breath. "I can't talk without crying; call me next week. OK?" My voice broke, and we said goodnight.

True to form, Jack called a week later. After reviewing how I was doing, he said he had news for me. "Exciting stuff happened here," he said. "Are you ready?"

"Sure." After days of long walks in the newness of May mornings, I grieved. The house was hugely empty without Penni-P's eight pounds of attitude. Talking to Jack was therapeutic and a welcome distraction.

"I made that side trip we talked about. Met a relative."

Chills ran up my arm. "Do you have a photo?"

"No."

I paced between the kitchen and the bay window. It was nearly dark, and I hadn't turned on the lights. I watched Jack's house in shadow. "Can you tell me about the relative?" How secretive was this place? "Did you give him any letters?"

"Well, he's in his eighties, and he is tall, bearded. A handsome man."

My father was alive, Jack had met him, and he'd crossed the Saraswati River. Holy smoke. "Can you tell me anything more?"

"No, you have to come to see him for yourself."

How many ways could I say no, before it felt like hollering into a well? I wept for hours that night.

Chapter 8 Obsessed

Every day I tried to accomplish something other than wallowing in grief. I mourned more than my dog's loss; I grieved the cruelty of disability more. My father was alive in a place stitched with magic, mysticism, and enlightenment, a home that welcomed me to visit, but I was born inside a body that would not allow the adventure. And he wouldn't even write to me. The frustration that dilemma presented haunted me daily, but I pushed on.

Fresh strawberry stands replaced roadside tulip bulb sales from the fertile Skagit Valley. Penni-P had passed two months before. I recalled her as a fierce, devoted soul who lived mightily with each breath. I had to show a little ferocity, so, damn it, I intended to move a stone-topped table room-to-room. I laid a towel under the table and flipped it onto its side. With my stronger left arm and hip, I shoved the table across the smooth surface of my wood floors to its new place in front of the couch. I took a breath and pushed forward to bring the table upright. A sudden pop in my lower back stopped me. "Oh, no. No, no, no."

After I explained to Carol why I wasn't going to the book club that evening, she brought soup for us to share. She fumed at me for living in a twenty-nine-hundred square foot house with heavy tables and stairs when she could find me the perfect home. She showed me photos of townhouses on her phone. I shook my head and cried. I wanted my dog, and I wanted Jack next door. I wanted my father back on a cloud in a mural on my bedroom wall. I wanted the pain to stop. I only mentioned Jack.

"Jack is a butterfly," she said. "He migrates. Butterflies are beautiful, but they are rare. That's why we all love him. Honey, he's never coming home to stay. And this house with you in it? Impractical."

"I'm not moving. Penni-P lived here," I said. "Mother lived here."

"Penni-P would have lived with you anywhere. Home is not a

building with a number on the front of it." She laughed with the cackle I always loved. "Don't breathe that to any of my clients." She stood to get her sweater. "One more thing before I leave—do you need a ride to the doctor?"

The doctor said I sprained my sacroiliac joint and would heal in weeks—maybe months, but I would get better. Jack made me promise on the memory of my dog that I would not move any more tables. He was quiet when I told him about Carol's suggestion that I sell the house.

"Can you imagine me any other place than here?" I asked.

"Sure, I can," he said.

Then it was my turn to be silent.

* * *

My old friend Joyce contacted me through Facebook in late August. She had retired in the Bay Area, and I told her about losing Penni-P and recovering from my sprain.

"Nothing to keep you in La Conner, twenty-four-seven," she said. "I haven't seen you in five years. Come on. Time for a visit."

I agreed, and we made a date to meet in San Francisco in late September. I kept thinking about the trip in terms of practice. But what was I practicing for? India leaped into my brain.

I found a travel website about how to pack everything you needed in a case sized to fit under an airline seat. I bought my ticket and ordered a taxi that took me to a shuttle that delivered me to Alaska Air at Seattle Tacoma Airport. The airport wasn't nearly as confusing as I had imagined, and the flight was relatively easy. As I deplaned, I studied the people at San Francisco's airport. People were going all over the world, and they seemed to manage. Look at me. A flight to India is just extended, I thought. I could sit for a long time. No problem.

On a Sunday, Joyce and I drove to Berkeley to relive some of her grad school memories from the sixties. The top was down on her VW canary convertible, and Leonard Cohen sang as we crossed the Bay Bridge. Over Thai food, we browsed through a calendar of weekend events that listed a show at the campus museum of Buddha statues from Nepal and Tibet.

"Perfect!" Joyce crooned. "Can you believe it? Just your jam."

We fed the meter and walked four blocks to the museum. Joyce was pleased that her laminated student card from 1969 got both of us in for free.

Warhol was in the corridor leading to the Buddha display. Joyce pulled out an artist sketchbook from her oversized bag and sat under a Campbell's soup can. With a nod towards the darkened room at the end of the hall, she said, "Have fun—I'm hanging here for a while."

The mood changed as I stepped away from the bright hall lights into the exhibition room. Somber lighting—quiet-sacred—I felt like I had entered a church. Glass boxes contained statues of Guru Rinpoche. I stepped back. How could it be? I pulled out my journal and paged backward to notes I wrote from Jack's visit home: "Padmasambhava, Guru Rinpoche. Traveled to Sangam; Sangam is that old. Eighth century." On a raised platform, the gold statue shone under a spotlight in the center of the gallery room. Its peaceful demeanor struck me first. Note cards, under the guru's likeness, told stories of his life. Like Gautama Buddha, Guru Rinpoche was born a royal, suffered, and through his suffering, became enlightened. He meditated across the river, beyond where my father lived; at least, that is what Jack told me; nothing about Sangam here. He was an advisor to a king and, in gratitude, was given a consort in the form of Yeshe Tsogyal.

Yeshe Tsogyal? The dedication of her statue was the event that precipitated our trip to Chamberlain Island. Had I dreamed this? I stood in awe, peering at her likeness.

Beautiful Yeshe Tsogyal's statues and prints adorned cases on the outer perimeters. Small cards under each display told her story as it related to Guru Rinpoche's. They lived high in the caves in Tibet or Nepal. *Aha, the caves!* According to legend, Yeshe could fly, and she understood Buddhist teachings at first reading. Like Guru Rinpoche left predictions for his followers, Yeshe left messages for hers. *Had I received one?*

Another coincidence? The exhibition of these two came months after the aborted statue dedication to Yeshe Tsogyal on Chamberlain Island. Joyce and I were stunned at the timing of these events. I made no mention of my connection to the abbess of the nunnery or my father, but it played in my mind.

* * *

Every year I bought a calendar from a Buddhist website that donated all proceeds to Tibetan relief causes in India. It was November, and my calendar for 2016 arrived in a tube. I loved the illustrations of Buddhist teachers and deities and looked forward to seeing what the artists had in store for the new year. I recognized Guru Rinpoche when I glanced at the cover image for January. April's art featured Yeshe Tsogyal. August's illustration had Guru Rinpoche and Yeshe Tsogyal together.

I had held hands with a Yeshe nun when she died. I met Guru Rinpoche and Yeshe Tsogyal at the Berkeley Museum, and the coming year's calendar featured them. I quit believing in "only a random happening" as an explanation for coincidences long ago. A year ago, I had not heard of Guru Rinpoche. The name, Yeshe Tsogyal, had not been in my vocabulary. Now, I met them time and time again. Their insistence that I pay attention to them reminded me of when I met Penni-P and how she jumped into my lap and pronounced that she was my dog. Something she knew, and I didn't. Yeshe Tsogyal and Guru Rinpoche knew something, too. And, possibly, my father understood, and that was why he didn't write me: something utterly beyond.

All I knew was that going to India was becoming more of an obsession, and each day, I found fewer reasons to stay in La Conner. If I managed here, I could survive there. My eyes followed jets, and my Internet searches focused on travel sites.

Christmas was coming, and Jack would be home. We had a date at Haliday's, and I had questions.

Chapter 9 Drinks to that

Haliday's faced La Conner Slough about six blocks from where Jack's house neighbored mine on the bluff above town. Shoppers crowded the small antique and art shops on Morris Street, and the lobby of the bar was full of people taking a break from Christmas over-buying. Happy hour well drinks cost five dollars, and on-tap beer, three-fifty—the best bargain these out-of-towners would see.

I had questions for Jack about La Maison Fortune in Sangla. Was it handicap accessible? Did it have an elevator? Did Dr. Jones, the inn owner, know of a guide to take me to the Saraswati River? Did such a person exist? I agreed with Jack about "Motu" Amul. After YouTube viewing his "spirit" channel, I had to laugh.

Dressed in white with elegant headwraps that matched his scarves and shawls, Motu stood out. Amul's large brown eyes melted the camera lens as his followers wept at his feet. His full white beard and delicate hand gestures completed the picture. The video I watched showed a small group that began their pilgrimage, so-called, at Amul's ashram in Rajasthan, a state in northern India. It looked like a movie set with high ceilings and lush fabric wall hangings. Amul sat on a platform while the travelers, who paid well over sixty-thousand dollars, meditated in his presence. I read the incense he used was laced with ganja, a legal herbal that heightened meditative experiences. These pilgrims walked for five hours on one day; they bussed or flew the other days. Motu ripped across one river in his high-powered motorbike. Throughout the video, a woman sang meditatively. My favorite frame was one showing Amul landing his helicopter. His followers looked to the sky as he touched the landing pad. The people who spoke described Amul as a "mystic" and the time spent in his presence "magical." I thought of Mr. and Mrs. Khaki Shorts and their willingness to pay over one hundred and twenty thousand dollars to make their idol richer. I noted most of the followers were European or American.

Carol kept pressing me to sell my house, and tours of one-level townhouses had their appeal, but I hesitated. I wanted to ask Jack about it. Despite what Carol had said, our houses, like Jack and me, were a pair. Without savings, a trip to India would have to be on credit unless I sold my house. I wanted that trip, and I wanted to keep Jack as my neighbor, even if he only visited La Conner on Mom-visits less and less often.

For as many months as Jack had been away, Yeshe Maya and the circumstances of her death were never far from my conscious thought or my Google searches. The museum exhibit and the Buddhist calendar directed my path.

If La Maison Fortune worked out, I had a place to stay in Sangla. My grandmother had been in Sangla, walked its streets, and gone into this far away village. My mother gave birth to me in Sangam. Yeshe Maya told me to go. What I had experienced on Chamberlain Island was real. I thought about Yeshe Maya. I taped the mantra at the end of the Heart Sūtra to my refrigerator and took up yoga to increase my balance.

At Haliday's, I stood, caught in the doorway, between two people jostling to get ahead of me. I could not see over the broad-shouldered woman with purple-streaked hair. The man she was with came in behind me. He put both hands on my shoulders and moved me sideways. I pushed forward like a football player willing to go one yard at a time to make a first down. As I lunged left, then right, Jack texted that he had scored a table by the window.

I made my way through the bar. Extra tables filled every serviceable gap, and the noise level created a feeling of organized havoc. But as I passed the last of the stand-up crowd, I spotted Jack staring at his phone. Beyond him were windows and an empty deck pelted by rain.

"Hey, Sunshine!" Jack stood as I got to the table. "It's a little crowded in here." He laughed and kissed me on the cheek. "You look so pretty. I love your red coat."

"It matches my house." I put my bag beside the chair and unzipped the coat. "It's hot in here."

Jack's jeans and pea coat blended with the other men's clothing in the bar, but his bright blue eyes and thick graying auburn hair garnered attention wherever he went.

The barmaid appeared as I sat down. She asked Jack if he would like more hot water for his tea. She was thin and a millennial who dug him. "Yes, please, and Maya, what would you like?"

"Tea sounds perfect," I said, "you have mint?"

She glanced at me. "Oh, hi," she said, "yes, we do."

"You have any cookies to go with the tea?" I asked. "Like shortbread?"

"Sure." She gave Jack another toothy grin. "Would you like some cookies, too?"

"I'll steal one of hers," Jack said. The waitress left.

You can't compete with Jack's blue eyes. "You must've just got home. But drinking tea?" I laughed. "So good to see you."

"I promised Haliday's." Jack silenced his phone and nodded. "I quit drinking. No one I know drinks in India, and it's lousy on your body."

"But you delivered Haliday's nevertheless! How was the flight?"

"Really, really long." His hand draped the phone, and he slumped in his chair, mimicking how tired he felt. "It takes ten hours to get to the Delhi airport itself."

"You came from India?"

"India for a few days, then Nepal, and home."

"To see the doctor who doesn't drink?"

"Her name is Natalie, and yes, we had Christmas plans. I have a gift from her to you. At home."

"Well, that was very nice of her." It sounded like Jack was serious about Natalie St. Ans, and I guessed that explained his long absences. "You must be tired. You want me to Christmas shop for your mom? We had a great Thanksgiving at my house. Her Trout Creek friends felt robbed—she likes her assisted-living posse, what she calls her pals there, and she misses you. Talks about you every time I see her." I was trying to remain upbeat, but it felt forced. The room was hot, conversations carried from table to table, Jack was distracted, and I missed my gin and tonic.

"Nah, I have Christmas covered—for you, too." Jack shook the ice cubes in his empty water glass. "I have a surprise—and I wanted to tell you first, well actually second. I'm selling the house—"

"Huh?" Selling his house? "Does Carol know?"

"Not yet."

"You're leaving permanently?"

The barmaid delivered our tea and frosted shortbread cookies and left.

"I hate these long flights. With all the delays, it took two days to get here." He yawned as if to emphasize his point. "I want to settle down. Funny, I think that place will be India."

"Not Greece?" I didn't know how else to respond, and the awkward pause escalated as I stared at my tea, then sipped it. My cheeks reddened as the reality of Jack moving away from La Conner sunk in. Even with frosting and sprinkles, I left the cookies on the plate. "Wow, Jack. Really? Are you going to go? I won't see you?" I pushed my cup on the wet paper coaster and made swirls on the tabletop. Life without Jack? Was he serious? What about his mother? He'd leave her like that? But what about me? Jack was my family. All I had. Gone? I cleared my throat. "Who'd you tell first?"

"My mom, about an hour ago. And you will see me again in May when I return to move her to Sangla."

My mouth dropped. "Your eighty-seven-year-old mother, too?" I took a sharp breath and released it. "Half a world away." I felt a dull thud in my stomach or maybe a carton of milk a week past its "best by" date. In his tortoiseshell glasses, handsome as ever, Jack just blurted his intention to desert me. And his mother was going to make the trip? I was mad at them both. "So as easy to do as selling your house?" I broke a cookie in two and offered half to Jack.

He popped it in his mouth and swallowed some tea. "Well, I may need your help on that front . . . you have always been so kind to see my mom, water the plants, oversee the cleaners," Jack said. "You're the best . . . don't look so sad." He knew he had delivered a blow.

"But you live in the house next door. You always have," I said. It had been a year of goodbyes, and I didn't think I was up for another one or two. I picked up a happy hour menu and pretended to read it.

"Maya. Look at me." He motioned with his index finger, eye-to-eye.

I raised my head to meet his gaze.

"You are my sister, you know that?" he said. "I loved your mom as if she were my own. You can blame her for my wanderlust."

A smile threatened to break up my stony composure. "It's the suitcase, isn't it?" I shook my head. "All of it. And Natalie. It's her, isn't it? I bet the owner of the hotel doesn't drink, either."

"Kismet, meeting Natalie. Then the other—and—" His voice lowered, and I understood his reference. "All the pieces I've shuffled around in my life suddenly fit. I moved to Sangla—"

"No more Corfu Town and goats on mountainsides?" I stared at my hands. "You're living in a hotel?"

"For now. Ravi lives in the coolest tree house, and when Nat moves to Sangla next summer, she and I will live in the tree house, and Ravi will come over to the inn. We have it all figured out."

"She's officially quitting her job to live with you?"

"Yes, ma'am. Her contract with the hospital ends in May. So, we'll live in Sangla, in a tree house."

"That seems awfully fast." I opened my mouth and shut it. Then laughed. Jack in a tree house? It made sense. My mother would have rejoiced at the novelty.

Jack continued. "Is that a smile? That's good," he said. "In part—the suitcase certainly opened up other doors, but you know all that's happened tells me that it is just time to sell the house—Mom encouraged me and is excited about a new adventure of her own. We'll have an apartment set up for her at the hotel. She wants me to 'settle down' her words, by the way. I guess sixty-six? About the right age for that?"

"Let me get this right," I said. "At sixty-six, you're settling down in a tree house with a missionary doctor who doesn't drink?"

He shook his head and shrugged. "I don't know." He sighed. "Novel, huh? I repeat it's time. Natalie is the one."

Of course, Jack, the capital-R- romantic, had found true love. I tapped his hand. "What sort of help will you need?" My voice tensed. I felt older than his mother, Avery Reynolds, and used. A convenience. I needed a drink.

"I'm not going to be in town long, and I thought you could oversee the real estate stuff. Mostly done online now, but you keep me informed— help my mom get ready?"

"Well, sure, if I'm still here." The words fell from my mouth before any rehearsal in my brain. "I'm selling my house, too!"

"Say what?"

"Carol's handling it."

"So, a townhouse then? Which is a great idea, one-level?"

"If I hear someone say, one-level, one more time, I might explode." My nostrils flared. "I have more to do than sit in a townhouse without fear of falling. I'm more than some old woman alone on a couch. Yeshe Maya told me to go to India. Plain and simple. And," I went on, "there have been signs ever since. I told you about the museum with the golden Buddha statue of Guru Rinpoche and Yeshe Tsogyal. Then the calendar where their images were all over it. When Penni-P—the queen of all little dogs died, it got clearer. She was my true companion." I emphasized, "true." I felt tears form, but they did not fall. "But, she's gone." Emotion choked off my voice. "It's time for a change."

"Oh, Maya, I'm so sorry about Miss Penni-P." Jack took off his glasses and rubbed his eyes. He was tired. "I should've said something first off. I know how much you loved her."

"You called me, Jack. And thank you for that." I was overly polite, still upset by all this news. How could he just leave me like this—and take his mother, too? "That was the longest night of my recent life. The night she died."

"Then, you sprained your back by trying to move that table."

"It healed, but Carol gave me an earful after about my house being too big to take care of and so on."

"She may have a point there." Jack motioned to the waitress. "Let's get soup or something and move out of the bar."

I wanted to rise from the table and shout, "Deal with your mother and your house!" But an inside voice less involved with the rat-a-tat of daily life and petty jealousy counseled differently. Jack had a right to live wherever he wished. He was a good son, setting his mom up and giving her an adventure I coveted for myself and a great friend who owed me nothing. He'd been the best friend I ever had. Jack's decision was as personal as I wanted to make it. He did tell me second (or third—I'm sure Natalie had known first). That was almost good enough. I held myself to this accounting as Jack ordered an early dinner.

We moved to the dining room, and the quiet was welcoming. Clam chowder and warm sourdough bread sounded soothing on a rainy night by the harbor. Our new waitress asked Jack if he was an actor. She thought she had seen him in an HBO series.

"What is it with you and women?" I buttered my bread, and the crust was crisp and the center soft, a perfect bite.

"Beats me. I stink right now. I have been in these clothes for two, three days. I've lost track." Jack took a bite of soup. "Really good." He peered at me. "Now, back to you. Tell me about selling your house. When did you decide that?"

"After seeing Joyce." I made up my response on the spot. However, it was a good story with a certain logic to it. "If I sell the house, I can get a smaller place and travel. I want to try to see all of India. You said you'd help me." I carefully avoided any mention of Sangam by name. "I have to try, right? I made it to San Francisco and back."

"Sangla will be helpful. We can work something out."

I continued to create a plan of action I had not been aware of ten minutes before. "You want me to set you up with Carol?" I was amazed at how easily I was putting this all together.

"Have her give me a call."

"OK."

When I returned home, I figured I would text Carol that Jack and I wanted to list with her—and then this feeling of panic snuck up on me. What was I thinking? After an earthquake, I imagine you momentarily felt that nothing had changed until you looked up and the roof was missing from your house. Was I willing to blow the roof off my house because of a suitcase in the attic? Maybe. I shook my head and patted my mouth with my napkin. If I decided I wanted out, I could back-track my words, say, gosh, I was just joking, and order dessert.

But then Jack gave me the same look he always gave his mother when he coaxed her to take his advice, and he shook his beautiful head and said, "Are you sure?"

"You only live once, Jack. And if I get to India, I can go anywhere." I took a breath and did my best to smile. "I'm thinking about going to Nepal, too." What the fuck? "I could meet Natalie." I gave him my most engaging smile.

After consulting with his phone, Jack air-dropped Natalie's contact information to my phone. "She'd be so happy to meet you and show you the hospital—but it is remote."

Standing, I zipped myself into my coat. "I've already started getting into shape. It's doable." I leaned over and kissed him on the cheek. "I'm going to run. I'll text you about Carol." As I turned to leave, my knees nearly gave out. I had to work a little more courage into this body of mine. As I crossed the threshold to the sidewalk on Morris Street, I realized I had left Jack with the bill. I looked up and down the street. Where the hell had I parked the car? As I hustled down the road, wind in my face, I saw my twenty-year-old Honda. Thank God it hadn't disappeared, too.

When I returned home, I poured a glass of chardonnay and then sat in my computer chair where Penni-P and I spent time and stared at the gardens between Jack's and my house. I thought about the pros and cons of travel. Irrefutable facts: Osteoporosis shrunk my body. Cerebral palsy created muscle pain and spasms that worsened as I aged. My back hurt most days. I was on Vicodin for pain. Death from whatever cause was not on hiatus by staying secured inside my red house on the bluff. Why not leave this world on an adventure?

Speaking of bluffing, I wasn't bluffing after all. I texted Carol and Jack and set up a meeting in my dining room for the three of us the following day. In a separate text to Carol, I said, "Oh, by the way, act as if you've already listed my house. I'll fill you in later."

· 2016 ·

CHAPTER 10 SOLD

I HIRED HELP TO GET MY HOUSE in shape to sell. Most of the furnishings, paintings, dishes, screwdrivers, snow shovels, my entire wardrobe, Mother's clothes, and on and on—were donated or trashed. We did the same at Jack's place. Along with Jack's cleaners, I hired a carpenter to paint rooms. Carol helped organize an estate sale for both our houses. We made $500, which Jack insisted I keep.

Six weeks later and four days after listing the houses, they sold. My new passport and the sage sticks arrived hours apart in late April; so many changes in such little time.

Jack's mom had died in March, and she would never see Sangla. On our last visit, I brought her a lightweight, wheeled carry-on for her long flight to India. She had me sort through her wardrobe for clothes that would go to donation and those she wanted to take. We packed the suitcase to see how well her things would fit. Avery showed me photos on Instagram of her new ground-floor apartment at Maison. She insisted that I stay with her during my visit to the inn. Over salami and cheese slices, we ended the evening by watching *The Best Exotic Marigold Hotel* for the fourth time.

Three days later, Trout Creek called me about her death. They were desperate to contact Jack but were calling his old house phone. I immediately texted him to call me. When I heard nothing back, I brought up the inn reservations number and dialed it. To my amazement, Jack answered the phone. I looked at the clock. It was nine-thirty at night in Sangla. "Jack," I said, "I am so glad I got hold of you."

"Is everything OK? What's up?"

I paced across my living room and back to the bay window, making slow loops as I spoke. "Honey, I hate to tell you this way, but your mom died. Trout Creek's been trying to get hold of you."

"Oh, God. Mom?" I heard the muffled emotion. "A stroke?"

"Yeah. It was sudden. Last night. She died in her sleep." I studied a squirrel as it sprang from a tall cedar in Jack's yard to my old cherry tree.

Jack was silent for a moment. "I'm all set for her here." Another pause. "Thank you, sweetie, for calling. Mom loved you like a daughter." He cleared his throat. "There's a plan in case of death. Trout Creek—they have the death notice and the order for cremation." I thought he was pacing, too. "Big favor, Maya. Trout Creek has the name of the mortuary. Will you be there for the interment? Next to my dad. I'd come, but right now, there're complications."

"Of course I will."

"I'm an orphan," Jack said.

"We have each other . . . family—you and me."

"Thank God for you," Jack said, "I mean that." The connection went quiet again. "She wanted you to have the living room clock—she gave me her rings last time I was home. Everything else goes."

"The clock?" I wiped a tear from my eye. "I loved her, Jack."

"We both did," he laughed. "Honestly, I think Mom loved you best."

"Well, you were my mother's favorite would-be son. Came home for her when she had cancer those last days—" The squirrel somersaulted from cherry branch to yew arbor across my side yard and back across to Jack's.

"Your mother changed my life, and that is all I have to say about that," Jack said.

"We were pretty lucky when it came time for having moms."

"Yes, little sister, we were." Jack said, "I'll ring Trout Creek. Do you have the number?"

* * *

Three weeks to the day later, I texted Jack in caps:

(ME) CONGRATS! HOUSE SOLD! BOTH OUR HOUSES! SAME WEEK!

(JACK) When are you coming to India?

(ME) Bags packed. Honda sold. First stop Matipokhara Hospital.

(JACK) What have you been smoking? Proud of you.

(ME) I went to San Fran—sold my house and yours. I think I can manage Nepal.

(JACK) You'll need help. All-day bus ride to remote hilly region. I get dizzy going there.

(ME) I AM going. Planning around 13 May. You said you'd help me.

(JACK) Ravi is going to the hospital around that time—will work to coordinate. You can catch a ride with him, maybe.

(ME) Thank you!

(JACK) No promises!! I need to confirm with Ravi.

In an hour or two, Jack texted again. Dr. Ravi Jones would enjoy the chance to meet me and would coordinate his schedule with my itinerary. "Tell him thanks, with a lot of gratitude attached," I texted back to Jack.

I settled in my armchair with a glass of wine. I probably should quit the drinking, I thought. After I get to India, that's when. Soon, I'd have money from the house and help along the way—what else would I need? Rice paddies and mountain peaks created the backdrop for fabled adventures, yet the people the hospital served were among the poorest on the planet.

When the house closed, I sent Natalie's hospital a thousand dollars, and I told her she might consider it a bribe: a good-natured one. She sent me a three-worded text: "We love you."

* * *

As I said, my passport arrived, and so did the smudge sticks. The empty house would soon be in the custody of a family with three teenagers. The new neighbors at Jack's had little guys—looked to be five and under—and a delightful beagle named Hilda.

I sat on the attic stairs one last time and pushed myself up with a lighter in my pocket and sage in my lap. I looked out onto the little town below the north dormer and remembered lemonade with my mother as she painted at her easel. The sage blessed the attic and sent the memories to rest. From room-to-room—floor-to-floor—I walked solemnly with my lit sage thanking each nook and cranny for holding my mother and me through hard and happy times.

The door to the trunk room was in the second-floor bedroom closet. I opened it to a waft of dust, making my sage stick bloom like a firework. I saw that I had forgotten to find a home for the antique mirror Mother had picked up at a flea market over fifty years ago. I waved the sage over it and hoped the new residents would be pleased to find such a hidden treasure.

Another secret room, a tiny prayer closet, was beside the staircase in the foyer. My mother used it to stack blankets. On the backside of the door was a small painting of the Virgin Mary. It had belonged to the previous owners. Beside Mary was a faded poster with curled edges. The metal tack held firm. The yellowed sheet bore directions about how to pray the Rosary. Hail, Mary, full of grace—I had memorized the prayers when I was a kid. When I was mad at the world during my teen years, I told Mary about it. Perched on blankets, I had my first beer tucked inside this cocooned lair and wrote poems to boys who never read them. In past years I opened the door to let Mary have a little natural light now and then.

While waving the lit sage stick, I apologized to Mary about the beers and said a few Hail Marys. During one of the prayers, my thoughts went to Jack and our mothers, Yeshe Maya and Natalie, at the hospital, and I paused, watching the sage spark in the air. Suddenly, the smoke alarm went off. I raced to the kitchen, extinguishing the sage in a pail of water I'd set out for that purpose. The smoke alarm shrieked as I opened the front door and began fanning a towel below it. Finally, the damn thing silenced.

Good enough, I thought. Good enough.

Chapter 11 Liftoff

With my red roller bag packed and my carry-on readied, I turned to look back before getting into the taxi to the shuttle for a red-eye flight from Seattle to Seoul. "Goodbye, old house." I wanted to go back inside. "I love you." My belly felt weak; I hadn't slept the night before. I enlisted Carol to organize the final cleaning for my house. However, that moment in the taxi, sweat under my collar, literally brought the reality of change home.

The taxi wound through festive streets filled with tourists gawking at flowers and sunshine. The airport shuttle stopped at a large restaurant along the busy highway outside La Conner. I pinched myself to check if this was all real. The next to last thing I did before leaving was to give Carol a final call. I had not sold or donated Avery's clock and gave it to Carol for safekeeping. I told her the clock was a gift from Jack and me. She thanked me profusely. I then texted Jack with that news. He sent a smiley emoji and said, "It's all about TIMING, kiddo! See you soon."

The taxi driver delivered me to the shuttle stop, and I stood first in the bus line, a smile washed over any concern. Checked in, I stumbled up the steep steps.

The driver yelled, "You OK?" He processed the next passenger.

"Yeah." I claimed the second row behind the driver, put my gear on the seat beside me, and watched the travelers board the bus. I texted Jack as the bus carried me and my bags to the airport. His response was immediate, which delighted me.

(JACK) Yay! You! Meet you at Delhi Raj on night of 22 May.

(ME) Can't believe I'm doing this—out-of-body experience.

(JACK) See you soon, Sunshine. Happy landing in Kathmandu. Everything set up for you there.

As we passed the Space Needle, I reread my itinerary on the bus: an overnight in Kathmandu and then a bus ride to Natalie's hospital with the doctor. I'm not good at talking to strangers, I thought, and was about to negotiate a world of strangers.

Sea-Tac looked cavernous that early evening. Sun beamed through lacy westerly clouds as I rolled my case inside the doors. I paused at the entry, and I found AsiaNow! Airlines check-in close by. A long queue formed, but I knew I had plenty of time since I was hours early. I tried to secure my carry-on to the top of my roller case, but it kept sliding off. Clumsily, I made it through the long line with a validated ticket as my reward.

A TSA person helped me shove my things into the little rubber baskets that moved right along. Beyond the conveyor belts, I found a bench where I slipped back into my shoes with a sigh of victory, having made it thus far. I took the elevator to the subway, which led to the international gates. Although I had four hours until flight time to Seoul, I bustled through the long hall until I saw my gate number—then, and only then, did I allow myself to relax.

I boarded early with passengers needing extra assistance, and a helpful hostess tossed my red case straight above my seat. Breathing deeply, I settled back: me—Maya Margarita Moore—jetting over the moon and into another world. I read the meal menu—and pulled out my moleskin journal to continue my notes. There, in Jack's elegant looping hand, was The Heart Sūtra. I whispered the mantra as the plane sped down the runway. The cabin noise escalated. Beside and behind me was a Korean family with three little children. Dressed in Disney motif pajamas, the kids looked adorable. The screaming, as we gained altitude, was another matter altogether. A glass of chardonnay helped. I took half of a pain pill, fell into a fitful sleep, awoke to a hushed, darkened cabin, and then went to the lavatory. Two flight attendants spoke quietly in the galley, just past the bathroom door.

When I returned to my seat, a passenger coming forward faltered as the plane lurched. I maintained my footing as we awkwardly advanced around one another, and when I plopped into my seat, the sign went on to buckle up. The Pacific Ocean spread for miles beneath the airplane, and I began to focus on how small this tin cigar was in comparison. Voices softened in the cabin darkness. A thin beam of light trailed down the aisle. Two rows forward, a man read from a self-lit reader. I leaned my head back and fell asleep.

I woke up again—nudged awake by an offering of breakfast from one of the flight attendants. After a meal that included a cheese omelet, hash browns, sides of broccoli and beans, a cup of vanilla yogurt, and sliced pineapple, I drank a cup of coffee. Comforted and full, I followed our flight path on the seat-back screen as we headed to Seoul, and a two-hour layover for me.

I looked at the Korean landscape as we prepared to land and thought about the cars speeding on the highways below. People like me were getting along on with their day. The plane taxied, and passengers jostled to get their possessions. The man beside me helped take down my carry-on from the overhead compartment. I realized I had not spoken to anyone during the nearly twelve-hour flight as I thanked him.

Many families, business people, and tourists whizzed by as I entered the airport proper. Everyone seemed to know where they were going and how they planned to get there, and the whole body of the airport was bright with light. The voice from the intercom was female. I could not understand anything she had to say in any of the languages spoken. I panicked, thinking I might miss my flight to Thailand, as I trotted behind a group of tourists whose leader raised a sign with Bangkok-AsiaAir! printed on it. I thought I might have made a good cow in another life. The tourist group went through customs first. With my passport stamped and help from the straight-faced customs official, I proceeded to the lift that took me down or up; I'm still not clear, but to the gates—mine was about a mile away—or so it appeared. The carry-on, which I started to call my watermelon bag, kept slipping off the roller case because of its size and bulk. I thought about getting a luggage cart, but the machine that spat them out looked complicated to use.

I caught up with the tourist group, but I went through them this time, counting the gate numbers down to mine. My feet felt warm and oozy as I traipsed along, but I finally made it to the gate. I found a seat that faced the departure door as if daring the plane to leave without me. The gaggle of tourists and their leader arrived shortly after and chatted excitedly about Bangkok. I prided myself on my itinerary—the jaunt to Matipokra, the road trip to Sangla, the Saraswati River, and beyond to my father. Only I was going there. Better than some old tour, I thought.

Carol had told me to bring slippers, a size too wide, for the flight. The slippers were now the only thing I could wedge onto my swollen feet. I watched people chat, and I grinned at a little girl dressed in pink. The planes on the field looked silvery in the transitioning light. I'm doing this! I thought.

When the first call was made for passengers with small children or passengers with disabilities to board the plane, I queued up with a man in a wheelchair and a lady with twin babies. A flight employee stood in the aisle by my seat.

"Can you please put this in the overhead bin?" I gazed downward at my red case.

She raised an eyebrow. Her demeanor was as unblemished as her red and yellow uniform or the perfectly bound bun at the nape of her neck. An English accent punctuated her words. "Not with my back." She checked something in the seat in front of me.

"I need your help because, well, because I need it." I stammered as passengers began filing down the center aisle.

She pursed her mouth. "You look pretty healthy." With no other words, she pitched my case into the overhead compartment.

"Thanks," I muttered above a whisper while avoiding eye contact. Go fucking figure—I work myself up to ask for help—and she says, no? I realized sweat dripped from my forehead. A disabled person appearing too normal—how ironic—I felt caught between two worlds. I was exhausted, I ordered a glass of white wine, which helped adjust my attitude, and I fell asleep for an hour.

We landed in Bangkok: another airport awaited. Here we go, I thought. I hope I can do this. The woman who initially declined to help me apologized as I exited the airplane. I guessed she saw me wobble as I navigated the aisle. I smiled and thanked the crew as passengers scrambled around me. When my watermelon bag fell off the roller case, I stopped to pick it up. People passed me as if I were my vintage Honda going forty in the fast lane of Interstate 5. I heaved the carry-on over my shoulder and soldiered on to my next gate.

The world came alive with a bevy of travelers with varying degrees of stress on their faces as they checked boards aglow with arrivals and departures. I asked a uniformed employee where I should go.

"First customs," the woman nodded at the parade of passengers queuing in front of me.

After stamping my passport, the Thai official gestured toward the concourses, which led upwards and downwards. At that juncture, I met a person who appeared to work for an airline, standing by a departure/arrival board. The animated board changed flights and gate numbers while I watched in confusion. "Can you tell me which gate for my AsiaNow! flight to Kathmandu?" I asked.

The woman pointed to the board as if I were daft and walked off.

I stared at the ever-changing board, willed it to speak, and prayed I would not miss my flight.

"Can I help you?" A woman in a blue uniform asked.

"These boards shift; I don't get it," I told the employee. "The flights change numbers while you are looking." I pointed to my paperwork with my flight number and shrugged. "I can't find my flight."

"You are about ten gates down in this concourse, number forty-three—you have twenty minutes. They have just begun boarding. Do you need assistance?"

Without answering, I took off, struggling with my watermelon bag banging against my back. I knew I should have asked for help, but I had something to prove and a gate to find. What the hell had I packed? Rocks? Panic laced with fear that the plane might leave without me caused muscles to tighten. The tendon in my right foot cramped, and I ignored it as I stumbled along the corridor, half-running, half-bungling forward. I slid into the gate and boarded at the very last. My bags slammed against the seats of travelers already buckled in as I moved down the plane's aisle. The strap of the watermelon bag slipped down my strong arm, my right arm too weak to assist. My hard case had to be stowed overhead again, and I spied a vacant spot. I retracted the handle and wondered if I could hoist the bag that high when a man across from me asked if he might help. I gladly accepted and then took my seat. I always tried to sit aisle-side because I was clumsy, getting in and out of confined small spaces. This time assigned a window seat, I rejoiced at the empty seat beside me.

My body screamed, and my foot ached.

I accepted a glass of in-flight wine and took half a pain pill. I tried to stretch my foot, and it froze in a spasm. The muscle finally softened, and the tense foot returned to a semi-normal feeling. Paging through an airline magazine, I studied hotel offerings in Kathmandu and fell asleep. I awoke to the captain advising everyone to look out the windows at the string of Himalayas.

"Holy God," I said aloud to no one.

"Quite impressive," a passenger said from behind me.

"Yes, it is." I pressed my nose against the window. Whatever else happened, I had now seen the Himalayas. The mountain peaks appeared to float atop a cloud-sea. How could Jack ever complain about a flight that included such a view? My father lived somewhere out there.

A crazy confusing crush of people met me as I worked my way through the taxi area outside the airport in Kathmandu. Before leaving Bangkok, I had bought some Nepali rupees at the airport; enough, I hoped to see me through my stay. Night had fallen, and a light breeze touched me as children begged and adults with open hands pleaded for money. Taxis gathered behind a temporary wire mesh fence, one edging out the other. Porters yelled, "Kathmandu, cheap!"

I followed the other people around the fenced area and watched for a van from Nepali Royal Hotel—a service Jack had arranged for me. Taxis and cars squealed in the night as I shivered on the sidewalk awaiting pickup.

A young man in jeans and a light jacket approached with a placard he held high. My name in bold letters seemed oddly out of place, but there it was: Maya Margarita Moore. I nodded vigorously.

The man said, "Ms. Moore? Yes, yes." Before I could answer, he took my luggage and motioned me onward. We wove through tourists and families and across a lane to a small van with its headlights on. I tumbled into the backseat with a deep sense of relief and gratitude for the quiet.

The world swam by, a mad painter's image of a time gone too fast. People dressed in white looked like walking ghosts. The vehicle sped on. The driver spoke on his cell in Nepali, and I heard my name mentioned. The jagged edges of the words spoken reminded me of the mountains I had just seen. The city bustled with people and dull lighting. I stared into the dark as we drove into a roundabout entrance to the pink-bricked Nepali Royal Hotel, with a lit sign in front.

As the young man stopped the van, I reached for the five-hundred-eighty-five rupees I had tucked inside my jacket pocket. Natalie had told me to tip at least five dollars for the ride, which the rupees equaled.

The driver nodded in appreciation, unloaded my luggage, and smiled again. "This way," he said.

We walked into the pale blue lobby with a Buddha at its center. Offerings of fruit lay at the statue's base. I paused and smiled, then followed the driver to the check-in desk. I signed the paperwork. The young man carried my things to a third-floor room. He opened my door, and I thanked him. Patiently, he waited for me to tip him an additional twenty rupees, then quietly shut the door. I collapsed onto the bed and immediately fell asleep.

I woke up cold. The air conditioning was on. Half asleep, I fiddled with the switch to turn the unit off. Congratulating myself upon completing this task, I lugged my bag onto the bed, brought out a nightgown, then ran the shower. I hung onto the sink to get over the bathtub's edge and finally felt water run over every aching muscle in my body. Afterward, I took another half a Vicodin as the sun began its journey into yet another day. I thought it still might be May 13, though I was unsure.

I woke from a deep sleep to my phone buzzing; it was Natalie from Matipokhara. Reality struck home. I was exhausted and I wondered if I could manage the bus steps. I took a deep breath and read her text.

Chapter 12 His Hat

> (NATALIE) Welcome to Kathmandu!
>
> (ME) Thank you. Looking forward to meeting you soon!
>
> (NATALIE) I'm leaving for Sangla tomorrow—but I will be here to hug you hello. Dexa Aha, new hosp. dir. will take excellent care of you. How are you feeling?
>
> (ME) Great! Got lost in Seoul airport, but I am here. Himalayas incredible!
>
> (NATALIE) Wonderful! Ravi will meet you at the bus station. 10:35 a.m. Same as we planned. He's an old guy in a hat, but he's tall. Has your picture. Get on the bus even if you don't see him at the station—he's always late. But carries through. Haha

I TEXTED BACK WITH A SMILEY EMOTICON and thanked Natalie twice. I prayed the old doctor guy would show up at the bus station—another stranger to meet. Natalie didn't say what kind or color of hat he would wear. Why can't I ask such a simple question? I struggled with that thought. He was responsible for me meeting my father. I probably should have gotten him a gift of some kind. Well, it was too late for that. Should I call him Ravi or Dr. Jones? My anxiety level escalated. Should I hold up a sign with his name on it like the hotel driver had? He knew what I looked like from a photo Jack gave him.

Even though I had plenty of time, I scrambled into a pair of khakis, a blue linen tunic, and sandals. I stared at my Keen boots. Jack told me to bring them, but my sandals offered freedom to my swollen feet and ankles; I ached in every conceivable part of my body. Natalie had asked how I felt? And I said, "Great!" I had a credibility issue there. But I did feel great about being here, yet fear rippled through me. The last hours—how many hours—I couldn't say—brought the reality of travel to me—clobbered me with reality. Airports processed me like cheese, and the physicality and mere strength travel required were beyond me. The soul of my identity lay in a little neighborhood high on a bluff far away. It scared me to be so alone. I wanted to go home with no new names to try to sort. My only possessions were those I carried, which were too heavy. Why had I given everything away? Thankfully, Jack had most of my poetry and other writings that I had given him, along with my mother's letter and books. No one knew that I had booked a one-way ticket. What the hell had I in mind? A sweet cottage next to my father's, on a cloud my mother painted when I was a kid?

Fears blossomed and bore fruit: What if Dr. Jones did not materialize? Or I got on the wrong bus? At the end of the bus ride to Pokhara, we were to be met by car for the last leg to Matipokhara. If we missed that connection, it meant a two-hour walk to the hospital. I stared at my aching feet and threw a pair of socks and my walking shoes into my shoulder bag—there was no way I could manage all this shit I had decided to take with me. And I failed big time; I realized because I did not ask Natalie what I could bring to the hospital that, they might need. Jesus, girl, you gave them a thousand dollars—but that was not in the spirit of a gift from a guest—I should have asked Jack what to bring, and now it was too late.

I brushed my hair into a ponytail and put on lip gloss, but the foreboding hung on. Jack came to mind. I decided to text him: "Hey Jack," I said, "—on the way to see Natalie—any messages to convey?"

That made me feel better—I hoped he'd write an inspiring message back. The jalousie window blinds remained shut. I felt safer with them closed. Dressed and packed, I lay on the bed with a pillow under my knees and stared at my phone. Simultaneously, thoughts about dying in strange, remote places danced the boogaloo in my imaginings, far less romantic here than when I considered the possibility in La Conner. I wished, to God, I was going home to my red house above the slough.

Jack's response made me nervous.

(JACK) Ravi might be late. Please be careful and ask for help when you need it. How are you doing?

(ME) FINE.

(JACK) If you are *really* fine after a 20-hour flight day, you're the only one who ever was.

(ME) I'm a little tired, and I haven't eaten yet. Hotel is nice.

(JACK) Commendable! I mean it. You get grumpy when you don't eat. Be sure to have breakfast, and if you feel dodgy and tired, that's natural. Ravi's a doc—so if you have any probs, let him know.

And he sent a smiley-faced emoticon as punctuation. I laughed a little and squeezed my phone, but I was worried. A bus ride across Nepal on vertical roads and sharp turns with cerebral palsy, swollen feet, and a bad back—what the hell could go wrong? The old joke made me laugh. For better or worse, I was about to find out.

To dispel the trajectory of my thoughts, I opened the blinds to a cobblestone courtyard. "Hello, day!" I said from the small balcony. A poinsettia tree, abundant in red bloom, caught my attention. Nearby, a woman sat on a white bench reading a tour book.

Despite the lovely visage of a Mary Cassatt painting just outside my window, my mind kept wandering back to the pertinent question of the hour: *What the hell am I doing?*

Jack was right—I needed to eat. I decided to find the restaurant I saw advertised in the lift the night before. The least I could do was to have a last meal. I laughed aloud at my inner drama. "Food," I whispered to the room as I left.

Sunlight beamed through a rooftop skylight straight above the stairway that led to the lobby. The lift was next to the stairs, and downstairs, I recognized the hotel desk where I had registered the night before. Small chairs abutted an area by the floor-to-ceiling windows. Tourists: men in cotton shirts and khaki shorts joined women in cropped pants, skirts, and t-shirts. The procession of travelers wound its way to breakfast. I was the caboose.

A buffet breakfast bar loomed ahead. It was always a balancing act, holding onto the plate with my weak hand, then serving said plate with my left. My wrist could not bear much weight, so I always had to be quick. I hustled to fill a plate of fruit, pancakes, and yogurt, and along with coffee, I sat down at a garden-side table and began eating. While dining, a kind waiter refreshed my coffee cup, and as I left, he brought me a bottle of water that I would save for the bus ride.

I checked my messages when I returned to my room to get my things together for the bus station. Nothing from Jack; this was all right. He had wished me well. My nerves were edgy as I wrote the bus station's name on a piece of paper for the driver and then the name of my destination on another slip of paper.

"So long beautiful hotel in Kathmandu," I said to the hotel as I waited outside for a taxi. I promised myself I would go home for good after the reunion with my father.

The people on the streets blurred. The stink of poverty surrounded me as the taxi wheeled into view. The driver did not have all his teeth, but his smile was engaging and friendly. The taxi we were in was a three-wheeler. We agreed on two-hundred-seventy-five rupees for the ride, which I paid ahead. I held on as the driver wove in and out around trucks, buses, and little lost dogs.

Ratnapark Bus Station: The Bus Park. Rain slapped the sidewalk as I engineered my luggage inside the station, and after perusing faces that might belong to Dr. Jones, I checked the time and headed to a ticket booth. The rain continued to fall. Where had the sunshine gone? I handed the ticket man the paper with Pokhara-Matipokhara written in evenly printed English. "I made the reservation online," I said, "for Maya Margarita Moore." I wondered if he understood any English. He said nothing. I thought he probably hated dealing with Americans, and I felt embarrassed that I did not know any Nepali languages.

The ticket agent consulted his computer, punched on some keys, and a document came out of his printer, which he stamped and not once asked me for identification. He handed me the ticket. "Your bus leaves now. Through that door, number fifty-eight." I was unsure whether he meant that the door or the bus was so numbered, but I followed the man's index finger and got outside to a lineup of coaches.

One bus was accepting passengers. I went over to it and showed the driver's assistant my ticket.

He nodded in reply. "Heavenly Peaks Run."

I pushed a few rupees into his open palm, then maneuvered my gear and myself on board. From the vantage point of the aisle, I studied every face, and no one fit Dr. Jones's description. No tall old doctors with hats on this bus. The driver's assistant asked if something was wrong. I told him I was meeting a friend. The assistant pointed to the closest seat and said, "Sit memsahib. Sit. The bus must leave now."

I sat. I looked out the window at people coming toward the bus, hoping that Dr. Jones was among them. The engine was on, and I tried to settle in. Somehow, I had thrust my hard case into the bin overhead. My watermelon bag filled my lap. Why hadn't I worn the walking shoes? I shook my head at the thought. With my feet this swollen, I doubted I could get into them. Sandals were more forgiving. I watched the last few passengers as they trundled down the aisle. An old Tibetan woman with a time-worn face sat next to me. She wore a traditional ankle-length dress called a *chuba* with a roughly woven green and purple cotton jacket over a striped patchwork apron called a *pangden*. In the old days, I had read, only married women wore the *pangden*; the colors and design of the patchwork squares indicated the wearer's village and region. I wondered where she was born.

Wherever this day took me, I was here, in this woman's land. I peered at her in revelation. She was my lodestar. I would be fine, and then I would be home. I am here. I smiled at the woman beside me. How awesome that I was on a bus going somewhere in Nepal!

The driver's assistant interrupted my thoughts. He spoke to the old lady. She giggled and walked behind the aide and into another seat closer to the front. A man appeared in the aisle and asked if I was Jack's friend, Maya. He spoke beautiful English.

I expected an old fellow. What I didn't expect was Ravi Jones. Ravi's chiseled cheekbones and bright eyes accentuated a full mouth. His thick black hair was interwoven with gray and banded back and tucked inside a topi, a hat worn by many Nepali men. His was a faded flower design, perhaps a favorite, and fitted his head neatly. He wore Western jeans and a loose white shirt. Although he was older, he moved agilely. Ravi smelled like cedar and soap and sunshine. I was captivated.

The driver shifted gears with a resounding crunch and eased the vehicle out of the bus park and through the confusing streets of Kathmandu as if nothing extraordinary had just happened.

Occasionally, I have what I call a "knowing," an instant understanding. I kept focusing on Ravi's hat. I had seen it before, sometime long ago, or in a dream.

"I swear we have met; something about you feels familiar," Ravi said.

"Weird, because when I saw your hat, I think I recognized it."

"My hat?" Ravi's eyes lit up. "I always wear it when I go to Matipokhara." He offered me a mint from a small decorative tin and took one himself. "So, you recognized my hat?"

I bit into the mint, which burst into a flavorful punch. "I had no idea what you'd look like—Natalie said (and I think Jack said the same) that you were an old guy in a hat. Your hat, I swear I've seen it before. Or you?" I blushed. "I didn't think you would be, you know . . ." I was going to say "sexy as hell" but blanched at admitting such a thought. "You know, as young as you obviously are. And in jeans. I thought you would be old . . . old." My voice dropped. *Just shut up*, I thought.

Ravi laughed. "I think I am complimented?" He stretched a little. "I apologize for my delay. I was hoping we could have caught a lift on the supply truck." He tapped the armrest. "They were to meet us at the bus park. I don't know where they are. I am glad you made it through the crowds and onto the bus."

"I was scared I'd get on the wrong one. The driver's assistant said this was the Heavenly Run, and I think that is the one that meets a jeep in Pokhara to take us to Matipokhara."

"Yes," Ravi said. "The problem is the supply truck would take us directly to the hospital and takes less time. Where the bus drops us, we will have a steep walk."

"That'll be OK," I lied. I pushed my swollen feet as far under the seat as I could.

"You will learn everything is a 'maybe' in transportation around here. How have your travels been so far?"

"Just finding my way through airports, you know?"

"I certainly do."

The bus stopped, and the driver came over to Ravi. They conferred for a moment, and Ravi stood, gathered his shoulder bag, and said, "That truck I was talking about—the driver just talked to ours, and they will pick us up here. Bless them. It will be much smoother and quicker to the hospital."

"All right, and thank you for taking me along. Are you sure they have room?"

"Of course."

I reached for my train case, and Ravi intervened, brought the bag down, and headed for the door. As we stood in front of a rundown hotel, the Pokhara bus, on its heavenly run, jammed its way into traffic, and off it went. I didn't see a truck anywhere.

Chapter 13 Use my Head, Then my Hand

"And there it is. On-time!" Ravi whooped, one arm waving at another imaginary truck.

I laughed at the joke. We played a spontaneous game of fake truck sightings for thirty minutes and counting. We had only been in front of the hotel a few minutes when Ravi pointed down the street and shouted, "See! The truck. And in good time."

I jumped to attention, "Really?"

The truck zoomed by, leaving the smell of diesel.

Ravi shrugged. "Sadly, no."

I stared down the road, and, in the distance, I saw smoke belching from a vehicle. "Is that the truck?"

Again, a truck lumbered on. Ravi shook his head. "Sadly, no."

We then paused between pronouncements of glee that our truck had arrived. Then one of us would point to a taxi or a bicycle or even, one time, a fellow carrying a wardrobe on his back to exclaim, "There it is, the truck!" The refrain remained consistent: "Sadly, no."

The city street wheezed with traffic, so we had many fake sightings, but Ravi was genuinely optimistic that the truck would be here "very soon." I hoped he was right.

"Wow! Look at my luggage compared to yours," I said. The lineup was impressive. My watermelon bag stuck out. Slouched next to it was my traveling purse. It housed my tablet, camera, connectors, a pen and notebook, a change purse, a copy of *The Connected Traveler* and a water bottle. Outside the bag, individual pockets held my passport and a paperback novel. My red train case centered on the display. In comparison, Ravi's single-shoulder bag nested beside the others. It was big enough for a laptop, identification, and probably lunch.

"Just how long were you expecting to be gone?" Ravi asked.

"You know? I don't know, but I really took too much crap." I shook my head as I eyed the roadway for the truck. "Everything I own."

"What?" Ravi cocked his head towards me.

"Don't ask," I answered. "I think I got carried away cleaning out the old house." I shrugged, "This is it."

"You travel very lightly, then," Ravi said.

"From how my shoulders feel, I think I could have gone lighter." Meanwhile, I noticed the pocket that should contain my ID was empty. I had the passport out at the bus station, but the ticket man never asked to see any identification. I feared that I had forgotten it. After flipping through the contents of my bag, I pulled out my passport and held it in the air, exhaling a sigh of relief. I noticed Ravi watching me, so I explained, "My passport—thought I might have left it on the ticket counter." I returned my identification to its proper pocket.

"I share your relief!" He wiped his forehead to show his solidarity. "In your search, I noticed you are extremely left-handed."

"You can say that again!" A flock of birds sailed down and lit on the roadway attacking food scraps and other debris while a group of people, a woman in a red sari and a man with a ball cap, trailed behind uniformed children on a school outing. A motor scooter passed them, scattering the birds. Bell sounds permeated the air. "Jack said he told you that I have cerebral palsy." I averted eye contact. The street seemed louder. I hadn't wanted to admit what was all too obvious; something was wrong with me. "I have learned that there is usually a walk-around to do almost anything except for doing the limbo. And in second grade, a boy broke his leg. The kids took turns trying his crutches out. I fell flat on my face." I laughed at the memory. "But for ordinary living, there's usually a couple of ways to go about things." I took a breath and peered up at Ravi, who stood inches from me.

"Name two things you walk around?" That grin again; I wanted to touch him. I thought he was the most handsome man.

"Well, uh, when I cut my meat, I stick a fork in it with my left hand, then I hold the fork down with my right and cut the meat with my left." I laughed. "It's a neat trick." Two small boys chased each other, rounding us in figure eights, and took off giggling. "And, when I file my nails, I place the emery board in my right hand and move my left-handed nails around it." A brick wall divided the sidewalk from the hotel property. I pointed to it. "Walls become a third hand; I can lean against one to tie my shoes or steady my gait. When computers became popular, I soon realized that if I were patient enough, I could find another way to fix a problem when I got stuck. Computers are beautifully logical. I guess CP taught me that there're additional ways to do something if I'm patient. Use my head and then my hand."

"'Use my head, then my hand' that's sage advice for anyone." Ravi's held his index finger to his lips. "Shh," he whispered, "A butterfly just landed on your shoulder. Not surprising. Aw. He flew away."

A black butterfly, with red and gold markings, wove its way upwards into the sky. "I feel honored," I said. "What kind of butterfly was he?"

"Called a Krishna peacock. And you should feel honored. The butterfly tells me that you have an exceptional ability to enjoy the simple wonders of life, but I saw that first when you were smiling at the old woman on the bus. I am so lucky to make your acquaintance."

Was he talking to me of slick repartee? "Well, I think butterflies like salt on the skin, right?"

"That butterfly had lots of choices. You said you felt honored. Do you believe in signs like that?"

"Oh, God, yes," I answered. "I wouldn't be here if I wasn't following all the signs given me."

"Tell me," Ravi said. "We can speak candidly here, just not on buses, hotels, or the Internet."

"You know about the suitcase in the attic and the sunstone," I began, "then Yeshe Maya's death, her dying words were 'go' and 'father' –set things in motion in ways I could not imagine." After relaying the trip to the Bay area, the calendar, Penni-P's death, and Jack's announcement about selling his house, I realized I had spilled much of my life onto the sidewalk as we waited for the truck. "Forgive me for going on like that," I said. "We call that verbal diarrhea."

"I asked, and I want you to know that Yeshe Maya was a powerful force; she shaped the lives of many."

"Why is this place across the Saraswati River so secretive?"

"Sangam is like the headquarters of the largest lending library in the world. It lends prayers instead of books. And the people who live there see the outside world as a distraction from their work."

"Anyone can pray anywhere, right?" I thought about my prayer closet, Rosaries to the Holy Mother.

"Sure," Ravi said, "but prayers and direct communication with the spirit world are possible once across the Saraswati. People there pray for the planet. Your father is the patron and librarian, a holy man."

"A holy librarian? There's a literal library—you weren't being metaphorical?"

"Oh, yes; a library like no other. You will see," Ravi paused and shook his head. "I cannot believe I am talking to his daughter. You were a surprise to most of us."

"He was a surprise to me. I had no idea he was alive, even his name. My mother kept all that quiet; she painted a mural on my wall that featured a fairy prince riding on a cloud when I was a child. For me, that was my father."

"You never did a DNA search for him?"

"By the time Mother died, I was in my sixties, so I figured he had to be dead. Were there brothers or sisters? I wished them love, but I wasn't interested in the odd family reunion. Jack has been my brother since we were kids; he's the only family I needed. So long story short, I wasn't interested in DNA. I liked the flying prince on my wall."

"You lived in a protected bubble," Ravi said.

"You're not the first person telling me that," I said with a grin. "This place, Sangam, Jack calls it, is it connected to Mt. Kailash?"

"Yes. You know about Mt. Kailash?"

"Oh, yeah. My mother told me about Mt. Kailash being the center of the earth since I was a little kid. And I've arm-chaired traveled and done imaginary circuits around the holy mountain. Watched dozens of times."

Ravi checked the road to see if the truck was coming, then glanced at his phone for messages. "You took what Jack told you about the region's geography and the proximity of Kailash and put the location together?"

"There've been all these stories about tunnels under Kailash; that's not new. What's new is that they might be true."

"They are," Ravi said. "You are in for the reunion of your life."

"God, does my father dress like Motu? I saw him in a video taking these rich dudes to someplace in Nepal to peek at Kailash. These guys paid over sixty grand to go on a thirteen-day trip. And Motu Amul's ashram was like bling-central."

"That man is the antithesis of your father. Motu spent a week at the hotel—he wanted to buy it. More groups; more money. I gave him a flat no."

"Jack told me about that. As for my father, I feel dissociated. This whole experience is unreal, unlike anything I ever conjured."

Ravi patted me on my shoulder. "I see a likeness between you and your father; meeting him will change your life."

I nodded.

A monkey discarded a banana peeling from high up in a palm tree across the street. The flock of birds reappeared and dashed away as a truck grounded to a halt in front of us, no fake sightings this time.

The driver hopped out of the converted bus. The front sported rows of seats ending with a homemade metal plate fitted across the back of the sixth row. The bus's rear stretched into an open flatbed, with all the supplies strapped down. A tarp secured the haul. Ravi piled my stuff with the rest. He kept his case and my purse containing my papers and passport and returned to where I waited on the sidewalk. My shoulders were relieved of duty, and I felt better without the additional weight.

With no steps to enter the vehicle, I was at a momentary loss about how I would board. Ravi jumped in, turned towards me, and lifted me inside. Had we done this before? Another lifetime?

"Well, that was easy," I said. "Thanks."

"Happy to assist." He gestured towards the seats. "Take any you like; I think we are the only passengers today."

I realized that I might be acting as if we were a couple, and the thought embarrassed me. I said, "Oh, sure," and chose a seat in the last row while Ravi spoke to the driver.

On the truck's floor sat a bin of water bottles near a box of oranges and another box with bagged macadamia nuts. Hospital supplies, I imagined. I peered at Ravi as he continued his conversation with the driver. Ravi was an asked-for escort, not a date; I shook my head. He seemed so familiar. Weird, I thought. What was this meeting going to be like with my father? He was French, not Tibetan, and yet was the patron? How did that happen? I turned my attention to the street outside as the truck pushed out into traffic.

Ravi turned away from the driver. "You should come up in front, better sightseeing," he said. "Take a water, and will you bring me one, too?"

The loneliness vanished. However, I realized managing two water bottles would be difficult in a careening vehicle, so I took one and moved down the aisle toward Ravi. I handed him the water bottle and took a window seat. He sat by me.

"I apologize," he said quietly, "I failed to see that you cannot carry two water bottles at the same time, and yet you gave me the one you were able to carry. I am impressed. And thankful."

"Who said it was for you?" I giggled— "I'm teasing now. Of course, the water's for you. Like you said, extremely left-handed."

Ravi got up without a word and brought back water bottles and two oranges in a small box that he placed in the empty seats across from us. "Any time you need something, only ask." He smiled. "You make cerebral palsy look easy. And I must say, with limitations on your right side, you have chosen an interesting culture to explore." Ravi peeled the orange into one piece and tossed the skeleton into the box. He gave me half of the orange.

"I do that, too." The orange was sweet and warm on my tongue. "Try to peel the orange into as few pieces as possible," I said between bites. "Tell me, what makes an overly left-handed woman a curiosity in Nepal?"

Ravi ate an orange segment, then answered, "In Nepal, people use their right hand to eat and their left hand for other matters."

"I use my left hand for all matters," I said.

"Oh, that creates a terrible picture." Ravi shook his head in mock despair.

"Why?"

"People wipe their bottoms with their left hand in the countryside, especially. And use the right hand only to eat."

"Oh, my God. Are you kidding me?"

"No!"

"You mean no toilet paper?" I asked.

"Yes!"

His amusement made me laugh. "And people will think I am dirty or something because I am left-handed?"

"Expect prejudice and accept compassion and let both go." His laugh was so good-natured. "I love that look of surprise on your face!"

I furrowed my brow. "I brought a roll of toilet paper just in case."

"You came prepared."

"I've been concerned about the squat toilets, but I thought the hospital would have Western ones."

"They have both," Ravi answered.

"Like you said, an interesting culture to explore."

"With both hands," Ravi said. "When we stop, there will only be squat toilets. I will find a woman to help you out. Just telling you ahead of time. You seem to worry a lot—" Ravi opened a water bottle and handed it to me.

As I reached over to receive the water, I was never so self-conscious about using my left hand. "Thanks," I murmured under my breath.

"Did you happen to bring a wrist brace?" Ravi asked. "Or walking stick?"

"Nope."

"We will find something suitable at the hospital. You will find a cane useful, especially in Sangla. Where you are going, nothing is level. People will change their expectations if they see you in a wrist brace. You really should be wearing one when you handle luggage." He drank water.

"Yes, I should've thought of that," I said. "Can I ask you something?"

"Certainly."

"What do normal left-handers do here?" I asked.

"They find it much easier to wipe their bottoms."

"And harder to eat?"

"And harder to eat . . ." Ravi echoed. "Did you prepare for your vacation before leaving home?"

"Not in preparation, exactly," I laughed. "But I sprained my sacroiliac joint a few months back, and it turned out to be a blessing. My doctor suggested I do something like chair yoga to regain my strength and increase my balance. Have you heard of that?"

"Yes, yes, I have," Ravi answered. "Yoga is an excellent choice."

"I found a program on YouTube—hour long—and I began practicing. I'm getting good, too!"

The bus bounced and bounded across the road as we veered around a hairpin curve. Rocks skirted one side of the narrow lane, and God resided on the other. "Is this usual?" I asked. "The way he's driving?"

"No. I will have words with him. He is trying to make up for time."

At the front of the bus, Ravi spoke quietly to the driver.

"Whatever you said, it appears to have worked," I said when Ravi returned.

He shrugged. "I told him to slow down."

I laughed. "The direct approach," I said. "So, tell me why you are going to the hospital."

"We have new computers and software to install, and I'm introducing Dexa to the system."

"And Natalie leaves tomorrow?"

"Yes. Natalie has been at Matipokhara for five years, an intense job. She's moving in with Jack and looking forward to quieter days."

"What kind of problems do they see at the hospital?"

"A lot of mending—broken bones and farm accidents. But we have a growing group of NCDs." Ravi leaned into the seat. "Do you know what that is?"

Our driver skidded around another truck and quickly turned onto the street leading out of a roadside village. Truck horns blared. "No," I answered, clinging to the armrest. I bit my bottom lip to keep myself from complaining. "You were saying about NCDs?"

"NCD stands for noncommunicable diseases. The hospital is developing outreach in villages to treat diabetes, lung, and heart disease. Some of the programs in this software tutor volunteers in outreach."

"You are the IT guy?"

"Roughly speaking." Ravi laughed at the job description. "Mostly, I'm at home, talking to the monkeys outside my window." Ravi finished his water, squashed the plastic bottle in one squeeze, and then lobbed it into the box across from us.

"You were born?" I asked.

"Apparently." A grin flashed across his face. "In Delhi. My dad was an American missionary, and my mother was Indian, a doctor by profession. I went to medical school at UC San Francisco on scholarship." He rubbed the back of his neck. "Were you an excellent student?"

"I did pretty well," I admitted. "English lit. major. The first year was tough at the University of Washington. I nearly flunked out. I protested the war—you know—Viet Nam—and I was homesick." I nudged Ravi's arm with my elbow. "How'd you like the Bay Area?"

"Study and surfing. I protested the war, too. Tried psychedelics. A student of the times."

"Once, on break, Jack gave me a tab of LSD, and I protested the war in sixty-eight and sixty-nine. Hell, man, I'm road-tested."

He laughed. "Do you believe in the soul?"

What a weird question from someone you've just met. "Everything has a soul. And I didn't necessarily pick that up from the acid Jack gave me. It's a knowing. Trees in the woods talk to each other. I think there was a study about that."

"So, you are an animist?"

"A Christian animist quasi-Buddhist, sayer of the Rosary, and open for the experience of relating to—I don't know?"

Ravi sighed. "You are your father's child. Tell me about the trees talking to each other?"

"Trees share a network of roots that mingle. They share water and notions about coming droughts, like giving each other distress signals. Natural things, of course, communicate. And are just as likely, therefore, to have souls as I am, or you are. They just talk in a language we don't understand." I studied the contours of rocks and broken pavement outside the window. "I saw a documentary about it."

"And your version of heaven?"

"Includes rocks and slugs."

"And you do believe in heaven?"

"Absolutely. But does it matter? This moment outside. When I saw the Himalayas flying into Kathmandu, I WAS in heaven—forgot all about how exhausted I was; it just filled me with the living beauty of those mountains."

"And God was there?" Ravi asked.

"Well, you asked what I believe. And I believe God is always along for the ride. And occasionally, if we are lucky, we get to see the totality of the world, and the beauty then is astounding."

"Do you think you must accept that evil is at work in the world to see the world's goodness? It's beauty?" Ravi stretched his arm over the top of my seat.

"Yes." I quivered slightly as the driver sounded the air horn at a truck coming straight at us. The over-packed vehicle swerved around us. Two men clung to the top of the load. "Wow, that was close," I said.

"Do you think this truck ride is evil or good?"

"I think it is a truck ride." I laughed.

Ravi laughed, too. "You know, Buddhists don't believe in souls."

"Well, they believe in spirit; that's like a second cousin. Right?"

"Where have you been all my life?" Ravi burst into happy laughter. "You are exactly right."

I rolled my eyes and mimicked: "Where have you been all my life?"

"An old come-on line," Ravi said. "But honestly, you make me wonder."

"Well, I was in a small town for most of my life. As you know."

"You were always meant to travel." He patted my knee, stood, then took an unopened water bottle to the driver.

"Did you take philosophy in college?" Ravi asked as he sat back down.

"A minor. Did you?"

"Double major," Ravi said. "Philosophy and pre-med. My mother, the doctor, wanted me grounded in humanism before attending med school. I loved it. And science, too."

Our conversation went from philosophy back to boomer politics. We drew comparisons between Seattle and San Francisco in the nineteen-sixties, and we chatted about Abbe Hoffman, the Seattle Seven, the Seattle Liberation Front, and the Students for a Democratic Society. We agreed violence was never a solution to anything. The US election was in November, and we both looked forward to the first elected woman president.

As we entered the Kathmandu Valley, Ravi pointed to rice paddies etched into the valley's steep sides. The roof of a distant red teahouse shone in a ray of sunlight. Our driver blasted his horn, then passed a woman driving a tractor.

"Did you see that flower vase on the tractor's dash?" I asked. I turned forward, and a truck burned rubber as it raced towards us head-on. More horns blasted, and both drivers applied their air brakes; with a screech, we were back in our lane. "So, how many people die on this road a year?" I asked.

Ravi shouted something in Nepali to the driver. The driver punched the air and nodded.

"What did you say?" I asked.

"I said, 'Congratulations, we all lived today!'"

"Don't encourage him . . ." My sweaty hand clung to the armrest.

Ravi patted my hand. "We will live."

Finally, the truck/bus stopped for a toilet break. Westerners from a tour bus picnicked on the side of the road. I noticed how laden they were with cameras and bags, and I felt less like a tourist and more like I belonged here. Ravi led me to the toilets behind the tea house, a rude storefront with a rickety porch. Two women sat on their haunches as their children played. Ravi said something to them, and the younger woman rose and nodded at me.

"Hold onto her with your right hand, and don't touch anything. Everyone pees on their shoes when they're rookies."

With cerebral palsy, sometimes muscles seize and spasm, and sometimes when you want to pee, you can't. At least, this had been my experience.

As I followed this woman to the toilet, I prayed that my muscles and bladder would be relaxed and in agreement. I did as Ravi advised, and everything went well. The stench from the toilet was awesome in its putridity. The woman nodded and smiled as we left the restroom. Ravi was there to collect me, with some rupees for my helper. I gave him a thumb's up.

The motion of the bus and the afternoon heat made me sleepy as we journeyed on. Ravi was shocked that I did not know how to play chess. As he explained the game, I put my head back on the seat and fell asleep. I woke up with Ravi's head on my shoulder. He had dozed off, as well. The scent of sunlight all about him and this incredible ride across Nepal lent another knowing; I was as happy as I ever hoped to be, anywhere.

Chapter 14 Sharp Edges and Steep inclines

THE TRUCK/BUS STOPPED, and the empty water bottles, orange rinds, and wrappers jostled in the box across from us. I surveyed outside the bus. Shit. Another set of stairs. I didn't know if I could stand, let alone climb worn stone stairs at an angle that might challenge a goat. What do old people do here? I wondered. An elderly woman in a light purple-flowered sari descended the stairs. The woman's scarf revealed thin gray strands of hair fallen over a deeply lined forehead. So, that's what they do. I felt compelled to perform. Somehow, I had to try to make climbing these steep stairs appear natural, normal-like. Inside I cringed. My stomach tightened with stress.

"Time to stretch. And there's sunlight; we made good time," Ravi said. "Watch your step." He grabbed the refuse box across from us and moved to the exit.

My right foot was asleep. A zip line of pain extended from my left hip to my left foot. I needed to take half of a pain pill. Only half—I never overdid it. I didn't think I could stand straight after the six hours inside the truck.

"You haven't said a word, you OK?" Ravi turned as I stumbled-stood with a hand on the seats on either side of me.

"I might need some help getting out of here." I begged my voice not to ring with the panic rooting in my belly. I didn't belong here; soon, Ravi would see how weak I was.

Ravi jumped from the truck to the ground and extended his hand. "There you go." He lifted me down. "Aw, look. Here comes Natalie."

I saw only a blur of light race down those many steps. Natalie's red hair could not be contained in the barrette doing its best at the top of her head, and her smile appeared too large for her face. A splash of freckles danced across her nose; her glasses hung on a glass-beaded thong around her neck. She greeted us both with open arms and hugs. "Namaste," she said. "Brilliant that you two managed to find one another!" She shook her head. "Jack won the bet. Ten dollars and a foot massage."

"What was the bet?" I asked.

"Jack said you would find one another; he claimed 'kismet.'" Her laugh filled the air. "I bet that you, Maya, would be the efficient, responsible person Jack described and be at the bus station and on the bus. And that you, Ravi, would miss the bus altogether." She shrugged. "Kismet wins." She shook her head, and strands of curls popped out of the barrette. "I'm glad to see you, Ravi. It's been a busy day. The computer finally gave up altogether. And Dexa is in surgery on her first day. An emergency with more to follow. An appendectomy—I would have done, but Dexa wanted me free to greet you."

Natalie was a mountain breeze on a spring morning. I knew that Jack must be in love with her. I'd only been here a few minutes, and I was smitten. Her green eyes sparkled, and that hair, nothing would contain it. She wore a cinnamon-colored wrap-dress and the same sneakers I had seen in the photos. The woman glowed. Her energy reminded me of my mother's—carefree, elegant, and exuberant. My mother once said, "Love wins out if you allow it. The trick is to allow it." I was happy for Jack.

Natalie said, "I'll get Ronny to help." She dashed to the top of the stairs, and I heard her yell his name. She darted back down with Ronny, a tall thin man with gray hair, accompanied by two younger men.

The road feathered into a pasture where I hoped I'd see a yak. Instead, I saw a bent old woman dressed in faded yellow, carrying a load of straw in a large basket on her back. She seemed the only beast of burden. I wished she had a yak to help her out. I leaned against the side of the truck and peered upwards. Beyond the stairs would be the hospital, and three hundred feet upwards was the village of Matipokhara. I knew all this from the photos and emails I had exchanged with Natalie.

Everyone began to unload and sort boxes. I figured the ones wrapped in coolant aluminum material were drugs of some sort. Bins of oranges and flats of bottled water, macadamia nuts, applesauce, first aid supplies— splints and bandages—and a crate of melons, all of the supplies lay on the road. Three new computers lay on the side of the road with DONATED in red print across the top of each box. Ronny and the other workers carried the freight to the hospital. A train of human endeavor. Hand to hand.

My feet throbbed. When I looked at how swollen and purple they appeared, I wondered if I could walk. My body found small comfort in the rounded front of the bug-splattered vehicle, but it held me up. Could I stand on my own? That was a good question. The nine-thousand-foot altitude on a tired oxygen-depleted body had made an impression.

Ravi was busy organizing equipment, goods, and medical supplies. He heaved boxes, helped load them up, wiped his forehead, and laughed with the workers. I admired his lean body and undeniable strength.

The stairs formed a specter in my mind, a harbinger of what I could not do—climb them. Overwhelmed and in amazement at the agility of the workers and this doctor, I wished I might be boxed and carried up those frightening steps.

Ravi came around with an opened bottle of water. "Drink this," he said. "We nearly have everything off the truck. How are you doing?"

I gulped some water, and a little dribbled down my chin. "Tired." I shook my head. "A little dizzy."

"And jet-lagged as hell." Ravi rolled his shoulders back and stretched. "Oxygen is thin up here. We're almost three kilometers high. Can cause all kinds of symptoms."

"Before anything else, a little rest," Natalie said as she joined us. "Are you OK on the stairs?"

"I'm going to need help." I began to cry.

"Why the tears?" Natalie's arm stretched around me.

"Stairs are hard for me." I wiped my nose and mouth on a tissue Natalie handed me. "I hate to admit it."

"May I escort you?" Ravi offered his hand.

"And I will lead the way!" Natalie said. One of the helpers, hefting all my bags, Ravi's backpack, and two boxes, came up from behind, circled us, and then disappeared up the steps.

Ravi slipped his arm around my waist, "Fifty-two steps. It will go with a click of fingers."

My stomach tightened. I clung to Ravi, afraid to look down and determined not to show any more fear. I set my eyes on Natalie, who glowed as the sun shifted in the heavens. A deep frustration threatened to darken the bright afternoon. I felt inadequate, weak, and despaired at being dependent on the good graces of others. *What the hell am I doing here in a world of sharp edges, steep inclines, and stairs?* I longed for my old house with Penni-P in my lap and Jack's light on next door. No, I fairly screamed to myself. That's gone. What had Carol said about a house only being a building with a number on the front of it? She was right about that, but the conflict remained. Better said, the grief remained.

"Keep your eyes upwards," Ravi said. "Here we go."

Natalie chatted in front of us. "Jack said the Holland tulips arrived!"

"You can plant them yourself!" Ravi answered.

I tripped over an uneven step.

Ravi's grip tightened.

"Sorry," I said.

"No apologies necessary. These steps need straightening. Next year perhaps," Ravi said. "A railing, too."

"Yes," Natalie chimed. "Next year. Dr. Aha is aware of the problem. The tulips were for Jack. A housewarming."

"We grew up with them," I said. "God, I would have brought some from home."

"You couldn't because of the restrictions placed on them in customs. I looked into that when you sent me your confirmation details."

"Last stair," Ravi said. "High five."

"Wait until you see the view!" Natalie said. "I will miss it most at sunset."

Son of a bitch, I made it. My body shook in released stress and fatigue. Open-mouthed, I viewed terraced hillsides, fallen in shadow, and edged in sun-brilliant amber. Above, a large bird whistled as it flew over—its outstretched wing redolent with light and the rest of its body in shadow. I pointed skyward. "Wow!" was all I could think to say.

In the distance, footpaths between the village and the hospital braided the backside of the facility. Two small buildings made from reinforced steel and concrete blocks completed the campus. Murals painted over the outside walls led villagers to outpatient services and the hospital proper.

The three of us stood there, Ravi's arm still firmly around me and my arm around him while I held hands with Natalie.

Below us, the workers carried the boxes up the stairs.

"Oh dear, look at your feet!" Natalie said. "No compression socks?"

"Sadly, no."

Ravi laughed. "A good one, Maya. Like this morning when we waited for the transport?"

"Yeah," I said. "I didn't pack what I needed for this trip—and I tried hard to do that."

"We have everything you need here," Natalie said. "You are brave to make this trip."

"I can't thank you enough." My body needed drugs, my arm a brace, and my feet, compression socks, and for balancing myself, I needed a walking stick. I failed to bring any of the latter. I licked my salty lips and involuntarily leaned into Ravi. He didn't mind.

"Let's get you settled first. I think rest and some oxygen before anything else are required," Natalie said. She took one arm and Ravi the other, and the three of us made our way to a dormitory at the rear of the hospital that housed guests and staff. It included a dining room that we passed on the way to my assigned room.

"I have computers to unravel," Ravi said. "I have had a delightful day with you, Maya. Thank you for that." He nodded toward Natalie. "I'm leaving you in excellent hands."

"Thank you for everything," I said

Natalie and I watched him leave. "He used to have my job; did he tell you that?"

"No," I said. "Ravi's an incredible person, isn't he?" We walked down a quiet hall. Some doors were slightly open, and others closed. A peek inside showed the rooms to be living quarters; photographs and desks were prominent.

"A man of many talents." She opened a door. "Here's where you will stay." The small room had an opened, screened window, a small bed with a blue bedspread, and a desk. "I want to get a reading of your oxygen level, so let me grab my bag and a portable unit. Do you have something light to change into?"

"Yeah, I have a cotton nightie."

"You change your clothes, and I'll be back in a jiff."

After changing to a sleeveless gown, I crawled under the blankets; the sheets smelled like sunshine, and I breathed in the quiet. With my watermelon bag under the pillow, my back felt comfortable, and I closed my eyes and immediately dozed off. A rap at the door woke me; Natalie appeared with a bag and a small oxygen unit.

"Good to see you in bed," she said. "What's under your pillow?"

"I can't lie flat," I said, "My bag serves many purposes."

"You lucky girl, the bed's adjustable. You need your feet elevated too." She cranked the bed up at the top and the bottom while I told her how it felt. With the bed adjusted, one slim pillow was perfect.

As she took my blood oximeter reading, I answered her questions about my aching head and fatigue. She took my blood pressure, too.

"Your oxygen level is pretty good. You have mild altitude sickness on top of jet lag, but you don't need oxygen. I think we'll give you paracetamol for your headache; it's an anti-inflammatory. How's your appetite?"

I shrugged. "I don't feel like eating. Sort of a sick feeling."

"I'll give you some promethazine, too. You need to hydrate and rest. I am delighted you'll be here for a week; it will give you time to adjust to the altitude. I'll have Aarti bring you your meds and a light meal, and she will massage your legs, too. That will benefit your circulation—much needed for swollen legs and feet." From her bag, she pulled out a large bottle of water. She poured some into a glass on the nightstand. "Drink this 'til the bottle's all gone, and keep one going at all times."

"I'm such a lot of work," I said. "So sorry."

"No apologies; you have a magnificent heritage, and it is an honor to help you on the way to your reunion. Getting you safely there is our job. Not another word from you about being sorry."

Ronny, the man, who helped with the supplies, arrived with my bags. He gave me a generous smile and left.

"I wish I were stronger, more like Jack," I said.

"And he wishes he had your insights or capacity for contemplation. And I wish you'd both be quiet about all your wishes. We love you as is. Now get some rest."

"Jack's my crazy brother," I said and smiled. "I am so happy he has you and so grateful to be here."

After she left, I thought about my father. Natalie knew about Sangam, and she probably had met him. The words "magnificent heritage" spun in my imaginings. What kind of man was my father? My head felt tight, and although amazed at the sheer miracle of being here, I was worried about what might happen next. What might he think of me? I had to stop crying and being wistful. No one loves a crier.

A knock at the door brought Aarti, a young Nepali nurse bearing a dinner tray and the paracetamol. "Water very important to drink." She unloaded the tray onto a bedside table. "Soup and apples will make you happy," she added. "I'll come back in an hour to treat your legs."

Creamy-corn curry smelled appealing, but I was too tired to eat much other than a few sliced apples. I drank half a liter of water, put my head on the pillow, and drifted to sleep.

I wasn't awake for long when Aarti checked on me again. She insisted I drink more water, then she gently massaged my feet and calves with eucalyptus oil. Before she left with the tray, Aarti adjusted my bed so that my feet were higher than my head.

I got up to get my pain med, took half a Vicodin—a large half—and crawled back into bed. I didn't mention to Natalie that I was taking Vicodin. I didn't think she would approve. Tucked inside a quiet room, I felt safe and secure. And somehow, I had made it up those stairs.

Where am I? I awoke with a jolt. Sweat drenched my pillow, but I was cold; day changed to night outside my window. Oh, the hospital—at Natalie's hospital. My memory jogged to Ravi and that truck ride, and it seemed as if we were old friends, just meeting. *Why had I cried about those stupid stairs?* I picked up my journal and put it down. I attempted to shut the window, but I couldn't make it move, so I changed from my nightgown to a sweatshirt and sweatpants. It was only eight o'clock, but how could I be sure about the time? I didn't think my phone adjusted automatically to time zones in Nepal. It's eight o'clock somewhere, I mused. I tried to go back to sleep. Still awake, I rechecked my phone: an hour had passed. Swollen feet conflicted with a mindset about going for a walk. I pulled the blanket around me and wiggled my toes.

I heard an animal screech through my screened window, maybe a monkey? I sat up. I wasn't going anywhere. Jack was right about the vertical geography, and I felt dizzy. *Perhaps tomorrow, Mr. Monkey.* Lying down, I shut my eyes and tried to meditate myself to sleep—that did not work out well, so I turned my light on to read. I plumped my pillow and opened my reader, but footfalls outside my room diverted my attention.

"Hullo?" Ravi opened the door an inch. "Your light's on. You OK?"

"Hi." I ran my fingers through my hair.

The hall light shone on him. "May I come in?" Ravi asked.

"Sure, I can't sleep."

I sat up, and my Kindle fell to the floor. Tossing the cover aside, I sprung up to retrieve it.

"You're completely dressed!" Ravi said.

"I got cold."

"You want to take a walk?"

"I think I heard a monkey, and I wanted to go see—I would love a little walk."

"That's Aama," Ravi said.

"Maybe Aama will be up!"

"What are you looking for?" Ravi asked.

"My shoes—this room is tiny, but I keep losing things." I leaned over to search under the bed.

"They're here." Ravi pointed to where I had stashed them behind the door. "Your feet are still quite swollen. A walk will be good."

Two small trails of clouds bore light as they played over the valley below us. I breathed in the scent of flowers and welcomed the cool breeze. "What kind of flower is that? Not a rose—but so sweet."

"Called daphne. They have poisonous berries." Ravi extended his arm, and I took it. "The ground is not even; I will be happy to escort you."

"Well, I thank you," I sucked in the night air as if it could save me. "A beautiful night."

"Look this way," Ravi gestured with his free arm. "Just a shadow of Annapurna."

"Oh, my God." The massive mountain left a trace in the deepening twilight—a traveling mist lingered in the distant sky—teasing me. "I've never seen a sky like this or a mountain like that. Like Archangel Michael."

"The Guardian—" He patted my hand. "And a reminder."

"Of what?" I asked.

"That angels are about—"

"And like they're telling us—don't stop believing even when darkness comes." I shook my head.

"What do they have to say about sunrises?" Ravi asked.

"'See. I told you we'd be back.'" I shrugged and pointed to the sky. "Meanwhile, we have a star!"

"That's Mars," Ravi said. The mountain melded into darkness. As he spoke, the sky became a kaleidoscope of stars and planets in varying degrees of brightness, but Mars stood out like a showman in a top hat and pink diamonds. I wanted to hold Ravi's hand and hoped he would reach out to mine, but instead, we stood side by side in quiet awe of the night sky that belonged to Nepal. Ravi then took my arm and guided me along a path from the hospital's front to the back. He matched his step with mine, and the warmth of his body triggered a receptive response in me.

We explored the courtyard, and Ravi showed me where a line of patients would gather in the morning. We strolled under Natalie's window, and then he pointed to a window on the first floor. "Now, do you see the light still in this room?"

"Yes," I said.

"Our VIP suite," Ravi answered.

"Really?" I asked.

"Your room."

I laughed. "I feel better."

For a long moment, Ravi stared at me as if he wanted to speak, then touched the lobe of my ear and said, "Shh. . . Up there," he pointed, "in the crook of the banyan tree—our monkey friend, Aama has gone to bed."

"Does she sleep there every night?" I whispered.

"Yes, and in the morning. Be careful. Aama eats breakfast in bed and throws rinds at anyone close by."

"Like that monkey in Kathmandu?" I laughed. "Another local custom I will remember." I patted his arm with my free hand. "You are an excellent guide."

"A good doctor, too?"

"A good doctor, too."

We walked back in companionable quiet. When we entered the dormitory, Ravi let go of my arm, and at my door, he said, "What a nice walk. Thank you very much." With his index finger, he tapped my lips and gave me a generous smile. "Now, you sleep. And dream."

CHAPTER 15 AND THEN THERE WAS ONE

MY BODY ACHED, but my spirits soared the following day. This pod of guest suites shared shower and toilet rooms down the hall. I was the only visitor, and the wing was quiet as I went to the bath area. The water turned cold after a few minutes, and I finished quickly, shivering as I toweled off in the bright morning light pouring in from the high open windows. After dressing, I brushed my hair into a ponytail and drank water. My head hurt, but I felt better, and the last evening's walk with Ravi made me smile at my reflection. Had he been to Mt. Kailash? Had he ever been married? Hadn't Natalie called our meeting kismet? Oh, so many questions buzzed through my brain. It was going to be a great day, hopefully without stairs.

Aarti arrived with tea, more packets of paracetamol, and two more liters of water. She massaged my calves and feet as I reclined on my bed. "You missed the sendoff this morning," Aarti said sadly. "We will miss Dr. Natalie."

"Gosh, I'm sorry I didn't get to say goodbye," I said.

"We had balloons, and the village children sang to her. Dr. Ravi returned with her."

"I thought Dr. Ravi planned to be here a few days." My heart tugged.

"I heard he was called back to his inn."

"Well, OK," I said. "I'm so sorry I missed saying goodbye to both of them."

She rubbed the last of the eucalyptus oil into my calves and said, "Your ankles look much better today, then attached the oximeter to my fingertip and said, "normal." My blood pressure passed muster as well. She put her equipment back in a satchel she carried crosswise over her chest and asked if I felt well enough to eat breakfast in the dining room.

I said I felt much better than the day before, "And I believe I saw where it is straight down the hallway to the right."

"In an hour, the cook closes the kitchen to further prepare daily meals, so go before ten." Aarti pointed to her watch, and with that, she left.

I lingered in my room, wishing I might hide out there. I opened my travel journal to write a few notes. How could I have developed a crush on Ravi in twenty-four hours? I missed Natalie; I could talk to her; she was my link to Jack and home. I felt an emptiness I could not explain away. Had I misread the tea leaves about Ravi's attraction to me? It was the same old me, I thought. My right arm was still shorter than my left. My smile was still lopsided, and I walked with a limp—not the woman of any man's dreams, but damn, yesterday had been—magical? Wrong word, I thought. We didn't have to talk to be happy sitting side by side—our meeting was like a reunion.

I was at the hospital in Nepal to support the hospital, not moon over Ravi. Ultimately, I would meet my father, and I had to focus on achieving that goal; it would take all the courage I could muster. I had to self-correct my inclination to confuse romantic interest with gentle kindness. I wrote all these thoughts into my journal under MUST Remember: I checked my watch, and I had fifteen minutes until the kitchen closed; I put away my journal and left immediately.

Comfortable couches with reading lamps made for conversation areas ringed the tables that served the staff in the dining room. I went to the kitchen window and knocked as I was the last one arriving to eat. A small woman in a turquoise shirt and blue jeans, her black hair netted up in the back, lowered the window. "You hungry?" she asked.

"Yes, yes, I am," I replied.

"I'll bring you tea and porridge, OK?"

"Sounds lovely. I found a table close by, already washed after breakfast service, and sat. A newspaper was on an adjoining table which I grabbed only to find it was in Nepali. Well, naturally, I thought. The woman came out with a tray of cereal, tea, and toast. My appetite lagged; however, I felt compelled to eat, wishing I had my journal to write in or my Kindle to read. I was lonely. After finishing my meal, I returned to the kitchen window. The woman appeared again, this time draped in a large white apron. "Where can I return my dishes?" I asked.

"We will fix," she said. "You go see Dr. Aha?"

"I suppose that's in order," I answered. "Thank you so much for breakfast!" I returned to my room to gather my journal and bottled water. As I maneuvered out of the dorm area, I crossed through a courtyard to a small cinder block building containing offices. A young Nepali man greeted me from a desk central in the entry. "You are Maya?" he asked.

"Yes, I'm here to meet Dr. Aha if she's not busy," I said.

"Of course, " he said. "Come with me. You wait in her office. She returns soon."

With a serious expression, the young man opened Dr. Aha's door and stepped back for me to enter. He offered a chair facing the large oak desk. The door clicked behind me, and once again, I was alone. On the wall behind her desk was a photo of a familiar face; Yeshe Maya pictured twenty years ago, I imagined. A rhesus macaque grinned wildly through the screened, open window and jumped into a banyan tree. Maybe that was Aama? Perhaps, I wasn't all alone after all?

This curiosity aside, I wondered what I could do as a volunteer during the week I had scheduled here. With no language skills in Nepali, I could not help with patient intake and was not allowed in the ward with patients suffering from infectious diseases. Those boxed computers remained taped up on the floor of the office. I wished that I were technologically savvier. I was more in the way than helpful at a field hospital.

"Good morning," Dr. Aha slipped silently into her office. She peered at me and then at a stack of charts on her desk. "I finished with another set of these last evening, and more arrive?" She shrugged. Dr. Aha appeared practical, dressed in a white coat over a dark skirt with a stethoscope around her neck. Her bifocal glasses hung from a chain. She reminded me of a Nepali Ruth Bader Ginsburg in size and attitude.

"They want to keep you busy," I said. "Ravi didn't get to the computers, I see."

"We needed him in surgery," she said. "Then called away."

"Did he say why?"

"No one said." She plied through the patient files. "But, he returned to Kathmandu with Natalie this morning on the transport."

"The truck/bus. Oh, OK." What had come up? "Ravi said he worked until nine or so last night. I figured he put the computers together."

"No," Dr. Aha answered. "I assisted him in an amputation—a patient in his forties. Diabetes is becoming a real problem here. Then we consulted on a work plan going forward—which involves the computers." She took a deep breath and looked up at me. "How are you feeling today?"

"Much better. I slept well."

"Be sure to drink plenty of water, and don't push yourself as you acclimate."

"Yes, Nurse Aarti has reinforced that message." I paused, ready to apologize again, "You must be very busy—"

"I am delighted to meet you and to have you here."

"I've set computers up before," I said. "Maybe I could . . ."

Dr. Aha held her hand up and shook her head. "That will wait." She sighed again. "We're networking with a hospital in the eastern region of Nepal—complicated, you see?" She took off her glasses and drank tea from a large yellow cup with a chipped handle. "I have a busy morning, unfortunately, but I suggest you go on for a walk. Before you leave us for India, you must visit the Kaliaka Bhagawi Temple. It requires a bus ride, but I'm sure you will enjoy it. For today a quiet walk to Matipokhara this morning. Three pathways lead from the hospital to the village; the middle one is the most accessible."

"Sure, sure." Reality minus romantic fantasy exerted itself. "One more question if you have time?"

"Certainly," she said.

I pointed to the photo behind her. "Did you happen to know Yeshe Maya? I read that she started the hospital. Is that her in the photo?"

"Yes. Most certainly, Yeshe Maya." Dr. Aha smiled. "Not personally. Before my time. But she was legendary." Dr. Aha folded her hands under her chin with her elbows on the table. "She was a midwife in her early days, I have heard." She wrinkled her brow. "Some say a birth she attended went wrong, and the baby suffered. She felt it was her fault and left her home near Chitkul. That's in India." Dr. Aha opened the top file and then looked up thoughtfully. "She wanted to learn more and to improve practices locally. She volunteered here when this was only a clinic run by a missionary couple. She wrote many letters to the Nepali government and foundations and received funding to build this hospital. The hospital receives government funding and private donations. She started a birthing ward for difficult pregnancies, although, it is said, she never attended another birth herself." Dr. Aha laughed softly. "She saw her blindness as a message; it was time to leave. She committed to a life as a nun. Her monastery is in Nepal, but she grew homesick for the hospital and returned here."

The doctor finished her tea. "That woman was tireless: a tiger for her patients. When she wasn't harassing donors for money to support the hospital—especially for her youngest patients—she made house calls—wellness visits teaching locals about nutrition and childcare. In her eighties, the monastery asked that she take charge of a group of Yeshe nuns in Canada. Where she died, at over one-hundred years of age."

Yeshe left Sangam when Mother had left with me. I stared over Dr. Aha's shoulder. No wonder Yeshe wanted to meet me; I'm happy. I'm OK; I prayed to Yeshe Maya while through the window, Aama cavorted on a tree limb and disappeared into the canopy of the banyan.

"You look as if you have something to say," Dr. Aha said.

I caught myself smiling at the photo of Yeshe Maya on the wall.

"Has something amused you?" Dr. Aha squinted at me over her bifocals perched on the end of her nose.

"I saw a monkey jump outside the window—it struck me funny." I shook my head. "What a wonderful woman your Yeshe Maya was."

"I wonder from time to time what happened to the baby?" Dr. Aha said reflectively.

"What baby?" Well, look no further, I thought.

"The baby who caused Yeshe to reexamine her skills." She sighed. "Probably long dead, but a legacy, nevertheless. That baby helped so many people. Think of that. One baby." She adjusted one of her small gold earrings. "I would like to chat more, but I have duties I must attend to."

"She gave that baby life—if the baby lived, I am certain that she, the baby, that is, might be eternally grateful to Yeshe and humbled by her achievement." Yeshe Maya listened in my bones.

"Naturally. Naturally," Dr. Aha repeated. "Now, before you go on your walk, I insist you use a cane, and you need to put that wrist brace back on."

"It made my hand ache," I said. "That's why I took it off."

"Did you sleep in it?"

"Yeah," I answered.

"Always take it off at night. That's why your hand aches. Wear it during the day only. Promise?"

"OK," I said.

"And I will meet you for lunch at half-past twelve. Right here." She stood, then straightened her hospital jacket. "Cane is on the handle back of the door," she added. "Short, suitable for you."

"Fine, yes, thank you," I said. "I'll see you then. At lunch." I took the cane and raised it in a little salute.

"Have a lovely morning." She disappeared down the corridor. "Beautiful village."

The sun blinded me. Yeshe Maya wanted me here. Being here was the hardest part. I walked through a courtyard filled with people lining up for outpatient services. A young mother in loose red mid-calf-length pants and a pink patterned blouse carried a sick baby in a boxlike basket on the back of her bicycle. I watched as she leaned the bike against a flowering, silky oak; she gently unwrapped her child. The sleeping baby, now fully awake, screamed. His hair stuck out from a face so sweet that I smiled. I said a little prayer for his health. His lungs sounded fine.

A young man had his hand wrapped in a bloody towel. He moved his head back and forth, either in pain or confusion about which way to go. I knew where the hospital entrance was. I tapped him on the shoulder with my right hand, and he jumped.

With the cane as a pointer, I gestured for him to follow me. I led him across the plaza and to the door that accepted patients needing emergency services. A nurse I had not met glanced up from her desk facing the door. I pushed the young man forward.

The conversation was in Nepali as the nurse took the young man through the double doors, leaving me alone in the lobby. It was time to go for that walk.

A large stone marked the entry to Matipokhara. Terraced hills surrounded the village; Matipokhara perched on a lower rung. Below me, the hospital glowed like a beacon in the morning light. I sat on the rock and drank water as I studied villagers going about their daily lives. Two men haggled over the cost or weight of green beans while a woman nearby sat on her haunches making pottery. A young woman in jeans, with kids tagging along, stopped at the vegetable stand, waiting for the business between the stand owner and the bean customer to have completed. Two middle-aged women in tattered saris shooed a thin, short-haired dog aside and headed down an alley between two buildings. People stared at me and turned away. A few children approached with open palms for money. I shrugged and smiled. Muttering, "Nothing, I have nothing." One little boy in shorts and a dirty yellow t-shit tried to grab my cane. I pulled it towards me. He pointed at my wrapped wrist and laughed. I studied the walking stick laid over my lap, loosened the Velcro on the wrist brace, and closed my eyes, letting the sun go through me. I imagined the mountains rising behind me, and from memory, I heard Yeshe Maya instruct me: *Go. Father.*

With my eyes shut, a shadow dropped in front of me. Startled, I gazed skyward to see a brilliant blue bird crowned with golden feathers dart upwards to the high mountain peaks. A Himalayan monal—the national bird of Nepal? I had seen one! I texted Jack to tell him, but the message did not go through.

I rose from my perch and strolled inside the village, taking the route of the women in saris. Inside the alley were paths leading to houses tucked one beside the other, fronting the alleyway, all lost in shadow. The street I entered contained a hostel and a bus stop; perhaps the bus for the temple stopped there. The road led out of the village. I photographed the terraced cliff side; a suspension bridge nearly out of view caught my interest as did a little dog who accepted a piece of my energy bar. I missed Penni-P, my constant, ever-ready companion. My feelings zigzagged. I felt restless and out of context, but I knew it was right to be here. I thought about meeting Ravi and how he described my father; a wave of anxiety woke all my inadequacies. Then it occurred to me that it was too late to worry about what anyone might think of me. I was here; the plane had landed. I kept checking my watch as if it were an accurate measure of time. A goat butted me in the back, and two boys played a game with stones in the hard, dirt-packed street.

American kids on bicycles zoomed past me; I filmed them wisecracking and laughing as they sped by. The green world surrounded me. A macaque skirted in front of me as an old SUV puttered along. I might be disabled, but I was still alive. Shortly after twelve, I went back to the hospital.

Dr. Aha thanked me for leading the young man to surgery. "He would have lost that finger if we had waited any longer," she said as she showed me the hospital wards where I saw medicine practiced in the most rudimentary ways. Many of the patients suffered from farm work injuries. Children came in with pneumonia and flu, and doctors admitted older people with strokes and heart conditions. "Old" for Nepali country people was a relative term: you simply didn't see women in their fifties and beyond here—they died younger than that. Men lived longer. However, again, age was a misleading term. A man in his fifties had the look of someone decades older. Life was harsh in this beautiful land, and doctoring required calm and adaptability to local customs. These small hospitals were difficult to fund, so it was challenging to acquire proper equipment and generators to sustain them. Community outreach was a flexible term—this hospital had four high school-age students studying for university entrance exams— farm kids that the hospital supported. Staff tutored as time permitted.

The ward rooms were large and bustling in Matipokhara. Volunteer nurses, a mix of Buddhist and Catholic nuns, came from all parts of the world. Family members slept on floor pallets and helped with patient care.

The week passed quickly. I filed charts, answered correspondence from English speakers, made tea and folded laundry, sterilized equipment, and took many walks. The village became familiar, and I was never tired of seeing those magnificent peaks.

The day before I left, Dr. Aha walked with me to the bus stop, where I boarded a bus to the Kaliaka Bhagawi Temple, about an hour away. I felt bathed in serenity as I ambled down the long entry into its center. Forest paths and tall birch trees banked the temple grounds. Before going in, I stopped at a brick wall; water poured from it, and I watched people stop and wash their faces before proceeding further. Yellow and maroon posts connected with bells along the way, and I did, as others had, rang the bells like I was announcing my arrival, asking to enter the sacred grounds. A gentle rain fell, and the clouds drifted away. Women in silk saris watched children running around, their laughter in the breeze. A bazaar formed a circle around the main temple building, and the fruit and colorful scarves caught my eye. Gold and maroon banners festooned the grounds.

Dr. Aha told me that I must not miss the bus returning to Matipokhara as there was only one a day. I leaned against a tree and dutifully waited, remembering the day in Katmandu with Ravi. I texted Jack while I waited. The bus driver who left me off picked me up, and I relaxed as we drove these narrow roads. Late afternoon settled in; I pinched myself to see if it were real.

That night I texted Jack, and he had received my earlier texts from the temple and the other messages I'd sent him during the week. They came in a bundle. How pleased he was that I had found my way to the temple and back! He said that Natalie was finally home.

I knew he was happy. What would La Conner be like without my lifelong friend? Carol, from La Conner, texted me. The reception was good momentarily. She wondered why I wasn't posting more on Facebook. The Internet was dodgy at best, so I told her that. However, this experience was beyond my imagination, and I didn't know how to say that in words. My silence seemed the best response.

"You look tired," I passed some hummus to Dr. Aha, who joined me for dinner as she had each night of my stay. "I wish I could have helped more." After its latest run, my transport would take me back to Kathmandu in the morning.

"A busy day." She spread the honey onto her bread. "We are all grateful for your help."

"I wish I could have done more."

Back on the truck/bus, I retraced the miles to Kat and recollected my first ride to Matipokhara with Ravi. That was love, and it's gone, I mused as the miles rolled onward.

At the airport, I said goodbye to the truck/bus driver and, with help, found my way to the departures lounge for my flight. Next stop: Delhi. Then, on to meet the father I never knew I had.

As the plane gained altitude in the Nepali skies, I congratulated myself on boarding the airplane without incident. I told myself that soon I would be going home to La Conner. I had stories enough for the rest of my life. They weren't stories told to me but my very own. I thanked Yeshe Maya and took a pain pill, only half, and downed it with a glass of wine.

Chapter 16 Meeting Motu

> Down below in the valley of the Indus, in the teeming swells of
> men and women and children in the markets of Delhi, in the alleys
> where beggars lay in shadow in parks with goat herders and the
> bleating of goats amidst the traffic horns and the rise and fall of
> people making their way . . .

I reread my journal entry as I waited for Jack, clipped my pen to
the page, and put the notebook on the side table. Jack had texted that he
was on his way to the hotel, and that the line for a car rental was long. Child
beggars, who had surrounded me yesterday when I arrived, circled a taxi
on the street below, a passenger disembarked. The children's singsong pleas
sounded mechanical, except their distended bellies were real enough.

Cool-quiet separated the hotel world from the sidewalk diorama.
Inside, dark mahogany framed the doorways and the windows of the living
area of the two-bedroom suite. The settee had a tufted, high-backed ornate
frame and pink Asian-inspired brocade upholstery. To its side was a red
recliner, with a pole lamp between the furniture pieces. I wondered who
the decorator was. I was more inclined to use the red recliner. I left the
television on for company, although, from the back of the suite, a laughing
cacophony of monkeys and birds made their presence apparent through the
screened terrace that overlooked a palm garden below. After fourteen hours
of rest, I felt better and was curious about what had gone on in Sangla that
had called Ravi away.

Jack texted he was parking the rental car and was on his way to our
rooms. Alert to hall noises, I waited for the elevator to arrive on the sixth
floor and was at the door to greet him. Finally, Jack arrived. "Hey," I
laughed, "look what the cat drug in!"

"Been a day. A long day." He rolled his backpack inside, leaving the door ajar. Jack opened his arms. "Give this old man a hug." Sweat lined the collar of his midnight blue Polo shirt. His face appeared flushed, but it was a hot day in Delhi, so as we hugged, I put aside concerns for Jack's wellbeing. "Is there something cold in that mini fridge?" he asked.

"Sure is," I said. "You want a beer?" I pulled out two Buds and offered one to Jack.

"I was thinking of bottled water." He plopped onto the red recliner. "This is comfy."

"That was my spot!" I returned to the fridge, inserted the beer, and returned with two Aquafinas, handing one to Jack. I settled on the settee, propped my bare feet onto a matching, ornate footstool, and tried to open the water. I held the bottle up. "Will you do the honors?" Jack unscrewed the lid and handed me the bottle. I held it up. "Salute!"

Jack reached over, and we clinked bottles. "I had company on the flight down." He took a deep drink of water. "But before I get to that, do you remember me telling you about Motu Amul and his visit to the hotel?"

"Yeah, of course. I saw some of his online videos—"

"Motu returned to the hotel about the same time you arrived at the hospital."

"Was that the reason Ravi left early?"

"Yes, it was. This guy showed up unannounced in his frigging helicopter. Someone on board tells us through a bullhorn to clear the playing field so they could land." Jack shook his head and stared at the bottled water. "I gave him the best suite available, but he starts quizzing me about hidden valleys and local secrets and that he wants to buy the hotel. I got Ravi on our satellite phone, and he got back. That was last week."

"You think our legendary guru learned something about Sangam, but how?"

"You know, if you go online, you see all the stories and rumors about hidden valleys and ancient secrets in Tibet and the Himalayas. That's the bedrock, but La Maison Fortune has a fabled history, too, because of your grandmother. She's the one who constructed it."

My mouth dropped.

"Guess Ravi didn't tell you that part of the story." Jack laughed.

"Failed to mention."

"After she experienced Sangam, she had a brief life as a nun, returned to France, married your grandfather, brought him to India, and built the hotel. Your grandfather wanted to go back to France. She agreed and deeded the hotel to the front desk man who guided her to Sangam years before. All of the managers are part of Sangam. Ravi intends to make the hotel a meditative retreat for all people of good works. I'm being generic here, but that's the plan." Jack peered at me and shrugged. "The world's in pretty rough shape."

"And don't we know that."

"Amul knows the rumors about the hotel. He came with questions the first time he got here—two days ago; he interrupted a closed-door meeting between Ravi and me. The sunstone, old hotel photos, and your grandmother's book were lying on Ravi's side table. He started quizzing us, said he'd heard stories about secret local villages and told us a story about the sunstone that wasn't far off the mark. He knew I had arrived recently— wanted to know if I was an interested buyer. Saw your photo that I clipped to the book, and he wondered who you were. Ravi interrupted and said you wrote to him about the hotel because you were curious about your grandmother. Then added, after meeting you in person, the two of you became romantically involved."

Not far from the truth, I thought. "So, how'd you explain you were meeting me in Delhi, Jack?"

"I said I was living in Corfu when you told me about Ravi and the hotel and became intrigued and protective about your interests. I explained we'd been friends and neighbors for most of our lives, truly the only sister I never had. I came to Sangla to check the hotel out for myself. Met Natalie through Ravi."

The suite phone's ringing interrupted Jack's story, and he answered it. He repeated "sure" a few times and "we'll meet you then, say in twenty minutes?" and hung it up.

"Was that Amul?"

Jack raised an eyebrow and nodded.

"Go on with your story."

"I said that Ravi had to return to Matipokhra for a few days, and I volunteered to be your Delhi guide. Motu asked where I had booked in Delhi; I told him this hotel, and he secured the penthouse for himself and his aides. Said he'd give me a ride down."

"So, like I'm his golden ticket to Sangam?" I sighed and drank the rest of the water.

"He wanted to meet you, invited you to stay at his ashram to get acquainted; he was interested in your family's history."

"Jack! He didn't buy it but figured out I'm somehow connected to the puzzle. Is it safe for Sangam for me to meet my father?"

"Your father says yes. Jethro Zane, I hope you get to meet this man: he's a messenger between your father and Ravi—he contacted your father yesterday. We devised a new plan, which is still formulating, by the way. Ravi is refining the details. You're leaving Delhi tomorrow night, and if we get you in, it will only be for a few days, at most. Out of Sangla, too. I'm so sorry to cut your trip short."

"Right now, we are meeting Amul? Where?"

"In the bar."

"The guru in a bar?"

"He'll likely be in jeans and have tea with his aide," Jack stood and stretched. "You, my dear, act innocent. You are here to see Delhi."

"Well, lead-on. I am having a real drink in that bar, OK?"

"That's fine." Jack went to find the suite bathroom, and I walked over to the open window to the garden centering the hotel. My father was risking so much getting me to Sangam. My personal story, the one I had carried for six decades, was upended, and I had only a clean slate and a blank stare at palms filled with a loud monkey tribe. I didn't know what to think. I slid into my sandals, and off we went. "Did you get a key?"

"Yep." Jack held the key card in the air.

"Let's go," I said.

We had to go down two marble steps to enter the bar that centered the Delhi Raj Hotel's lobby. Reflexively, I grabbed Jack's arm. A spotlight shone over the bar—softer lights haloed tables around the circular stone counter. A black ceiling gave the feeling of perpetual night. Behind the counter, shelves displayed bottles with shiny labels, and the attendant manually rotated the display to whatever beverage he needed.

I perused the drink menu. "This is one swanky bar. I'd like a lemon splash martini. I don't see it here. But I think we better have tea, right?" We sat at a table facing the glittery, boozy display. Two Japanese businessmen conferred over drinks and documents on their table across from us. Otherwise, quiet prevailed.

"Yeah, that's a better idea." Jack fidgeted and drummed his fingers across the shiny surface of the black table. He checked his phone twice before the barman came over for our order.

I asked Sai, the bartender, if they had cold, iced tea, and he offered a smile in reply.

I grinned back and glanced around the room, glad that Amul and his aide were nowhere in sight.

"I will join my friend in iced tea," Jack said.

While waiting for our drinks, we chatted about the hospital and my stay. I told Jack about the bus ride with Ravi and how much I liked him. He listened intently but said nothing in reply. Sai arrived, and Jack and I clinked glasses and said, "Cheers." Jack offered me a cinnamon-dusted star-shaped cookie from a small basket Sai had brought with the drinks.

As I chose one, two people jogged down the marble stairs. I immediately recognized Motu Amul. His thinning mass of white hair pulled back into a ponytail—his large brown eyes and smooth mocha-colored skin gave his face a distinctive appeal. His full white beard completed the picture, pictures I had seen all over the Internet. The aide was a lovely dark-haired young woman in a mid-calf length straight gray skirt, a tunic-styled shirt with a green silk scarf tied loosely around her hips. Amul's belly bulged over his belt; he lived up to his nickname. He sported a diamond-studded watch that sparkled under the bar's spotlight.

We rose to greet them, and handshakes and smiles sufficed for introductions. Amul slid into the booth beside me. He smelled like spicy vanilla; Rachel Weatherby, the aide, sat next to Jack.

"I am so honored to meet you," I said. "Jack, you're so thoughtful to arrange this."

"What are you drinking?" Amul asked.

"Iced tea."

"Have you followed my work?" the guru asked.

"I'm humbled to be sitting with you," I said. "Your talks inspire us to take better care of ourselves, most certainly." Jack kicked my foot under the table. I didn't know if he approved or disapproved of my overly appreciative remarks.

The guru opened his manicured, soft hands as if bestowing a blessing. "The gift of giving contributes to good karma." Rachel nodded and lowered her head; I noticed her half smile. Sai came to the table with lemonade for the guru and Rachel; I guessed the bar service knew he was arriving. "Tell me, Maya; Jack tells me you were a guest at a hospital in Nepal at Matipokhara. Were you named for the nun who was its first director?" Motu quizzed.

"I don't know who my mother named me for," dumbfounded at how much this slick impostor knew.

"Hmmm," the guru said, "what brought you to the hospital?"

"I'm a donor," I said.

Amul turned his body toward me and calmly stared into my eyes. "Interesting," he purred nearly under his breath. "May I be so bold as to inquire about the nature of your disability?"

Again, I realized Motu knew far more than we thought. "I have cerebral palsy. The right side only," I added.

"I have many friends around Matipokhara, and a story I have heard from a very old man concerns the hospital. Its first director was a nun named Yeshe Maya. She delivered a baby somewhere around Sangla in a community cut off in the mountains; the birth was difficult, and the infant suffered a birth injury. I believe the couple was French and returned to France sometime later. Yeshe Maya left India and started the hospital in Nepal to improve the birthing skills of midwives, although she never delivered another baby."

"I was at that hospital and missed that story altogether," I chirped. I didn't think the guru believed me.

Jack peered at his watch and then at me. "Gee, honey. How's your headache?"

"I do have a headache, and you're a darling to ask about it." I turned toward the guru. "Yes, I think we better take our leave. Again, I'm honored to meet you, Amul, sir, and you, Rachel."

I scooted out of the booth. Jack put his arm fully around me and gave me a side hug as we exited. I whispered, "Shit," under my breath.

Chapter 17 Lots of Layers

I STARED AT MY REFLECTION in the mirrored wall of the elevator. I appeared as gobsmacked as I felt. "Maybe, I should go home?"

Jack slouched as he scrolled through his phone. He squeezed my hand and put his phone in his back pocket. " I just ordered butter chicken on room service; Ravi sent three texts during whatever that was at the bar. Let's see what's happening with Ravi, and you know you love butter chicken."

"That's my favorite," and despite my anxiety, I smiled.

I took off my shoes and ran some cold water on my face in the suite's bathroom. Before meeting Motu, I imagined him as a caricature of a yogi, someone easily dismissed. Charm and charisma oozed from Amul, and he could stare down a snake. He knew that I was the child Yeshe Maya delivered. And I should have figured, I thought, as I sat on the toilet peering at my phone, that stories about Yeshe Maya would be widely circulated. The woman was a legend.

"It bears repeating, Jack," I said as I joined my friend in the lounge. "We are in deep shit."

"Indeed, we are, Sunshine." From his chair facing mine, Jack sipped a lemon-lime soda.

"I think there's a chardonnay in the fridge, and I'm having it; how can you drink soda pop at a time like this?"

Jack burst into laughter. "Sit. I'll get you a glass. Dinner should be here any minute." He opened a can of peanuts, also resurrected from the fridge, and offered me some with a glass of chilled white. He popped a few peanuts in the air and tried to catch them with his mouth.

"Hey, you missed two." I grabbed a handful of nuts from the opened tin. I held my glass to Jack's soda bottle and said, "Cheers!" I took a long, cool gulp, immediately relieving some of the tension. "Hmm, that's better," I said. "What does Ravi think?"

Jack's phone buzzed before he could answer, and within seconds there was a knock on the door; dinner had arrived. Jack stood, then nodded towards his bedroom, where he intended to take the call.

I let in two servers who set up a table by the window.

Jack reemerged and poured more wine for me. "No one in Sangla thinks you should go home. Your father says it is divined that you go to Sangam."

"Divined?" I stared at Jack. "By what force on earth?"

"Your father's. Ravi says your father believes your travel to Sangam will protect it." Jack pointed to the table, "Let's eat."

"My father's divination?" I wanted to pack my bags and take the next flight from Delhi back to La Conner and that one-level townhouse Carol promised. "This sounds crazy, Jack. Does my father have a crystal ball?"

"I cannot explain your father's gifts, but rest assured he has them. You have to trust me."

"Are you sure he isn't an isolated old man wanting to see his daughter before he dies at anyone's expense?" I put my wine glass down. Jack lifted the bottle to refresh it, but I placed my hand over the top of the glass. I felt drunk, and I needed to stay sober. "Amul knows too much. He has people all over; they'll follow me. I'm the biggest threat Sangam has."

"Your father would never put Sangam at risk. I'm only repeating Ravi's message."

"So, if my father said to jump out of the garden window, would you do it?"

Jack pointed his index finger at me from across the table. "That's not the question. The question is: will you put aside everything you know about this situation and do what he asks? Go to Sangam."

I breathed deeply. "My mind tells me to go home that my father sounds like another fake guru who's convinced you that the sky is violet and the grass is blue, but my heart says to go to my father—Yeshe Maya's last request of me. OK—I'll put aside my knowing mind and follow whatever plan you and Ravi have concocted."

"We'll get into the particulars in a little while. Ravi's calling in a few minutes; for now, let's eat." Jack motioned toward the covered dish containing the chicken.

I removed the lid, and the earthy, spiced aroma of curry melted the air. "Who doesn't love butter chicken?" I loaded my plate with jasmine rice slathered with chicken steeped in curry and a cucumber carrot and mint salad. I took a bite. "Man, this is delicious." As beautiful as the food was, I still was confounded by the decision to go ahead with my reunion with my father. After a second helping of chicken, I put down my fork. "I gather we're leaving Delhi tomorrow night. Are we driving to Sangla?"

"I'm not going with you—my job is to sneak you to the train station. You're going alone."

"I'm what?"

"I'll get you on the train to a place called Kalka; Ravi will pick you up the day after tomorrow." Jack offered me a glass of lemonade that he'd ordered with dinner.

I sipped the beverage. "How far away is that?"

"Not far. You'll be going in a sleeper car and arriving in Kalka before you know it. Ravi meets you."

"I like that part. OK, I'm in. I'm going to bed. Will you take care of this?" I motioned to the messy table.

"Happily."

Jack's phone rang. He put Ravi on speaker.

"You like trains, Maya?" Ravi asked.

"I like trains," I answered. "I gather I'm taking one tomorrow night." I bit my lip holding back any mention of my reservation of the plan, but blurted, "I feel like a mouse chased by cats."

"A close analogy," Ravi said.

"Ravi," Jack said. "So, the train tomorrow tonight to Kalka will put Maya in at 7:10 in the morning. We are set on your end, then?"

"Yes," Ravi said. "Be careful tomorrow—I'll see you, Maya, the day after tomorrow, bright and early."

Jack took the phone off speaker and said, "I'll get her on the train tomorrow night."

The next day Jack thought it best that we stay in our suite. He had a quick errand to run in the morning for what he claimed was a surprise for me. We put a hold on calls, and I was not to answer the door. The cats were quiet, but Jack saw them reading newspapers in the lobby when he returned to the hotel.

Jack sat on my bed as I sorted through my things. I had washed out underwear to take with me the night before. The rest of my dirty clothes filled the laundry bag I laid under the clean clothes in my red train case. "Should I wear my boots?"

"No, but take them for the walk. Sandals are more casual."

"I was going to wash my stuff at your place or home," I sighed. "This is crazy."

Jack shrugged a response and adjusted the bed pillow behind his head. "Oh, and I'll take your train case with me to Sangla, and we will get your clothes washed." He raised himself to a sitting position, rolled his shoulders, and stretched his neck. He appeared far more relaxed than the day before.

I was going all alone on the train to meet Ravi. My heart skipped a beat. "Tell me again what the plan is?"

"I'm putting you on the train, and Ravi will get you off. I booked a sleeper car for you—you'll sleep the whole way. After you meet your father and see where you were born—I'll come into Sangam and get you to Delhi." Jack sat up as I finished packing. "You ready to close the train case?"

"Yeah. Everything I need is in my watermelon bag," I answered.

"I have a sari for you."

"That's the surprise?" My eyes lit up. "Thank you, Jack!"

"I got it for you to wear tonight to board the train," Jack said and grinned. "You'll look smashing. And well disguised."

"Where is it?"

Jack immediately left to bring me the sari. Folded, it draped like a sheet on its satin-covered hanger; a dark border embossed with tiny stars edged the peacock blue silk fabric.

"Oh my God, it's gorgeous!" I oozed with delight. "Imagine me in La Conner, wearing this?" I held the hanger up for the fabric to catch the light through the window, then hung it over the doorknob for later. "How long does it take to get to where Ravi's supposed to meet me?

"Kalka. You get off at Kalka. A little over ten hours, overnight and about twenty stops," Jack said.

Both Jack and Natalie had cautioned me that Ravi was always late. "He'd better be on time." I turned my attention to my ballooning carry-on loaded with boots, jeans, hiking shorts, a t-shirt, underwear, a dress, a nightgown, and all my electronics: laptop, Kindle, and phone. "Damn, I think I left my charger in Nepal? Do you have an extra one with the adapter?"

"You won't need anything electronic—none of it will work in Sangam, and they don't allow it, anyhow." Jack eyed my bag. "Can you lift that thing?" he asked. "After the train, you have a long walk ahead of you."

"Let's see." I gamely picked up my watermelon bag from the bed. My arm burned with the lift; I may as well have had boulders in that bag.

"Dump it," Jack said. "I'll help you pack."

I began dismantling the bag.

"While you do that, I'm going to put the Do Not Disturb sign on the door—almost forgot." He jogged out of the room for more than a few minutes.

I stayed inside my bedroom and repacked my carry-on, leaving out the jeans, laptop, and Kindle. The bag still felt too heavy. What if I get lost, or Ravi is late, and I don't have my cell? Certainly, I could take that. Were those voices in the hall? My mind wandered.

I heard the suite door open and close, and Jack reentered the room. "Rachel was just getting out of the elevator across the hall."

"Motu's aide? What did she want?" I asked.

"She offered to take you to the Chandni Chowk—I told her we were staying in—all day—that you had a migraine."

"Good. They're off our backs for now."

"Now for your bag. Extra clothes you can wear under the sari, including your nightgown. It will fill you out. Change your shape, an even better disguise. In the bag itself—toothbrush, toothpaste, the all-important roll of toilet paper, journal. T-shirt and shorts and boots. Nothing else."

"I know you left the books and Mother's letter in Sangla, but did you bring me the sunstone? I'd like it with me."

"Ravi has it."

"OK." I tried lifting the bag again. "How far are we walking?" I asked.

"Around ten miles, not more than that, and the bag will lighten when you're wearing the boots."

"Holy crap," I said, "ten miles?" I collapsed on my bed. "Are we doing room service all day?"

"Yes—neither one of us is leaving the suite."

"Is that ten miles an easy hike—I don't suppose it is, is it?" I rubbed my right shoulder.

"It's rough, but Ravi'll keep you upright. And, Maya, at the end of it, you're going to meet your father," Jack smiled. "I wish I could be there to see your eyes light up!"

Jack had me text Carol in La Conner that I expected to be in India and off the grid for a while. I added that the trip so far was "magical." Carol was the kind of friend who worried if she did not hear from me, and she had texted several messages that I had not answered because the shift in my reality had veered dramatically in Nepal, and I was still trying to put it into words. For now, "magical" would have to do. And I told her not to post anything about my trip on her social media accounts.

The day pressed on in slow motion. I settled in the recliner and tried to write but could not concentrate. I thought about my grandmother's travels to Tibet in the 1920s. Madeline Caron-Martin was short, thin, and, weirdly, I looked like her. We shared high foreheads and a slight Gallic turn of the nose. I suspected that her wide eyes were blue-green like mine. I drew circles in my journal, held imaginary conversations with her, and pictured her as a totem.

Room service delivered lunch, a platter of *paranthas*—a selection of pita-like stuffed bread filled with radishes, eggs, potatoes, or chili chicken. I drank a soda while Jack ate. Later in the afternoon, more food arrived.

Curry centered with the kebob platter, and Jack encouraged me to eat. I tried but was too nervous to eat more than a nibble.

"If you're not going to eat, I will!" Jack popped a kebob off my plate and bit off a chunk. "Why don't you soak in the tub for a while? And try for a nap?"

The water was too hot, and the air conditioning too cold. I could not settle. I dried my hair, dressed in my nightgown, and then lay down for a nap. The angels of sleep arrived, and finally, under a silk comforter in this fancy hotel, I slept.

Jake woke me up. "Hey, it's time to get you into that sari," he said. "We have to leave in an hour."

"Oh my God." I sat up straight from a deep slumber. My heart raced. "You should have gotten me up earlier."

"Good, you had some rest—I envy you this adventure!"

Jack had me wear khakis and a t-shirt under my nightgown. Over the nightie, I wore a sundress topped with a linen tunic. Then Jack wound yards of blue silk around me. With the sari in place, he draped the shawl and scarf over my shoulders and head.

"I feel like I'm a ghost on Halloween—you know when the mom dresses you way too hot so you won't get cold trick-or-treating?" I tried to lift my arms. "God, Jack, I can hardly move!"

"Trains are cold at night—you'll be grateful," Jack answered.

I tried to find that reassuring but could not. India does not get cold at night. Maybe in the Himalayas, I thought. I stood in front of my bedroom mirror. "Who are you?" I asked the small woman who could be any one of millions, but today it was me.

CHAPTER 18 DISGUISED

AT 9 P.M., JACK HAD ME TAKE the elevator to the lobby. The elevator doors closed, and a slight mechanical jolt made me jump as it transported me downstairs. I carried a skein of yarn and knitting needles that Jack gave me before I left the suite. He bought them when he procured the sari. "No one," he said, "would expect to find you knitting."

I sat in a conversation area across from the welcoming counter. The mirror that stretched behind the front desk allowed me to see who was coming or leaving the lobby. Jack told me to fake knitting. I did know how to load the yarn onto a knitting needle, so I did that, peering out from under the loads of clothing I wore, studying the mirror assiduously. Jack came downstairs dressed in a kurta pajama set with a Nehru jacket. He wore a wool hat and carried my watermelon bag.

I watched Jack go through the circular lobby door, counted to twenty-five, and put away my knitting, as he had asked me to do. According to Ravi and Jack's plan, I was to leave the hotel and meet Jack driving a red compact Suzuki at the corner, a half-block away. As I stood, I saw Rachel Weatherby and another person wearing a ballcap, get off the elevator and heading to the front entrance. I took off my glasses, put them in my knitting bag, and held my breath. Since I was standing, I had to go somewhere. I decided to go to the bank of elevators, crossing by them.

I stared at my shoes and hunched my shoulders; neither Rachel nor her companion acknowledged me. As soon as they left the hotel I took a couple deep breaths and followed them outside. I stayed in the shadows and eyed the sidewalk both ways. Everyone looked suspicious. I headed toward the corner where I was supposed to meet Jack and prayed his car would materialize. My heart sunk when I spotted Rachel and her friend speaking to a man in a red car, paused in traffic. Was that Jack? I couldn't tell. My glasses were in the knitting bag, and I assumed the worst-case scenario in the dark with myopic eyes.

As hard as it was to do, I held back until the man in the car left, and the other two headed back toward the hotel. A sidewalk canopy hid me, but I got a good look at them, and it was Amul's aides. The red car had to be Jack's. All I could think was that Jack would figure I was close, circle the block, and look for me. I waited for the late model Suzuki, and as I stood under a streetlight, I prayed Jack would be the driver.

The red Suzuki paused mid-traffic; the passenger door opened from the inside. "Get in, lady!"

I jumped inside and slammed the door. Jack put his hand on the horn and leaned on the gas, and we were off to the train station.

The train station's fluorescent lights shined brightly amid throngs of moving people. Jack told me he would help me onto the train and said, "Everything's OK." As he locked the vehicle, I gripped his arm. "As I told you, you did great. We figured Motu would try something." Jack's enthusiasm baffled me. He was having a great time.

"And you're sure they didn't recognize me?" I clung a little tighter to Jack.

"Yeah," Jack said. "That's why they went back to the hotel."

Jack told Rachel he was going to a poker game with some buddies while I slept.

"So, they are waiting for me to make a move at the hotel?" I asked as we stepped around an old man asleep on the sidewalk by the depot doorway.

"Well, I suppose they have called it a night, or one of them will be waiting outside our hotel room. Either way, we're good." Jack straightened out my scarf while a slight breeze lifted it from my head. "Come on, let's get you on the train."

"I wish you were going—" my words stopped as we walked into the colossal depot, which was a bevy of activity. Languages I could not understand, the universal cries of babies everyone understood, and the voice over an intercom that I struggled to hear, greeted us. I was grateful that Jack did all the negotiating at the counter. Early for the train, we roamed around the station, where many customers slept on floor pallets while they waited for their departure. Colorful blankets covered sleeping bodies. We chose to sit outside on a bench while awaiting the train to commence. When the conductor nodded, I followed Jack obediently into the sleeper car.

"A 2-AC," he said. "Second class comes with bedding and air conditioning. You'll hear mice. The other thing is someone might steal your spot if you get up. It's about eleven hours, so try and hold tight."

He helped me into a lower bunk. "The chai is good—but I'd stay away from fluids," Jack said. "Toilets are terrible. Would not advise."

"Well, you said someone would steal my bunk if I got up anyway," I said. A white sheet and small square pillow lay on a thin mattress, long enough for me.

"You need a blanket?" Jack laughed. He could see sweat trickle down the sides of my face. Those layers of clothing were keeping me mighty warm. "The air conditioning will be on as soon as the train starts."

"Where am I getting off again?" I asked.

"Kalka. Ravi will probably meet you on the train," Jack answered.

"Kalka, Kalka," I repeated. "I can't lie down in this getup," I said, "and if I do, I'll never get back up."

"Try this." Jack put the train pillow under my knees and my carry-on under my head.

People bustled by us, and the man in the upper bunk settled in. "Not comfortable, but doable," I said.

The train whistled out its departure warning.

Jack kissed me on the forehead. "Remember, this is an adventure. I'll see you soon. And, by the way, Ravi likes you, too."

Jack's acknowledgment made me smile. The train jolted me from reverie. I tried to wiggle my toes, but my feet were asleep. The man above me belched as the train left the station. My body lurched as the train switched tracks. Why did Jack tell me about frigging mice? Out of self-preservation, I decided to stop with that line of thought. I began to count the places I had stayed since leaving La Conner. I could not recall the name of the hotel in New Delhi, and then, I could not remember the town where I was supposed to get off—a word like Cal—Calcutta? Did they even call Calcutta, Calcutta, anymore? There was a new name: Kol something. Kalka, where I'm supposed to get off? I thought. I was going north and not east, but nothing was what it appeared to be. I was going to see my father; the mystery surrounding him compelled me like the clickety-clack of the train wheels carrying us deeper into the Indian night.

I woke to what I thought were scurrying mice but turned out to be the guy above me cracking peanuts. His bunk shook mine as he produced a loud fart or sighed after consuming more food. He came aboard well prepared.

A high squeal of the train whistle left ribbons behind us, or so I imagined. Oh God, what have I got myself into? My stressed-out stomach churned; I hadn't eaten much that day, and my bladder ached for release. Could I even get to a toilet or find my ass under all these acres of fabric? Why hadn't I used the toilet at the train station? My prayers morphed from universal peace into something more personal.

I shut my eyes and waited for sleep to come again, and it did. A conductor woke me and asked me something, to which I nodded without understanding what was said.

He looked concerned and said something else and left, briefly, bringing back a kind-eyed woman in a sari. "Are you well?" she asked. I guessed that the conductor had asked if I was sick and I answered in the affirmative. This woman was a nurse who spoke better English than her coworker.

"Oh, I am fine," I said, "but could you tell me where the toilets are?"

"Toilets are two cars down, next stop, five minutes." She paused and cocked her head, "Are you certain that you are 'fine?'"

"Just tired," I answered with a smile.

"OK, aunty." She shut my curtain, and I heard her leave the compartment.

I slumped back in my bunk and shut my eyes; a dark sleep fell over me. I woke up, licking my dry lips. The man snored in the bunk above me, and my clothing stuck to my skin. I felt shrink-wrapped. The scent of robust curries and flatulence overwhelmed my senses.

All the while, the train made stop after stop. Where did I get off? Kalka, that's it, I thought, with some relief. Ravi better not be late. In the cold reality of the train ride, the idea that I was somehow being transported to a mysterious Himalayan village seemed like something conjured on a psychedelic. I sweated in the dark as I watched the car lighten. Morning, I thought. My mind wandered into a tangle of thoughts, some directed toward my mother. What other secrets had you left untold? Oh, Mother, I love you, you crazy lady. In a sharp mental twist, I wondered if one of Amul's aides were on the train, snuck on, somehow, and then I did my best to disengage from that mental rabbit hole and fell asleep again.

"All passengers will disembark," a dream voice uttered.

"Aunty! Your son is here You are at your stop."

"What? Oh, hello," I muttered as I opened my eyes. My legs were asleep. I tried to focus on the short woman with a red dot on her forehead and hair bound back, the same woman who had made a wellness check— how many hours before?

"Your son is here," the woman repeated.

"Ravi?" I sat up and hit my head, and the world went askew. The guy from above me hopped out and sauntered down the aisle with a prodigious fart from his skinny backside. "Well, good day, to you, too," I said.

Ravi and the nurse appeared confused at my observation. "Steady. Steady," Ravi said. "Let's get you out of here."

I winced as I swung my legs over the edge of the bunk. Ravi offered his hand, which I took. I collapsed into a soft heap in the aisle when he let go. My legs were both sound asleep. Padded as I was, I was in no danger of harming myself. Foremost on my mind was my overfull bladder. "Can I use the bathroom on the train?" I asked, peering at Ravi from my vantage point on the floor.

The nurse shook her head, no. "The depot WC is much better." She grabbed my right elbow and began to lift me as my legs were barely coming to life while Ravi assisted me on my left side. "There, there, aunty," she said, "there, there." My legs felt rubbery and unreliable as I balanced between Ravi and the nurse.

"Can you get your mother off the train?" the nurse asked Ravi as if I had no cognitive ability.

His mother? I admit I was not looking my best, but his mother? People talk over old people, and I guessed an old and disabled person gets talked over a bit more. I would have cared more about this injustice if I hadn't needed to pee so badly. "Let's go," I said. "I'm not his mother," I added with as much defiance as a pile of fabric could offer.

Ravi had my watermelon bag on one arm and me on the other, and I hung on tightly.

At the exit of the train car, Ravi said, "Grab the railing." I watched him jump to the platform with ease, and for a moment, I thought he was going to leave me leaning over the steps, pee about to stream down my leg. He turned and smiled, "Now, you." And I stepped off and into his arms.

"Are you inside there?" Ravi smiled.

"I have about twenty-five layers of clothes underneath the sari," I interrupted. "And I'm about to pee through all of them." Alongside the brick depot, doors opened to the lobby. Each entryway bore paned rounded transoms. The gray sky was indifferent to my plight. A cleaning crew approached the train to give it a good going over before the train returned to Delhi. The fresh morning air was welcome. "Which door is closest to the loo?" I asked, tucked under Ravi's arm. We passed a flower stand where one woman wove marigolds into garlands while another sold them. "Aren't they lovely?" I asked as we breezed by.

"Yes, yes, they are." Ravi turned me as if we were about to waltz and led me toward Door Number One, which I thought was aptly named. "You didn't leave the bunk at all?"

"Jack told me not to," I said. "It was just too complicated."

Ravi hurried right along, and I appreciated the effort. A woman in white capri pants and a bright blue scarf coiled around her head nearly collided with us at the women's toilet door.

"Can you manage from here?" He handed me some rupees for the attendant inside the bathroom.

"Thank you," I said, "I'm fine now," feeling anything but fine. "I'll need my bag." Ravi handed it to me. Sweat rolled down my back. I wanted out of the confining layers pressing in on me.

The gods were with me, and a stall was open. I paid the attendant and locked the stall door. I bundled the sari over my right arm, freeing my able hand to find the front of my khakis buried under the sundress and the nightie. I unbuttoned the pants and managed to get the zipper partway down. I wiggled and pushed my pants down. I was giddy with relief.

I sat for a moment before reversing the process. I pulled my pants up as high as possible while sitting on the toilet; the sari spread around me. With the closed stall door to lean against, I wiggled the pants up and managed to button them. I had brought my bag in because I had hoped to remove one of the layers, but the narrow stall and one operational arm proved this an impossibility.

I opened the stall door to a lineup of women awaiting a turn. I put my scarf over my head to hide my unkempt hair and to avoid the scowls on the faces I passed. Outside I picked up two words over the intercom: "Kalka Station." Where was Ravi? He was nowhere in sight. He might have had to use the bathroom, too. I answered my thought, which I believed helpful, as I perused the crowd of passersby making their way through the station, rolling cases for some, while a few walked by with shoulders loaded, and one woman balanced a box on her head.

An announcement broadcast the final call for the Himalayan Queen, the famous UNESCO so-called toy train that wound its way through the Himalayas in cars made especially for the smaller tracks. The British engineer, born in the mid-1800s, designed the train to transport colonials to cooler regions in the hot, muggy summers of the early 1900s. The humid summers continued long after the British left, and local and global tourists now flocked to board the train to Shimla. Before coming to India and that fateful attic day, I had watched YouTube videos of the train, and I thought it to be an ultimate adventure ride. As I stood appraising the tourists leaving on the Himalayan Queen, I envied their day until I remembered where I was going. The letter from my mother and all it portended felt unreal, dreamlike, and the feeling of being drawn toward my father stronger as the adventure continued.

A blonde woman with deep brown eyes and a SUN/FUN bag over her shoulder tapped me on the arm. "Are you local?" she asked breathlessly. "You think I have time for the loo? I'm going on the Shimla train—you speak English?"

I jumped a little at her touch. "Yes," I stuttered. The woman could not tell that I was an American. A blue-eyed one at that. OK, this is a dream. "I don't know how long you have." I nodded towards the door. "And there's a long line in there."

"Oh, damn," she said and disappeared into the moving and ever-changing crowd of tourists.

Another woman approached the women's toilet door. She was Western, as well. I realized I appeared to be a gatekeeper as she, too, struck up a conversation. This lady asked, "How long's the line? Do I give you a coin?" She struggled with a money belt she inartfully tried to hide under a tight yellow blouse. She had a garland of marigolds around her neck and a large floppy straw hat on her head. The stem of her sunglasses hooked over her shirt between her large breasts. "Well? Tell me. I do not know the custom." She pronounced the words slowly in a high-pitched, pinched nasal voice. She wagged a rupee in front of my face. "You speak English?"

"No line, memsahib."

She thrust the rupee in my hand and barged inside the door.

Ravi was laughing. I had not observed him standing immediately behind the woman.

I burst into a fit of laughter, too. "Can I buy you a chai with my rupee?" I noticed he carried flowers. "Where were you?"

"I wanted to give you this," he said, and with a kiss on my cheek, put a garland of marigolds around my neck, adjusting the scarf as he did. "In Indian culture, marigolds welcome the traveler."

"Oh, thank you, but I'm local. However, I would enjoy a chai." I fingered the flowers, soft to touch, and our eyes met for a moment, and for a moment, we said nothing. Classically romantic, I mused. I wondered what a handsome man like Ravi would ever see in me, but right then, I didn't question.

We went to the tea kiosk across from the bathroom and received our chais when the rude tourist roared out of the toilet and spotted me. "You lied!" she yelled, "and if I miss my train, you'll pay for the ticket!" Off she ran, a bit of toilet paper clinging to her shoe.

"I better get you out of here," Ravi said. "Jack has your credit cards!"

We wove through tourists, clamor, food stands, and train whistles to the car park alongside the station. I slopped my chai all the way. Stands of evergreens on brown hills reminded me of the Pacific Northwest. The air away from people took on the sweetness of the outdoors.

Ravi held my arm. He matched his step with mine. "I think that woman is looking for you!" he said as we approached his dusty Toyota.

I thought he joked until I turned my head slightly, and there, several paces behind us, the woman charged toward us. "Oh, my God, how'd you know?"

"That's what I get paid for!" He opened the passenger's side. "Get in!" I tried to reach the driver's side to unlatch the door, but my layers of clothing constricted my progress.

Ravi unlocked his door and hopped in behind the wheel. The lady neared the car as Ravi pulled out of the space. The last I saw of her was with her mouth wide open and our car exhaust heading her way. And now we were off to God knew where; I sure didn't.

Chapter 19 And Then There Were Two

"A NARROW ESCAPE!" I laughed and removed the scarf from my sweaty head. I hung the marigold lei around the rearview mirror. The day promised heat, and I needed to get out from under a few layers of clothing. Soon.

Ravi had the sun visor down, and I noticed him referring to what appeared to be driving directions on two clipped papers.

"I guess you can't google coordinates for where we are going," I said. Curves and sharp turns wound through Kalka, where houses and businesses edged the two-way road. Drivers sped along in the center of the narrow way until challenged by oncoming traffic. Bright sunlight caused glare, and I squinted to see the dangers ahead.

Ravi looked quizzically at me. "Oh," he said, "I am looking for a place called Pinjore Gardens just after the rail crossing. A beautiful spot, but unfortunately, we can only stop briefly."

I mopped sweat from my forehead with the end of the scarf. "We just got started. Why stop so soon?"

"You need water, obviously. I have flasks in the back. And breakfast—I imagine you are hungry. And correct me if I am mistaken, but you appear to be overdressed. I thought you might like to," Ravi paused, "what do you call it in the States? Downsize?"

"You're not wrong, but I don't know if I can get out of the sari by myself." I was a sweaty mess under the sari and was afraid of what we might uncover.

"You will have help," Ravi said.

"Is there a chance that Motu or someone working for him has followed us?"

"Highly unlikely. Once out of the station, we are much safer. But we don't want to stand out, be memorable; we want to blend in, not raise suspicion, so think of us as a couple on holiday. This is tourist season up here."

"Jack told me that was our cover story."

"It's a logical one," Ravi said, "don't you think we'll blend nicely?"

"I couldn't write a better script," I said.

My thoughts diverted because a truck was coming straight at us. Ravi dodged around it as an SUV wheeled around our vehicle. My foot pressed against an invisible brake. "Jesus," I muttered, "—or maybe, Shiva! —these people drive—insanity!"

We passed the Himalayan Queen and drove a short distance to a large car park. Over the tops of vehicles that filled only a small portion of the lot, columns and arches rose in the early morning air. It was half-past seven, and a short lineup of people was in front of an entryway.

"Oh, my God, you have to pay to get in?" I opened the door, turned outward, grabbed hold of the edge of the dash and boosted up and out the vehicle.

"I am impressed with how you maneuver." Ravi stood back, allowing me the distance to stand relatively on my own as I wobbled slightly upon gaining an upright position. "Only a small fee. I'm sorry, only that we cannot spend the day."

I grabbed the open door. "I am impressed with what I see and that I have feeling in my feet—at least the left one," then blurted. "Can you help me out of this thing? I am dying inside here. I think there are pins on the shoulder, and as I recall—"

"I'll do my best to unravel the mystery." As Ravi unpinned the sari from the sari blouse I wore underneath, I stood stalk still. He placed the pins on the hood of the Toyota and rested his hands on either of my shoulders. "OK!" he said, "I will turn you around in a circle. Don't try to help. It's easier that way."

I held my arms out straight.

Ravi laughed. "Arms down," he said. "Just relax."

"I'm sorry, I just thought—"

"First rule. Do not think." That smile again as if he held all the answers in the palms of his hands. Indeed, he had only fabric—six yards to be exact. Ravi tinkered with the tie in the back. "Jack knotted this."

I breathed a sigh of relief when the fabric fell to the ground. "Phew," I said, "that feels good." Ravi unfastened the sari blouse, and I took another deep breath.

"May I introduce you to my tunic top?" I laughed and curtseyed, then pulled it up and over my head.

"And what is this, a sundress?" Ravi said. "It sticks to you—you must be so uncomfortable."

I shook the dress out a little, "Can you unzip it?"

"Most respectfully." Ravi's voice carried a teasing note. "I am curious about what comes next—under the dress?"

Some teenagers passed us with day packs. "Go, aunty, go!"

I bowed toward the boys and laughed. "The big reveal." I lifted the dress.

Ravi clapped his hands together. "A nightgown under the dress," Ravi said. "Most find India too warm for nightshirts."

"I'm new in town." I twirled in a circle. He unzipped the sundress and helped me out of it, and I grabbed the nightgown's hem and threw it off over my head.

"And what comes next? Khaki slacks and a t-shirt? Are you feeling better now?" Ravi whistled in mock relief. "I think we have reached the last layer!" He stood quietly with my sundress over his arm. "You are the most prepared woman I have met in decades."

"Thank you for your help. Wow, I wish I could shower."

"Our next stop—there's a wonderful shower—you'll like it."

"That sounds great. What a gorgeous day—"

"It is, and we have time for a walk and a good breakfast in the pavilion." Ravi folded the sari and the clothes before packing them in the car.

With my walking boots on I said,"I think I'm ready." Ravi offered his arm. After paying twenty rupees we entered a garden that spun out in front of us. A waterway serrated the grounds. Covered walks leading from building to building bore columns with elaborate archways. Vendors were getting their wares set up for the day. Marigolds bordered the straight canal. The restaurant was open; we sat on a terrace overlooking a field of fountains. From what little Jack had told me, I had expected that Ravi and I would be camping or eating in the car, not in this setting of exquisite architecture and formal gardens with seven mahals and palms set along the canal in an arrow-straight fashion. Ravi ordered *thali* for us to share. A platter arrived with rice in the center and bowls of yogurt *dai*, chutney, and roasted corn. I loved *patande* best—ghee stuffed inside wafer-thin slices of bread. Coffee and milk came after.

Too soon, we returned to the car park. From the rear of the Toyota, Ravi extricated two water thermoses. "These have filters" Ravi said. "And are lightweight. I have a gallon container for refills, and we will be close to water sources for most of our journey."

"I like that we aren't using plastic."

"So does the earth." Ravi handed me a light pink colored thermos loaded with water and ready to go. His was blue. "We are taking a tourist's route to confuse any pursuers part way."

"Well, I like your plan, and thanks for the explanation," I said and drank some water.

We then began our car ride northeasterly to Tashigang Village, at the border between India and China. The road was uphill through the Himalayan Shivalik foothills to Shimla, the famous endpoint of the toy train route from Kalka. We had already gained almost a mile in altitude, and my ears popped continuously. Ravi brought out a packet of ginger chews. My friendly doctor told me that hard candies help reduce nausea and other symptoms of altitude sickness. I popped one in my mouth.

"Where we will spend the night at Pooh is at twenty-three hundred meters."

"What's that in feet?" The ginger warmed my mouth.

"A little over seventy-four hundred." Ravi tapped the steering wheel, a nervous tick I noticed because he always seemed so calm. This trip across Himachal Pradesh was not all fun and games.

"That's a lot of hard candies," I said. "Won't we have to stop for gas somewhere?" As the miles passed by, I hadn't seen many petrol pumps.

"We'll top off at Narkanda when we stop for tea, about four-five hours away."

I wanted to ask him about the scar on his eyebrow, but I thought that might be too personal. "I cannot tell you how much better I feel without all the layers." I stretched my arms. "I'm a bird; I can fly." I fell quiet after, mesmerized by the changing scenery as we climbed higher. Buses and trucks stopped randomly along the road. Dogs and the occasional cow or goat meandered across the narrow highway, never in a hurry despite the rat-a-tat of car horns, trucks, and buses. The road had no guardrails, and erosion had worn the edges to a shine. Steep ravines and dense forest with the roiling Sutlej River below marked miles upon miles of sharply curved highway. Ravi tapped the steering wheel with his left hand as if listening to music. He drove well and never showed that he was upset by the air horns that made me jump each time I heard one.

"How did you end up in Sangla?" I asked.

Ravi breathed deeply, drummed the steering wheel, and exhaled slowly. His posture shifted into a straighter position. "My wife and I came from Manali to volunteer at Matipokhara hospital. Yeshe Maya was the hospital administrator at the time. She wanted us to stay on after our year's services ended. Brenna and I were indecisive, so we took a holiday in Sangla, at Yeshe Maya's suggestion, to rock climb, camp, and think over the possibilities." Ravi raised both eyebrows and cocked his head toward me. "This is a dark story—do you really want to hear it?"

He's married, or he was, I thought. "Yes, yes, I want to hear your story. Tell me."

Ravi tapped the wheel again. "Brenna and I were up in Sangla— picnicked, a day like this. Not a cloud anywhere. We began to discuss our options. She claimed she had always wanted to go to New Zealand and said she wanted to go on a cycling tour and perhaps move there. I had not heard about this before. She went on to say she was tired. 'Tired of it all,' her exact words. I told her we had a lucky life— 'Look around! We can bicycle here if you wish! We don't have to move to New Zealand.' Then she became more precise. She was done with the marriage. With me. Hospitals and especially Yeshe Maya, whom she claimed was a master manipulator." Ravi shrugged. "Brenna had everything all planned out—she would go back to Matipokhara alone, pack what things she needed and go to New Zealand. I could return to the hospital the week after she left, and stay or leave, whatever I wished."

"When did all this happen?"

"In 1995." Another tap on the steering wheel— "That's not the end of the story."

"I'm listening," I said.

"You can imagine it was a quiet ride back to Sangla. She left the next day. She had everything arranged. I got drunk in the bar at La Maison Fortune and listened to an old man tell fantastic stories about caves. Encouraged by drink, I set out on a borrowed motorcycle at four in the morning to find caves with a bottle of whiskey as a companion. I hadn't gone far when I missed a turn and tumbled, cycle and all, over a cliff. The bike and I parted company. Other than a bleeding forehead, I was uninjured."

"The scar through your eyebrow was from that?" I asked.

"Yes."

"What happened next?" I couldn't imagine the man I'd come to know acting out this way.

"I was out of alcohol and out of family. And as far as I knew, probably out of a job. And I had wrecked the bike. I curled into a fetal ball and asked the gods to take me. I slept but woke to a spotted eagle contemplating me from just feet above my head. 'Go for it,' I shouted. My voice echoed. I noticed that I had landed on an abutment above the river, the bike about ten feet away. Maybe my yelling shook the motorcycle off the edge, but seeing it free fall into the river terrified me. Annoyed by my situation, the eagle took off." As he spoke Ravi braked for a goat, and a truck blasted its horn from behind us. "And I don't know how, but I climbed down the cliff to the river—not sure why I didn't go up to the highway, but that is the direction I took. I fell into a pool of water. I remember thinking, enough, and I pulled myself out. That eagle was there again, and I followed it to a cave entrance—the one you will see soon. My head was bleeding, and I smelled like alcohol. I wandered some and met a man, who turned out to be your father." Ravi turned toward me with a smile. "How we met. Tenzin asked why I was there and asked me to tell him my story. I told him to kill me, and then I told him what had happened. I told him about Matipokhara, and he asked about Yeshe Maya. I was shocked that he knew her. Your father insisted I go with him—I was out of options—and that is how I entered Sangam."

"What happened to Brenna?"

"She sends me Christmas cards from Auckland every year," Ravi said with amusement. He touched his shirt pocket. "Have you seen my sunglasses?"

"I think I saw them in the backseat."

Ravi scratched the back of his neck. "Must have fallen out of my pocket."

For a while, we drove in silence. I smiled as I stared out the window at the ever-changing day. Growing up in a world where bodies of water lapped shores and seagulls flew in seaweed-scented skies, I reasoned that oceans and islands were necessary parts of anywhere I might call home. Mountains drew me out early in my life, but their mystery and majesty were illusory. In my father's world, the Himalayas were homey touchstones while oceans and scrolling seagulls were far away mysteries. Opposite of my experience. Could I live here? I asked the question to myself and shrugged it off.

We stopped for a break at Narkanda Hill Station. Passersby caught my attention as they did Ravi's. Our plan was to appear that we traveled as a couple. Obligingly, I offered my hand to Ravi. "Your hand is so soft," Ravi said as he held it. I walked closer to him, and he kissed me before we entered the new Pradesh Hotel and Spa's restaurant. We sipped tea on a patio overlooking a meadow nestled in the fir forests of Himachal Pradesh. I kept telling myself that this day was another elaborate play developed by Jack and Ravi, but not all of me believed that version of the journey.

"How high are we now? I can feel it, you know—like when you land in an airplane." The dark-eyed lady in the saffron-colored sari offered a small plate of dried apples and apricots, which we gladly accepted.

"About eighty-eight hundred feet."

Wildflowers dotted the field below, and tall snow-covered peaks cut across the horizon line. "Can we get gas here?"

"Definitely," Ravi said. "Are you feeling OK?"

"Yeah, yeah, I'm fine," My heart thumped louder, and when I breathed in, the air didn't go as deeply as it might. But I felt all right. The tea was fragrant. My ears continued to pop. "This is truly the Himalayas, right?"

"For truly," Ravi said.

"It feels like I've waited my whole life to see them." I touched Ravi's arm. "Being here makes me happy."

"This is a good day," Ravi said and unfolded his map.

I thought I could live here, with flowers and firs, sipping honey-sweetened tea, watching Ravi study his map, as I went back to scribbling in my journal. Too soon, Ravi peered at me, smiled, and raised his scarred eyebrow. Time to go.

"What have you been thinking about?" Ravi started the Toyota and turned onto the narrow ribbon of the broken highway.

I stuttered, "Well, I—" I nearly said how taken I was by his attention or something to that effect; this was what I wanted to say, but I willed myself to focus on why I was in this car with Ravi. My father waited for me in a village layered in secrecy, so I swallowed hard and started over. "How beautiful it is here—how my father lives with mountains, and I live by the water, and that somehow the water—the need to live by an ocean—becomes the same as the need to live by mountains."

"It isn't an either/or," Ravi said, "but a connection to nature, the nature of things."

"Not nature with a small 'n' but a capital 'n'—Nature. When I was a little kid, my mother took me to the ocean on the Oregon coast in the summer, and whenever I first saw the water that never ended, I felt like I was coming home. The sound of the waves, you know, they sing to you."

"Mountains sing, too. Especially up here," Ravi said.

I laughed. "The forests are quite talkative, too."

Ravi rolled down the window and asked me to do the same. He parked the car along the highway. "Let's see what our friends have to say."

In a moment, the choir began. "That's a macaque?" I asked.

"Aw, look, in the high tree, you see them?" Ravi pointed to a fir with long branches and an odd curve at its base. In the topmost of the tree, three birds noisily whistled. "Plum-headed parakeets—not monkeys."

"Parakeets? They're as big as parrots!" Another sort of bird piped in. "Who is that?" I turned toward Ravi.

"That's a flycatcher. Sounds like a drum, right?" Ravi drank some water.

As I took a swig from my thermos, a loud thump landed on the car roof, and when I looked up, a monkey stared back at me—upside down.

Ravi started the car. "These guys figured out we have snacks."

We watched the monkeys scamper to the other side of the road and got lost in that long-armed fir. "This forest is full of gossips and good-timers." I rolled up my window.

"Like you said, quite talkative." Ravi shook his head. "The government asks people to kill them. Farmers upset by crop damage and so on."

"I hate to hear that." I studied the moving forest scene as we sped along.

"Well, those two will be all right."

"Are you sure?" I asked.

"I promise." Ravi patted my leg. "Do you know about Hanuman?"

"Yes, of course, I know about Hanuman. Buddha's chief lieutenant. The monkey is said to be alive to this day."

Ravi laid into the car horn as we veered around a sharp twist in the road. A bus met us mid-point. We hugged the turn and drove on. "You're feeling a little nervous right now? First, the monkeys, and now the road?"

"Yes, a little, I admit—"

"In Hinduism, Hanuman is a shift-shaper, a devotee of Rama. Some say an avatar of Shiva. He did the impossible for Rama, organized the monkeys, and saved Rama." Ravi adjusted the rearview mirror. "He helps his friends face ordeals." Ravi smiled at me. "And conquer obstructions—so at this moment. Think of Hanuman—it might have been Hanuman peeking in our window."

"You know, I think you're kind of full of shit, but I love the story." I folded my hands across my chest. "I do like the story. I'll take it." I stretched my foot out of a spasm. "I read that Hinduism has a story to guide us through any human dilemma. Social psychology at its max."

"Are you being facetious?" Ravi asked.

"No, I'm not," I said. "I don't kid about spiritual paths or belief systems. You can trust that."

"Then why did you say I was full of shit?"

"Because you would ease my unease with a made-up story," I answered.

"Well, I might," Ravi shrugged and smiled over at me. "But quite honestly, when the rhesus smirked at us, the first thing I thought was Hanuman wanted our attention. Maybe an obstacle ahead or something to conquer."

"Then you saw my reaction to the monkeys, and it made sense. I'm the one trying to overcome a lot of learned fear while—" I paused for a moment. "I love being here with you. But I've been scared spitless, part of the time."

"You need only a little Hanuman love."

"He has my attention," I said. "Quite honestly."

We rode on. Ravi pointed at a Himalayan griffon, a vulture flying across the sky. We talked about the train ride from Delhi. I fingered my lei of marigolds that I roped around the rearview mirror, wishing that the flowers might stay fresh, but as natural things do, they began to wilt. Ravi and I would chat, then fall into silence, and I found communion with him in the quiet. It was deliciously, enchantingly easy to be in his company.

The road had flattened and widened during the last half hour or so. Ravi drove through beautiful Sarahan-Kullu village, where peaceful views from hilltops of white mountain peaks framed a perfect day. As we left the Sarahan, the Toyota pointed downward at a steep angle. I asked for a little bravery nudge from Hanuman.

"Aw, there it is!" Ravi said. "Altitude twenty-one hundred meters, in case you want to know—" and took a sharp turn on a mud-baked road that angled toward the Sutlej River. "The turnoff. A place called Sarahan Bird Sanctuary. Are you ready for a shower?"

Sweat beaded on my forehead, not from the heat but from the sharp angle of the so-called road. I felt like we could easily fall off it. "Yeah," I managed to utter. The hard-packed road ran above and parallel to the river. "We've come down about two-thousand feet, right?"

"Yes," Ravi answered.

My ears popped as I finished my latest candy. I guessed we were safe, and I was confident that I stunk. Long before we arrived at Sarahan, I had picked up the scent of sweat inside the car. I thought it had been Ravi who smelled a tad ripe. At our last stop, the smell followed me. I finally realized it *was* me. After being buried under all those layers of clothing, nature had won out. "I'm more than ready," I said. I imagined Ravi was more than ready for me to shower, too. "But where?" I saw no signs of any buildings whatsoever.

Cars parked alongside the road. Below us, along the Sutlej River, I could see inlets where Ravi told me springs formed. "People shower in their clothes and change afterward. Good waterfalls there. You get thoroughly cleansed. The rocks are slippery, so I will hold you up, OK?"

"Clothes get cleaned, too?"

"A thorough job!" Ravi previously wrapped his dry clothes inside a bath towel.

"I have hiking shorts inside my bag," I said.

Ravi held them up and passed them to me. "You have a t-shirt, you want that, too?"

"Yeah, that's great," I said, and along with my sandals, I was set.

Watching him ply through the backseat, I thought of a magician's hat. He had everything imaginable tucked inside four labeled boxes that lined the back—the first contained thermoses and towels. The second box contained foodstuffs. "What will lunch be?" I asked.

Ravi held up a linen drawstring bag, "Naan and cheese," he said. There were other cotton bags with pears and apples. And tea. "We'll eat after we shower. Is that all right with you?"

"Sounds good."

We followed a trail down the riverbank and then went around a bend where the river widened. Across from us, I saw a family gathered under falls that flowed over a broad stretch of rock. Ravi knew the area well. He chose a footpath that went up a hill where tall cedar and oak hid the river view. We angled down on a switchback. We held hands, which was not a romantic gesture, but one to keep me on my feet. Other falls appeared across from us.

"We're putting on a show for the birds." I looked upward to where Ravi pointed. In the fir trees overhead, rose finches and plum-headed parakeets peered down at us. A Himalayan monal flew low over the Sutlej. With its rainbow-colored plumage shimmering above the sunlit water below, and its plaintive call, the male bird was the star of the bird show.

"And cat calls from the monal! My mother drew them in a mural in my room when I was a little girl. God," I shook my head, "I forgot all about the bird in the mural until just now."

"We're going in his direction. You see the falls over there?" Ravi pointed to cascading water on the far side of the river.

"How do we get there?"

"The river is shallow enough. We will walk across. And," Ravi paused, "you need to change into your sandals. Take off the wrist brace; you won't need it today."

"Gladly." I released the sticky brace from my wrist. "I'm wearing a yoga bra, I said, averting my eyes and pretending to be ever so casual about stripping to my underwear. "Would it be OK to take off my shirt, too? I got so hot and sticky." Smelly was more accurate.

"Yes, most assuredly." He sounded doctorly.

I tossed off my shirt.

"Let me help you with your boots." He bent to untie the laces and I used his shoulder while he aided in getting the shoes and socks off my feet. "You have a blister on your heel," he said. "I have bandages in the vehicle. I'll run up and get one. The sandal won't rub as much."

Standing alone without the benefit of my shirt, I gazed at myself from the birds' point of view. Ravi and I were humans to be avoided and funny looking without feathers. As Ravi jogged back to where I was along the river, I thought he probably had more bird approval than I did.

Ravi covered the blister with what he called a plaster. "I'm sorry—it still may irritate." He rubbed my ankle in the palms of his hands, then took the other foot and did the same. "Your feet are still quite swollen. We'll get you propped up in the car." He offered his hand, and we stepped out into the water.

The day had to be in the mid-seventies with bright sun. I had not thought about the temperature of the water. "Wow, that's cold," I said as I took the first step into the river.

"You'll get used to it. It will help your feet." Ravi took another step, and I gamely followed.

"This is painfully cold," I said.

"It feels great."

The gravel and rocks were uneven as we walked across the waist-high spring to the cascading water from above. Ravi stayed close, and his grasp on me was firm until he zigged, and I zagged, then lost my footing. I fell into the water and had total body shock from the cold. My head went underwater, and my eyes were wide open. Ravi had me up within seconds.

"I guess that's one way to get used to the water," I said. "God!"

"You OK?" Ravi hugged me close with one arm. He kissed the top of my head.

"I'm fine. Fine. I fall easily." I laughed again. "God works in mysterious ways. I'm getting used to the water. Hanuman says I am fine."

"You are a good sport." We took a few more steps, and we were at the falls. "We just find a good spot and let the water clean us."

Water flowed and spun rainbows around us. Ravi and I lifted our hands to the heavens, and the falls poured over our heads, faces, and bodies. After getting over the cold, it refreshed every square inch of me. Ravi took my other hand, and we danced, well, we tried anyway, as the water washed the train ride away.

We walked cautiously back to the beach. Ravi dried off and I turned away as he slipped into a dry pair of khaki hiking shorts and shirt. I dried off, but I wanted out of my wet bra and needed some privacy.

"Will you turn around while I get dressed?" I asked.

"Of course," my companion replied with teasing eyes.

I hustled into my dry clothing "OK, you can look now." I bit my lip when our eyes met and we both laughed. I was falling in love, and that worried me. This journey was about meeting my father; Ravi was my guide. This couple thing was an act.

I sat in the car while Ravi brought out a small scalpel and some ointment from his medical bag.

"What are you going to do?" I asked with eyes on the shiny small knife.

"I'm going to sterilize the needle, then remove your foot."

"You bad man!"

He struck a match and burned the end of the scalpel. "I'm going to lance the blister. You ready?"

"Go for it," I said, "I guess I'm going to trust you with sharp objects. You need your glasses?" Do you wear glasses?"

By the time I had finished my sentence, Ravi had lanced and applied an antibiotic. "You will not need a bandage until we walk again. We'll let it air out."

"You are very good at what you do," I said. "You have good eyes, too!"

"One more thing," Ravi said. He reached over me to open the glove compartment from which he removed a small leather pouch looped on a braided beaded strand made from soft leather. "Your sunstone's inside." It warmed at the touch of my skin when I looped it around my neck.

"Thank you," I said. "The beading is beautiful."

"That is a gift from Yeshe Maya's sister. You'll meet her soon." Ravi stretched. You want lunch?"

"Who's the sister, and yes to lunch."

Her name is Deva Tara; she manages day-to-day concerns at Sangam and keeps Tenzin on track." As Ravi spoke he handed me a slice of cheese.

"Gosh, I didn't know Maya Yeshe had a sister," I said between bites.

"She's remarkable; you'll love her." Ravi answered.

A couple parked by our vehicle and spoke to Ravi in Hindi. The woman smiled at me and I at her.

Ravi explained that they wanted directions to the falls.

"I cannot believe I actually showered under a waterfall," I exclaimed. "It's hard for me to wrap my head around all the changes in the last few days. I look forward to meeting your Deva Tara, and right now, I feel rejuvenated. The pear was a perfect dessert!"

We cleaned up after lunch, and Ravi adjusted the front seat to its furthest back position so I could use the dash as a footrest; then we took off.

"What happens when we get to the hiking part? Jack said it was about a ten-mile walk after that."

"You're right. We have about a four-hour drive. We'll camp tonight at Pooh and get an early start in the morning. You'll love it!" Ravi said. "It's a nice spot, and I'm all prepared."

"Jack didn't mention anything about being out overnight," I said.

"You can ask him why he didn't tell you tomorrow morning."

"What? He's meeting us out here?"

"He'll be with Natalie." Ravi said, "They will come from Sangla, the more direct route, to retrieve the car and lend us a motorbike."

"So, this was the final plan you guys came up with?"

"Yes."

"Jack told me we weren't going through the Indian access point to the Saraswati Cave; is that right?"

"Correct," Ravi answered.

"Does that mean we go through on the Chinese side?"

"We are getting help from a Sangam friend in Tashigang."

"Tashigang? Where is that, anyway?"

"About an hour away on a motorbike from where we camp. Then we walk."

"On the Chinese side?"

"It's safe. Our friends in Mahamaya keep us informed about Chinese patrols, and they've been inactive the last year or so."

"Oh, cool! I have always wanted to go to Tibet!" Who was this relaxed traveler with feet propped on the dash? I was getting acquainted. I figured Hanuman was helping at the moment. I wondered what I could do to make myself stronger. "I always wanted to ride on a motorcycle," I said aloud, totally out of context. My old self unkindly exerted an internal complaint about camping and motorbiking, but I kept mum.

CHAPTER 20 MOSES OF THE CAVES

DEEP PLUNGES INTO VALLEYS marked our route as we ascended a pass. No railings skirted the narrow roadway. Trucks, motorbikes, buses, and dust-covered farm vehicles shared the highway, each edging upon the other. Occasionally, a goat or water buffalo meandered along.

I told Ravi more about my chair yoga. "I can do this pose called cat-and-cowl," I said. "Before I left La Conner, I was getting pretty good."

"It's called cat-cow pose," Ravi said.

I laughed. "The teacher has an accent—so that's what it's called? That makes sense! The cool thing is I can do it!" I said. "And you know what else? I can do the tandem pose and warrior pose. That takes good balance, you know?"

"I do know—and I think doing a yoga workout was a smart way to prepare for your trip."

"It helps with breathing—I've missed it—doing yoga, not breathing. I still do that!" My back hurt, but I delayed taking a pain pill. I didn't think Ravi would approve of Vicodin. He was so robust, and I didn't want him to think I needed it, so I talked more about the benefits of yoga.

I peeled oranges for us while the trees disappeared from view; no more monkeys today. After a patch of silence, Ravi asked, "I'd like to understand what you knew about your father growing up. Certainly, you must have been curious?"

I bit into an orange segment and considered my answer. "When I was about four, my mother told me that she found me under a periwinkle shell, and then I asked her if this were so, how could she be my mother? Later, she amended the story to say that a prince had come from a cloud with me bundled in his arms. The prince told my mother that he had heard her prayers for a child and that I was handy." I shrugged. "I thought my dad lived in the clouds. Maybe I was right?" I licked the juice off my lips.

135

"Anyway, I don't know. My father felt like something out of a fairytale, and my mother never left me wanting more."

"I think I missed out on not meeting your mother," Ravi said. "A periwinkle shell? Well, the cottages in Sangam are shaped like shells; they're yurts, and your father communicates in the clouds."

"Do you know how my mother met my father?" I said.

"Your mother was older than your father—he turns eighty-four this fall. He was fifteen when they met in Paris at the Sorbonne. Your mother was studying art on a scholarship. The attraction was immediate."

"I never knew she had done that—gone to Paris. I knew she was from Seattle and that her parents were dead. That's it!" I shook my head. How many secrets did Mother have? "Tell me what my father looks like?"

"Tenzin is well over six feet, with eyes like yours. He spent ten years in meditative isolation in the caves. His guide is Guru Rinpoche—Jack says you are well acquainted with Guru. I think you will get along with your father." Ravi took another steep curve as we headed upwards. "The only woman he ever spoke about was your mother."

As I listened, I tried to imagine this spiritual man. "Does he laugh?" I asked. "I want to get this image of Moses out of my head."

"Moses of the Caves," Ravi grinned. "His heart is light." We drove through a tunnel; a valley emerged on the passenger side. I sucked on candy, and my ears popped as the scenery took on something like an astronaut might see on the moon.

"Can you go to Mt. Kailash through underground tunnels from Sangam?"

"I haven't but others have," Ravi said.

"Do you know I have a painting of Mt. Kailash on my living room wall? Or I used to have." I laughed. "I used to have a house, that is, but I sold it." The admittance made me pause: "What else can you tell me?"

"I'm going to let some of it surprise you." Ravi squeezed my hand. "Why not try to sleep a little? I think it's going to rain." Heavy clouds gave way to raindrops as I closed my eyes.

Ravi sang a song that I thought might be in Hindi, or it could have been in Tibetan. His sweet low tones blended with the rhythm of the rain as it beat down upon us. I grabbed a blanket from the backseat and wrapped it around myself.

I hadn't had a Vicodin in two days, and listening to the rain and Ravi's song, I decided against a pain pill. My back ached, and my nose felt dry, but the old world seemed far away. When I woke up, the Vicodin would be there. Listening to Ravi sing was enough. I closed my eyes, and the day fell into quiet, undisturbed sleep. In my dream, I flew, and I had no pain. A woman with wild black hair floating in the wind took my hand and brought me back to earth. Lotus blossoms bloomed upon a pond by which we sat. "You have followed me," she whispered in the jasmine-scented air. "I am here to guide you." I understood in the dream that she was Yeshe Tsogyal. "Go. Father," she repeated the last words of Yeshe Maya. She faded, and I slept deeply.

I woke up in pitch darkness as we veered downward, where the road narrowed and divided. Ravi nosedived left over a rutted goat path through a field. I prayed Ravi was not having a flashback with him on that motorbike. I sucked in my breath, and my eyes widened. "Oh my . . . how long have I been out?" I lurched forward. The car came to an abrupt stop.

Ravi checked his phone. "It's almost eight—time for dinner." He sat back with a sigh. "We're here. The Sutlej River runs way down there." He patted my hand. "No worries. This is a flat place. It stopped raining a while ago."

"This is Pooh?" Nothing appeared flat to me.

"A few kilometers away."

Ravi's satellite phone rang.

Jack was checking in with us. He and Natalie were ready to leave Sangla before daybreak. Ravi handed me the phone, and I chatted happily about the monkeys and the birds. What I hadn't told Jack was that right then, my back hurt like hell, I felt a little breathless, and my head ached. Plus, I was concerned about getting out of the car on such a steep hill. We said goodbye, and then I turned to Ravi. "Where will we sleep?"

"The car. As you can see, the seats go back—and I have sleeping bags for an additional layer. We will be comfortable." Ravi put his phone into his shirt pocket. He put on his coat, a high-end jacket meant for mountain camping that matched the one he had brought for me.

An animal screeched, and I jumped. "What was that?"

"A wood owl; they get quite chatty at times. Let's get you walking, and we can explore a little."

I could tell Ravi liked this camping business. Hanuman was nowhere in view.

"I threw your boots back here." He got out of the vehicle, and I saw that he used the door to steady himself on the incline. The field slanted downwards. "I'll bandage your foot, too." He held up my boots. "Here they are."

"Thanks." When I turned to receive the boots, sharp low pain in my back left me breathless. My hand cramped at the same time as my foot cramped. I tried to breathe, locked temporarily, in a rounded-over position like an armadillo.

Ravi opened my car door. "You're in pain! Just ask for help when needed, please." Ravi put down the boots and knelt to look closely at my contorted foot. He rubbed my foot, tenderly stretching the tendon. "We are over a mile high. Altitude plays havoc sometimes."

"Don't know that's it's because we're so high up. I feel this way when I am tired or cold. The weather's changed." I wrapped the blanket tighter around me. "I haven't had Vicodin in two or three days." I reached for my bag on the floor of the car. "They're in here."

Ravi put his hand over mine. "I told Jack to get rid of the pills."

"What?" I stared at him in disbelief. "Why?"

"You don't need them—they should never have been prescribed. I've watched you—you move well."

"How dare you tell me what I need!" My Ravi fantasy blew up in tiny little bits of confetti. "You don't walk in my shoes. And Jack knows better." I rose to sit as straight as possible and winced in pain. I gritted my teeth. "I only take Vicodin when I need it, only half a pill at a time. And, boy, do I need it right now."

"How long have you taken it?" Ravi was still on his haunches, a boot in his hand.

"Six years," I said. "And I'm not addicted."

"Fact: You are addicted. I suspect your head hurts, and your stomach burns."

"Maybe," I said. "But I just woke up, and I'm still getting used to the food. And, as you said, altitude. If I had a Vicodin, I would feel much better in twenty minutes."

"Fact," Ravi said in the same quiet voice. "That is the drug talking. You are going through withdrawal. I am surprised you slept as well as you did." He took my foot, which had begun to cramp again. "The good news is your feet are less swollen. Let's get a plaster on your heel and you into the boots and walking a little. I have some acetaminophen. You'll feel better in a while."

"Fact," I retorted, "my doctor prescribed them."

"Then, your doctor was not acting in your best self-interest." Ravi began stretching the other boot.

"My doctor likes me very much," I said defiantly.

"No. Your doctor was doing what was expedient. Doctors hate treating chronic pain. Drugs quiet patients down." Ravi put the boot on the car floor. "Look," he said, "You might not like the message, but just as I said before about trusting me, trust me here. I am telling you the truth. I believe in your ability to deal with pain. Your doctor did not."

"Well, you're a very mean doctor, and I can get my own feet into my own boots." I twisted my body away from Ravi and winced.

"OK," Ravi said. "Let me know if you want something for your headache—regardless—drink water." He stood and stretched, leaving me with water, boots, bandage, socks, and attitude.

My foot continued to spasm. I doubted if I could stand on my own. I wasn't going anywhere. I knew I needed help with the boots and that probably Ravi was right about the Vicodin. I had been uncomfortable being on an opioid, although I'd swear on a Bible, I had never abused it, for Christ's sake. But how dare they? I remembered before I went to sleep when Ravi sang, and I felt comfortable and thought I didn't need anything else. Ha! "Ravi?" I said.

He was a few paces away, setting up the cook stove. "Yes, my love?" His voice was light.

"OK. You might be right about the Vicodin, but you had no right. And I'd like three acetaminophens. My foot's still spasming."

"Two and an acid reducer, and it's a deal," Ravi said.

"OK, you win."

"Foot, please," he said. He massaged the rigid arch on my foot. "I know it hurts." He then applied the bandage.

"I'm sorry I yelled," I said, "I've come to believe that I hurt more than anyone else. I know that's not true." I swallowed hard. "But every time I think about you and Jack stealing my pills without telling me, it makes me so mad."

"It was not theft, and you don't need them," he said without apology. Ravi brought acetaminophen and an acid reducer tablet from his pocket and then filled our thermoses. He handed mine to me. "Drink lots of water."

I rested my forehead in my left hand. "I'll try."

"Let's get you standing up; it's steep here, only here."

"You guys thought of everything," I said. "High places with sheer drop-offs," I whispered. "Thanks a lot." My snarky tone surprised me only a little.

"You won't fall. You are such a brave lady," and he kissed me. His lips on my cheek seemed natural to me. "And you always will have help despite being a drug-addicted-homeless lady."

"Very funny!" I said, "I'm going to miss those little pills."

The homey feel of my boots boosted my confidence. The area Ravi had set up with the cook stove was level. After a dinner of lentil soup, more naan bread and cheese, and date candy, we drank hot tea.

On a night where brilliant stars competed for space and heavenly bodies touched each other, we told stories about the first times we ever camped, drove a car, painted a picture, and went off on our own—all fairy-lit under this magnificent sky. "First time ever I showered under a waterfall is today," I mused. With my eyes adjusted to the dark, I braved up and, with the walking stick as an assist, claimed "the woman's peeing station" by a hillock on the other side of our campsite. I didn't ask about the men's room.

Below us, the Sutlej filled the air with river music. We talked until after ten. Ravi brought out sleeping bags and suggested we sleep under the stars. I placed my watermelon bag under my knees, and Ravi's down vest became my pillow. We slept separately in our sleeping bags with a woolen blanket as an additional outer layer. Somehow, we managed to hold hands. I don't know how exactly that came about, but I do know how it felt. I told him I was still a little mad about the Vicodin but that the night was too pretty to waste on grudges.

When we said good night, I kissed Ravi on the cheek.

Ravi touched his cheek, "First time, ever," he said and kissed me in return.

The smile on my face that no one could see told that part. I didn't sleep well; my back hurt, and my neck ached, but it didn't matter. It just didn't matter. I didn't want to return to La Conner because I had found a home here. The thought nearly broke my heart, for I had to board a plane that would take me far away. I prayed to God that I might remember every moment. "Every moment," I repeated it like I was saying a mantra. "Please hear me, Yeshe Tsogyal," I added.

Morning came when Ravi's phone went off. "An hour?" he said. "See you then."

"Was that Jack?" Blue sky peeked through clouds. I wanted to stay in the sleeping bag, but I needed to get up.

"Yeah," Ravi responded. "I'll make tea."

"What time is it?" I peeled off the sleeping bag, stood, and opened my arms to the brightening morning

"Just after six."

I leaned over to grab my coat and got stuck halfway down. Slowly, I stood, grateful that I could. Damn, if I just had a pain pill, I thought. Chills, acid stomach, and headache were bitter reminders of the wake Vicodin left. My boots were tucked upside down to prevent critters from finding temporary homes. Wrapped in my coat, I sat on the sleeping bag and began putting on my socks and shoes; I tried to ignore my aching back.

"What are you thinking about?" I hadn't heard Ravi arrive.

"Vicodin," I said. "I'm cold, and I hurt."

Ravi got down on his haunches and held my chin so I could meet him face-to-face. "I said, let me help when you need it. I know this isn't easy. But we had fun last night, yes?"

"Yes, I had the best time." Ravi took my arm and helped me stand. He walked me over to the Toyota while he made coffee. Instead of a second cup, I drank a cup of heated water chased by an acid reducer and acetaminophen. Ravi brought out collapsible walking sticks for us and told me how important they would be on our day's walk ahead, and I found mine helpful when I walked over to my tree to pee.

Ravi told me that Natalie and Jack, dressed similarly to us, would take the Toyota back to Sangla. If anyone had followed us, they would find it difficult to tell who it was in the vehicle.

Ravi and I were chatting next to the Toyota when we heard Jack and Natalie arrive. They popped off the cycle, and Jack removed his helmet. With a big smile, he said, "Hey, guys, how are you doing?"

"Somebody took my Vicodin without telling me—and I'm kind of mad about that," I said.

"Hey, it was for your own good," Jack said.

"Well, this is for 'your own good,'" and I kicked him in the shins.

"She's kind of ticked at us," Ravi said.

"You mean you did not discuss this with Maya first?" Natalie asked. "I'd kick you, too." She opened her arms, and we hugged.

"Great to see you." I turned towards Jack. "I'm OK with it, but I don't want to hear another word about Vicodin from either of you."

They both agreed.

"What's new with Motu?" Ravi asked as we ate sandwiches Jack and Natalie brought. They also brought extra water bottles for the driest part of our trek across Tibet.

"Amul called our room yesterday morning," Jack said. "I told him that when I returned to the hotel, I found a note saying that you had taken an early train to Sangla, anxious to see Ravi. He offered me a ride up on his helicopter, and I took it. He quizzed me about La Conner and our families. He's far too curious about you, Maya."

"Well, I was supposedly at the Matipokhara hospital to help Dr. Aha with the transition. I doubt he believes that story, yet it was accurate." Ravi said. "You may have been followed this morning, so guys, you better hit the road. Nothing unexpected so far."

"You are in for an awesome adventure—I wish I could be there when you arrive at Sangam," Jack said as we hugged goodbye. "I love you, kiddo, and I'm coming into Sangam a few days after you—so I'll see you soon. I'm your ride out."

"What?" I asked.

"I'll be taking you back to Delhi early next week." Jack sat behind the wheel in the Toyota.

"Gosh, I lost all sense of time." The sudden realization that next week I was saying goodbye, forever, to Ravi socked me in the solar plexus. I hoped Jack could not read my face. "I love you, too, Jack," and I nudged his arm. "I truly am grateful for all you've done to bring this about."

Jack started the old white Toyota, punched the gas, and with a flume of exhaust, he and Natalie boomed up the hill. They were gone, leaving Ravi and me with light gear. My mind was not on the day ahead but my companion.

I watched the dust trail and stood motionless. I didn't know, but Ravi stood behind me, whisper-close. He wrapped his arms around me, and I leaned back into his embrace.

"Next week?—"

"I know," he cooed, "I know. Let's live this day, OK?"

I tasted salt from tears free-falling and wiped my face with the back of my hand. "I'm going to enjoy every bit of it. Every little bit." I turned to face Ravi. "Even the littlest bit."

His reply was a kiss.

"Especially that bit."

Chapter 21 Taylor

"Hang on," Ravi said as he gunned the motorcycle's engine.

That every "little bit" seemed like a daunting task when he explained the art of riding as a passenger on a big motorcycle, once positioned, not to let go, no matter what. That "no matter what" concerned how nervous going straight up the steep dirt path to the highway made me feel. It would only take seconds to get up to the top of the grade, but it only took one of those seconds to upset the bike's balance by upsetting Ravi's balance.

Every tenth step I took on this trip came with some degree of confrontation with a body, however marginally affected, disabled by cerebral palsy. Balance issues and my inability to hold on with a tight right-handed grip were the issues Ravi and I faced today. Thank God I was past trying to be better than the best I could perform. In other words, I finally understood my weaknesses and was not trying to pretend them away or pretty them up. Right then, I had no time nor patience for faking that both sides of my body were equally functional. On the side of the motorcycle were saddle bags for our walking sticks and day gear.

I wrapped my arms tightly around Ravi, and my full-faced helmeted head pressed to the back of his leather jacket. The jacket was Jack's, and I was wearing Natalie's. Short jackets on a motorcycle made sense.

"Holy shit." A flume of dust slapped the helmet as we zoomed up the steep dirt path to the road above. I was sure I was going to fall off the bike. My heart sank into my chest, but I hung on.

Ravi paused the engine as we rounded over the road's edge. "How are you doing back there?"

"Holy fuck," I said through a mouthful of ginger candy I was supposed to suck on while we gained another seven thousand feet. "Holy fat mama."

"That's all you have to say?" Ravi was laughing.

"That's it." I decided not to add details.

"Here we go!" He accelerated the bike onto the road that angled upwards. He loved the bike. I could tell by the tone of his voice. There was a teasing quality, too. Men! I thought back to the night in Delhi, where Jack enjoyed our secret ride to the train station when I was unnerved. I did have to admit to an adrenaline rush when we pulled it off. And so far, this motorcycle ride was, without hyperbole, exciting.

My thoughts distracted me momentarily, and then my visor cleared sufficiently to appreciate the sheer drop-off on this narrow road carved out of the tall rock we drove along. Deep below us, the Sutlej River ran; across from it was Tibet. In the far distance, the Kailash Mountain Range flirted with clouds. Ravi sounded the horn at every corner in this road that only knew hair-pinned curves; he hugged the bike to the stone wall. At one point, fine gravel cascaded over us. My ears finally gave out, and the engine noise sounded distant. I barely heard the two cars that passed us coming from the village, I presumed.

I started to enjoy myself. As it rolled by, the jaw-dropping view of brilliant sky and rock demanded attention. I saw rock change color as the sun splayed rays that suddenly fell into shadow. Breezes dropped in temperature, and icy patches slushed along the broken road. Some potholes filled with water, and mud and water pattered against my legs. I shoved Vicodin withdrawal to the back of my concerns. Holding Ravi close, I rested my hands on the top of his belt under his jacket. I didn't need much else to complete the day, but the day expanded as we rode along. The road dropped into a field, and the way became mud and gravel. I saw some white buildings on top of a rock, and I figured it must be Tashigang.

Ravi pointed to the left of us and stopped the bike. "Blue sheep," he said. The sheep were grayer than blue, but their coats under the brilliant sky had a bluish quality. The four or five we watched brushed and charged against each other. One had a mustached-shaped set of horns. At our proximity, the sheep scattered. "Are you OK?" Ravi asked. He squeezed my hands; I kept my head nestled on his shoulder.

"Yeah," I said.

"Just a short way more to the temple," Ravi said, "hang on!" He revved the motor, and off we zipped to the village carved out from a mountain. A dirt path led upward to cave entrances; the temple was inside one. Ravi walked the bike, and I trailed behind using a stick. The footpath was steep but accessible, although I might have panicked if I had seen it a week or two before. The one drawback was the altitude. At fourteen-thousand feet, my pace slowed, and my breath felt labored. Not far along was the first entrance to the cave. A gaunt young monk in maroon robes and a slight overbite met us and nodded at Ravi. He bowed in my direction. Ravi unloaded his day pack and my watermelon bag and gave control of the bike to the monk, who quickly disappeared inside the cave with the cycle.

"What happens to the bike?" I asked.

"We'll collect it some time," Ravi said.

I caught what Ravi said, but my ears remained plugged.

Another monk appeared and beckoned us inside to a chamber featuring cave wall paintings from a thousand years before to current times. A youthful portrait of the fourteenth Dalia Lama sat on an altar. I thought Shiva was in the mix. My heart skipped a beat when I noticed one of Amul down low in a corner. What was that doing here? The mix of Hindu gods and goddesses with Buddhist monks and yogis was not surprising, Ravi told me earlier that day; the higher you go in the Himalayas, the more the beliefs blended. Prayer flags and banners attached to the ceiling hung over the bright display. The monk said nothing to Ravi, and Ravi asked no questions of the monk, but both acted in sync. With a glance from Ravi, I took his cue to follow the monk with Ravi behind me. Ravi took control of the walking sticks. We crawled through a passage covered by banners at the rear of the temple room. The floor was worn smooth from those who had gone this way before. After a short time, the monk turned toward me; I noticed his penlight as it flashed against the stone that circled us. He smiled and turned back. It was black-dark now. I could barely hear and didn't know if we were supposed to talk. Ravi patted me on the shoulder and moved around me; our bodies touched at awkward angles. "A ladder," Ravi said.

"A what?"

There were many rungs down, and the gaps were sizable between them, and I heard the old ladder creak as Ravi descended. I sucked in a breath, and was about to take a step down wondering if I could do this on my own. "I'm going now," I called to Ravi.

"Wait, let me guide you with my voice," he said. "When I say 'step' go to the next rung." Natural light emanated from below, and the smell of dampness carried on an upward breeze, but I could not see Ravi. In a moment he yelled, "Ready? Step." And I took the first one.

"Ten steps," I said when I got to the bottom. "I did it!" The light waffled over an underground waterway, inches from us. A boat tied lasso-style around a rock bobbed in the inky water.

Ravi hopped into the boat with our gear. "Take my hand," he said. Two planks lay across the boat's interior. Bench seating, I presumed.

Ravi unknotted the line and pulled it inside the boat. He took the oars from the floor and began to row against the current.

Eyes stared down from the ceiling of the cave. "Are those bats?" I asked.

"Yes, and probably annoyed bats. They like to sleep in the daytime."

"I saw a picture of Amul, at least; I thought I did." The tall stone cave's walls extended heavenward as we rowed through the cave's exit. We paddled close to the shore of a small tributary of the Sutlej River. Above and growing in the distance from behind us, I could see Tashigang Village.

"I saw it too," Ravi said. "Near the floor—not to worry. Tourists come up here to see the temple and leave tokens." Ravi shrugged as he rowed on.

"All right," I looked around. "Are we in China?" The far-field and mountainscape fell out of a montage of photographs I had seen of Tibet.

Ravi nodded and raised his scarred eyebrow.

"You look like a pirate!" We paddled along until we reached a shallow rock bed with bursts of whitewater rippling across where the stream merged with the Sutlej. Another monk hailing us from the rocky shore.

"This is where we exit," Ravi said as he maneuvered to the holy man. They bowed in greeting, and both men offered hands to help me out of the boat as it rolled gently. With our two bags unloaded, the monk got into the boat and began rowing back to the cave. A boulder the size of an eighteen-wheeler extended into the river, and it appeared that we would be going over it. I saw a path that wound upwards over the rock. Ravi handed me my walking stick.

The pathway had no edges but gently angled up to the rock's apex. I stared at the way downward; the backside of the rock sheered off. "Welcome to Pahaad Aaramapasand," Ravi said.

"This boulder has a name?" I asked. Panic oozed from my brain to my limbs. My hands shook. How would I manage this descent?

Ravi stroked his chin. "In English, it means Mount Easygoing."

"And you just made that up!"

"Grant you. But a good name?"

"An excellent name, but I've never gone down anything like this." I saw the Sutlej—white water washed over rocks. The wind picked up, and a chill ran down my arms—another tenth step. The day would warm quickly, but cold winds and temperatures were unfriendly at high altitudes even inside my jacket. "Looked OK at first."

"Yeah," Ravi said. "Use the stick. Follow me."

We started down, and the path loosened into gravel. I wedged the cane into the ground at every step. Then, the trail stopped. A ribbon existed; I could see where a blue sheep or a mountain goat might find it passable, but not me. "How do we get down from here?"

"Yes, yes . . ." Ravi picked up my watermelon bag, his backpack, and my walking stick, then heaved them below.

I stared at him, my mouth agape.

"Now for you." He stretched and took a deep breath. "You have heard of the fireman's carry?" Without waiting for me to say a word, he pulled me in a half sling position and hurled me over his shoulder.

My body bobbed along over his. I tried to act nonchalant, but nothing in my experience had prepared me for a moment like this. Nothing. I noticed a spray of dust as Ravi secured a foothold, carefully anchoring the walking stick as he side-stepped down. We slid a few inches while Ravi found the next anchor. "I wish I could do something to help," I said when Ravi paused.

"You're doing fine," Ravi said.

"I'm not doing anything," I said to the back of Ravi's shirt.

"And I am grateful for that." Without notice, he swung me back to my feet, where a path emerged, and stopped to pull our thermoses from his pack. Next, he tethered my watermelon bag to his backpack and heaved it over his shoulder.

"Thanks. I'm released from duty." I stared upwards and could not tell exactly where we had been. I again marveled at the idea of being here under any circumstance.

The river walk was flatter and the shore broader. Soon we left the river and headed to a canyon above it. With Ravi's arm around me, I never felt uncertain. He told me where the Sutlej River originated at Lake Manasarovar at the foot of Mt. Kailash. The sources for three other holy rivers, the Brahmaputra, Karnali, and the Indus, come from Manasarovar. Hindus and Buddhists revered the lake and joined pilgrimages with Jain and Bon people to Kailash and Manasarovar to pay homage for ages. "Understand," Ravi concluded, "Sangam is part of the complex, a holy place. Kailash protects it."

He had said that the day before, and Ravi was not one to waste words. I understood he wanted me to recognize the importance of Sangam. "I hear you," I said. "Yesterday, I dreamed of this place. Yeshe Tsogyal was in it. The river feels holy, and I understand where we are going is holy. I truly mean it when I say I am humbled to be here." The chills I felt were not from the breeze but from realizing where this journey would end.

There was joy in the day. Gophers darted, and the distant mountain peaks changed colors as the sun warmed us. A flock of sheep from the high country filled the horizon as herders and dogs drove them to lower ground. The fields that cut between the river and our path grew noisier as they proceeded by. One of the herders spoke to Ravi, and the fellow waved to me. A young man with a camera hopped over the walkway's edge and took photos of the herder. I was startled when he spoke to me in English.

"You're American?" he asked.

Ravi peered over his shoulder at the young man and continued to chat with the herder in what I thought was Tibetan.

"Guilty," I smiled. "What brings you here?"

"I'm doing a thesis on nomadic shepherding; Name's Taylor. And you? How'd you wind up here?"

With a whoop, the herder returned to his flock, and Ravi stepped over to me. "Honey, this young man is traveling with the sheep," I said. "Isn't that something?"

Ravi and Taylor shook hands, and the young photographer said, "I better catch up with the flock. Have a good holiday."

"You think he's following us?" I asked Ravi when we were out of range. Ravi shrugged in reply.

Chapter 22 Angels and The Goddess

The winds howled and painted our skin and clothing with dust. I licked dirt off my teeth and thought about how this environment equalized us all.

"Tell me about your parents," I asked. "Your dad was a missionary, you said?"

"Yes, he was assigned to Manali—arrived to teach hygienic practices at a school his home church in Santa Rosa, California sponsored." He squinted upwards at a flock of white birds. "Funny thing—he met my mother on a home visit—she was attending a birth—and she shooed him out. He was gobsmacked by her. They argued about politics and religion all the time but fell in love. Were married fifty-seven years."

"Did your dad stay a missionary?"

"He remained devout, but out of respect for my mother's Hindu beliefs, stopped proselytizing, " Ravi said. "My mother's family lives in New Delhi, where they were married. My mom always said I was 'job enough.' I was an only child—like you. We vacationed here annually, and I never got the high country out of my system."

"Where'd you go to secondary school?"

"Switzerland. Then after to the States for university."

I paused to take a drink of water. "After medical school, you came back to India?"

"Eventually," Ravi said. "Brenna's student visa was up—so I followed her to Dublin. She loved being home—we were both doctors—we established practices. Meanwhile, in India, my parents got old, as you noticed, we all do, and they necessitated the move. They retired to Manali, where they died. Old age, basically."

"You took care of your folks, then?"

"Yes. It was a good year, that last one with my parents." He appeared wistful as he wiped the sweat from his brow. "Brenna and I moved onto Matipokhara after—something my mother asked me to consider."

"It turns around the whole relationship, doesn't it?" I asked. "I mean—my mom and I laughed more times than I can recall when things switched around, and I was taking care of her the last eighteen months of her life."

"She had cancer, Jack said." Ravi put down his backpack. "Let's rest."

I breathed a sigh of relief. My feet were tired, and the sun was getting hot. "Yeah, yeah. Esophageal. Bad stuff," I said. "I loved being there for her. She still told me magical stories, and I took on all the household responsibilities."

"I thought you were always cared for—protected from the world."

"I always ran for cover from a world of bullies, maybe, but I tried not to complain much," I reflected. "My mom saw a new side of me when she was sick; maybe a new part of me emerged. I became interested in Buddhism—because it helped me respond to each day rather than to outcomes—and I had dreams of a monk who guided me. Recurring dreams that helped me sleep at night." I stared up into Ravi's marvelous brown eyes. "I am not a weak-minded woman, just one who comes with wobbles." Stunning, sometimes, the moment a truth reveals itself; this was such a moment.

"You took care of your mother throughout her illness?"

"One time, she offered to go into a nursing home—she worried that the lifting and so on was too hard for me. I looked at her and said, 'A nursing home would kill you'—one of our best laughs."

Ravi handed me a honey-nut bar and took another for himself. "These are quite good." He ate silently.

"Hmm. This is delicious. I think food tastes better up here."

It was time to continue our trek. As my energy waned, the road became tougher to traverse, and speaking to one another seemed an additional burden. My feet felt hot and swollen. Sweat ran down my back, and I didn't know how long I could push one foot in front of the other. I kept looking into the distance for any sign of where we might be going. The ring of mountains appeared to grow taller, and I swore we passed around them more than once. Tinnitus made river music in my head. "For now, I am here," I whispered aloud. Ravi did not hear me.

On our next break, Ravi asked, "You've been quiet. Everything OK?"

"Sometimes I get a little lost in my thoughts," I started to explain. "This is hard stuff. But the nature is wonderful. And I'm tired. But wonderful."

"Wonderment? Outside your common field of things accepted?" Ravi asked.

"Something like that," I answered. As harsh and beautiful as this landscape was, it made me happy. Perhaps, it was the closeness I felt toward Ravi. More than that, I felt at home. I had no words for either feeling. *How could I ever leave?* I wanted to say but didn't. Would I be talking to the mountains or the man, or was one the other?

"I know!" Ravi jumped to his feet. "I nearly forgot!"

Ravi's sudden burst startled me, and with wide eyes, I asked, "What?"

"These!" Ravi pulled out a bag of multicolored button-shaped candies. "Jack said you loved candy—especially American chocolate. He gave me these before he and Natalie left."

"I'm glad you remembered!"

He handed me the bag. "You have to share, and I get all the green ones."

"Did you know they used to use bug juice to make the candies shiny?" I asked, my mouth plugged with candy.

"What?" Ravi popped a green one into his mouth.

"Yes—it came from the rear end of a beetle. And I think they called it candy shellac or something," I said.

"You are the holder of many facts." Ravi stretched his legs out. "Really, from a beetle's butt?"

"Yeah, isn't that weird?"

"I will check that out."

"Ever eat chocolate-covered mints at the movies?" I asked.

"You're kidding." Ravi raised an eyebrow.

"Dried beetle butt made those little mints very shiny. You can look it up, too." Sugary chocolate warmed my mouth.

"I am not opposed to eating dried grasshoppers. But I want them to look like a grasshopper, you know?" Ravi said thoughtfully.

"I can't believe you just said that." I shook my head. "Jack had me eating chocolate-covered ants once when we were kids. He dared me—and it was OK because I pretended the ants were raisins inside the chocolate. I did not want them to look like real ants."

"I guess we are different in how we want our bizarre foods served." Ravi tapped my arm. He kept looking at the sun as if it held secrets, or maybe he was tired and peered at the skies for relief.

I nudged his arm. "Time to go?"

"Yes."

In another half-hour, we began to climb a bit, and there in the distance, I saw a dun-colored outpost. Sunlight streamed on this building in a burst of spear points, or I saw things, a notion I took seriously. As we traveled closer, I saw black holes for openings in the building, and sunlight glanced off them. The three-tiered structure took on the character of a shiny honeybee hive with doors and windows.

Ravi had said little the last while but smiled when the building came into full view. "Time to stop."

I didn't need much encouragement. I sat in a heap on the ground, my back against the side of the structure. Startled birds flew out of openings in the wall.

"Drink water." He handed me a water bottle. "And this." From his pack, he offered me a wrinkled piece of dried meat. "It's yak jerky, really quite good—it looks exactly like what it is. Try it." He had a broad grin across his face.

"It's still pink," I thought I might gag but gamely took a bite. "This is really good." It was more tender than beef jerky. Sweeter, too.

Ravi took off his backpack and put it alongside my watermelon bag, then wiped his forehead with the tail of his t-shirt and sat next to me.

"You've got to be tired, too," I said.

He nodded and shrugged.

My nose ran, and stinging pain coursed through the circuit of my nerves from foot to neck. I did not see how it would be possible to stand upright again. I closed my eyes and dozed for a few minutes.

Ravi patted my leg, and I opened my eyes. I shook my head and drank some water. I noticed Ravi had field glasses in one hand.

"You see something?" I asked.

"Behind us, about eighty meters, I noticed sunlight glinting off something moving." He smiled at me. "Let's go explore."

"Shouldn't we hide? Is it Taylor, do you think?"

"Someone has eyes on us; let's find out who it is." Ravi offered his hand and helped me up. He kissed me on the cheek.

"OK, what if they have guns or are robbers or something?" My voice wavered.

"Let's see what it is before we discuss what it might be," Ravi answered; he was a few paces in front of me.

"Wait up!" I said. "Remember, we're a couple."

Ravi laughed and held out his hand, which I grasped. He cautioned me to be quiet. The sunstone felt warmer inside the pouch, and I didn't know what to make of that. My back ached as we traipsed close to the path's inside edge we had gone down an hour before. We approached a switchback, and Ravi put his index finger over his mouth and motioned me to stay. I watched him move stealthily like a wolf approaching its prey; he disappeared behind the bend.

Ravi came back around, where I hugged the path's side and Ravi held up a stainless steel bowl. He cautioned me not to speak, put the bowl in his backpack, and offered his hand to me. I patted the pouch around my throat for courage; my fingers tingled as we continued to the beehive house. "Well, I'm glad that was nothing," I said. "Someone forgot their bowl."

"Maybe." Ravi took a drink of water. "But we have to be cautious. He checked the door to the structure. "It hasn't been disturbed." He searched the area with his field glasses, "We'll carry on. Are you ready?"

"Ravi," I said, "before we go, my sunstone heated up when you went looking for the shiny object, and it heats up at this little beehive house. Is there something special about this place?"

"What you call a beehive house is a Buddhist temple. In the old days, a sect of Yeshe nuns lived here. Your grandmother may have stayed here, and it's not surprising that the stone heats up. Mine, too."

I took a step back to see the entire structure. "Erosion has done a number on it." I watched as a small bird left through a high opening in the cone-shaped edifice. "I thought those were windows." With my hand flat on the side of the temple, I felt stinging—beehive, bees stinging, I know—not meant to be the same. I felt a sharp pain, and the stone was hot. "There was trouble here, wasn't there?"

"In the sixties, the Chinese destroyed many of these mountain temples—the Revolutionary Guard did not miss much. We'll cross the Sutlej in about five, ten minutes. We have a narrow bridge—narrow planks—you'll see. We're going downhill to the river. I'll get you across."

I was getting adept with the cane, and he used his stick as well, both of us poking ahead for potholes and loose rock. The steep path did not bother me nor the river below us. Large rocks littered the shore, but even my fear of falling headfirst into certain death and destruction became a mere annoyance. Egrets sailed across the Sutlej. My body tingled not with pain but with life. The stone buzzed slightly against my skin; its temperature cooled. As tired and worn as my body felt, I was not suffering. I exalted at this moment, like on a day when my mother was doing well.

My new self-confidence waned as the narrow railing-less bridge came to view. Across the bridge was a waterfall that obscured a small rocky path that Ravi said led under a mountain.

"How do we get across the river?"

Ravi took my walking stick. "I go first—hang onto my belt—we count together to thirty, and when we finish, we will be across the river."

I positioned my hands around Ravi, held onto his belt, and hugged into the gear he carried on his back. "I'm ready."

"Let's go," he answered. "We go as one." Our steps were in sync. Thankfully, the wind died down, leaving the air and river still. By the time we had counted to twenty, we were standing on river-slick stones at the mouth of the waterfall. The falls pelted us with flumes of spray and soaked our clothing; I did not let go of Ravi.

"Your second waterfall shower!" Ravi shouted. "Thank the river goddess, Saraswati."

I was awestruck by the power and the brightness of the white water free falling into a pool at our feet.

The late afternoon sun melted the western sky as it settled over the distant mountain peaks. Ravi held his sunstone like an offering to the waterfall; the stone glowed in violet shades, and rainbows sparkled and faded through the mist.

"Wow," I said, "It's like the sunstone was talking to the waterfall."

"Something like that." Ravi's voice rose over the noisy falls.

"My stone warmed up, I swear!" I touched the wet pouch that hung from my neck.

Ravi shook his head. He didn't hear me. He then took my hand and led me behind the waterfall on a trail that went into the cave about twelve feet from the falls. Pathways opened to the left and right of us. If he had anything else to say, I couldn't hear him. The ground itself shook from the thundering water. The falls shimmering ever-changing roaring bursts shot out rainbows like fireworks.

Ravi motioned for us to the left; the path widened on a steep descent.

"Isn't the waterfall something?" Ravi said as we stopped at a natural rock formation shaped like a bench. "Sit, sit here." He plunked my watermelon bag on the rock.

"I have never heard anything that loud or seen water move with such focus. Yet graceful, and then the pools below sparkled. And the stones; mine vibrated." I burbled on like the water in fits and starts; my hand placed over the pouch.

"A lot of water in motion!" Ravi said.

I closed my eyes and took a breath. As soon as I stilled myself, my muscles stiffened.

"How are you feeling?" Ravi asked.

"Baptized." I laughed.

"A religious experience. Yes, maybe that." He turned directly towards me so that we were eye to eye. "I, ah . . ." Ravi stopped then said, "We're both soaked, but we'll dry out quickly." Ravi offered his hand, which I took, and we began our journey.

"Finally, the Saraswati Cave. Wow." Anxiety and excitement mixed at being so close to Sangam, where I would meet my father. At that moment, I watched light sparkle on the interior cave walls. "Where does the light come from? A kind of rock like the sunstone?" I asked.

"Yes. An interesting phenomenon—curious to this cave. A good thing because caves get awfully dark as you saw."

After a quarter-hour, the cave floor flattened as we continued walking onward, and the noise of the waterfall's thunder receded into calming sounds that echoed off the craggy stone walls on either side.

"The breeze feels warm in here," I said.

"Why we will dry out quickly," Ravi said.

I stared at the top of the cave, which I figured was about the height of my living room. In places, water ran little rivulets down the walls. I thought we must have been walking under the Sutlej River. "Well, you are right; this is much easier. I don't mind this at all." My clothes were nearly dry. "Where's the Saraswati River?"

As soon as the words left my mouth, the path veered sharply up, the ceiling lifted, and we stood at the edge of a stadium-sized arena. Below us was a river. "So, this is it?" I whispered. "The Saraswati? My stone is vibrating again."

"Yes, Maya. We are here."

"Sangam?"

"No, we cross the river to go to Sangam."

"Look at that!" A white fish broke through the skin of the river and dove deep.

As we stood at the high point of the arc, clouds appeared above us and moved like apparitions. "Did you see that?" I asked.

"The river creates its climate, some say, the source of the breeze." Ravi pointed with his walking stick to a cloud. "Doesn't that one look like an angel?"

"Breathtaking," I whispered. "Like a real angel."

"So, you believe in angels?"

"Yeah, I always have."

"I like that." Ravi stopped. We had reached stone stairs that spiraled downward over the river.

My mouth dropped in utter amazement. "I know I should be scared to death. But the water sparkles in the dark, the angels, and the goddess."

"The sparkles are fireflies. They love it here. I am glad you are not afraid."

"And the cave walls seem threaded in gold—is that what creates the light?" I felt holiness all around me. I pointed downward at the river so clear that even in the dim light, I could see black stones on the bottom and golden koi that moved languidly along.

The stairs stopped, and the passage snaked upwards.

"The last part's most strenuous, but we are nearly there. Take my hand, love."

I felt my heart in every step as we walked a zigzag path at a steep angle. I kept visualizing tumbling backward. My mouth went dry. The river grew distant, and the ceiling loomed low over our heads. We wound around a steep corner where the path divided downwards to the left and right of us. "Which way?" I said.

"Straight ahead."

"But that's a wall," I said between labored breaths.

Ravi held up his stone, and a seam of sunstones shone in the shape of a circular doorway. "This way," he said

"What is that?" And then I paused, "That's the way inside, isn't it?"

Our feet moved in sync; the cave was behind us.

Chapter 23 Sangam

Ravi and I stood together on a natural granite platform as the clouds filled the valley below. Quiet. The square we stood upon was wide enough for us if our bodies met. A diver's platform against a field of white. My knees wobbled as fear of falling froze my feet into place.

"I can't," I whispered.

"You can't, what?" Ravi asked.

"Can't move. My legs won't work."

"You can and you will," Ravi answered. He wrapped his arm around my waist. "Together. The stairway's right here." He pointed with his walking stick. "Let's go."

"I'm not moving," I turned slightly to see the cave entrance, but it had closed. "I want to go back," an instant failure, but an alive one. All my fears coalesced; my new bravery and insights vanished.

"I am going down these stairs." Ravi pointed with his walking stick. "And you are going with me."

"I honestly can't move. Everything feels lopsided; the clouds make me dizzy. "

Then, I'll leave you here."

"You wouldn't, would you?"

"Give me your stick and take my arm."

I did as he asked and watched as Ravi secured the walking sticks through the loop that tied our bags together, amazed at the load this man carried.

"Let's go," he said.

I trembled as I took the first step into nothing I could see, and twenty-seven steps later, we alighted onto a graveled landing hidden in a cloud; my shaking did not stop. A river of cloud mist flowed lazily through the air. Water pearled on my forehead and dripped in my eyes. "Holy God," I said, "how far is it down?" I turned my head away from Ravi and vomited.

Ravi reached into his pocket and pulled out a cotton handkerchief. "Face me," he said, then wiped off my mouth. "Any more coming up?"

"I don't think so."

"Drink some water." He pulled out a water bottle from his other pocket, which he opened one-handed. I was in awe of his natural dexterity.

"I can't hold the bottle in my right hand." The left one clung to Ravi.

"Trust me. I have you. Use your strong arm."

I edged my arm around and out of Ravi's embrace and grabbed the water. On the way to my mouth, I spilled the contents on myself but took a solid gulp. Water never tasted that good. "Thank you," I said.

"Breathe," he answered. "You're doing fine."

If by magic, the clouds lifted from above us. A thinning layer remained below while the sky struck the colors of a richness I had never experienced. Ravi glowed in tints of red and gold and shades of blue. It was like seeing him through a kaleidoscope. I stared at the fading sun as it oozed rose gold and Aegean blue across the skies. The brilliant colors made me dizzy. "I think I might throw up again." I closed my eyes and began to pant. "I feel stoned."

Ravi held me securely to his side. "Breathe with me nicely and slowly."

I took a breath and looked up at him. His huge smile broke up his face.

"Good. Count to four and take another breath. I haven't lost you yet. Trust me, Maya." He kissed me on the cheek and made a face. "You still have puke on you, girl." He dampened a clean corner of the handkerchief and washed my cheek off. "Let's go, OK?"

I think that may have been the moment I knew that I was in love with him—wiping puke off my face—go figure. "Yeah. Let's go." Wispy clouds hugged us and changed colors as they slow-danced and disappeared. "It's astonishing—the colors." My voice shook. "Totally stoned."

"Stunning, isn't it?" Ravi said.

A bird darted and zeroed in on Ravi. "Watch out!" I yelled. My heart sped up.

"That's Dial." Ravi took a walking stick from the gear and held it out for the magpie. He landed and hopped up the cane to Ravi's shoulder. Dial's green breast, red beak, and feet made him distinctive; his black mask added mystery.

"Hello, hello, hello." Dial repeated, and then he flew loops into the kaleidoscopic heavens.

"A welcoming committee," I said. "Dial has a gravelly cartoon voice." The bird's antics eased me—he was inquisitive and, obviously, smart. "And he talks?"

"He has no bad habits," Ravi said, "and he speaks French, too, but he always greets me in English."

I pointed up to a ring of lights under the passage into Sangam. "What are those?"

"More caves," Ravi said. "In the old days, most people lived in them. Used for meditation now." He brushed my bangs aside. "How are you doing?"

"My heart's racing, but I'm OK." I hoped I sounded braver than I felt.

"Why don't we begin to go down? The stairs are shallow—not bad."

"How many steps?" I took his arm.

"Let's just take them one at a time," Ravi said.

I felt like a passenger in an airplane coming in for a landing, waiting to see what lay below. High icy peaks, like tines on a crown, surrounded the valley. Sunlight glanced and shimmered while shadows grew more abundant and the air warmed.

A grunting sound interrupted my reverie. A takin and her kid lumbered up the steps. "More greeters?" I asked. The horned mama had a massive snout and little eyes carefully trained on Ravi. The baby trotted in front of her mother. "God, the mama goat is big!" I thought they might attack us. The tawny-colored animal appeared more like a yak with its long hair, broad shoulders, and muscular body. The mama suddenly nudged the baby in the butt, and they jumped off the stairs.

"Off to bed," Ravi said. "They like rocks."

Now I focused on what lay below for other critters that might be lying in wait. I noticed a statue on a second platform, maybe thirty steps away. The "statue" raised an arm to say hello, and I realized this might be my father.

And then, there we were.

"*Mon enfant.*" The tall man with sea-blue eyes, wet with tears, placed his hands on my shoulders. Tenzin Neil Caron-Martin wore brown trousers with green suspenders, a red and black plaid shirt, and well-worn boots. I cataloged every detail as I peered into my father's face.

A memory from years and years ago came to me. We stood in this very spot, and I cried as my mother took me from him when we left Sangam. "I'm home," I said. "I remember you, Papa." My voice broke. "I remember."

He held my hands and kissed me on both cheeks. I was happy that Ravi had wiped the last of the puke off my face. The thought grounded the moment.

Ravi released me to my father. "Shall we go?" he asked.

My father's delicate touch guided me; we walked at the same slow pace. Ravi led a step below, and the panicky feelings abated.

"*J'ai attendu ce jour,*" Papa said.

"*Moi aussi.*" My father was not Moses in the Clouds, but Papa, the librarian, with a quick smile and a steady arm. I knew him. A veil lifted. My father.

He laughed. "*Parler français?*"

"*Je ne parle pas beaucoup de français,*" I replied.

"Then we will speak in English," Papa answered, "but you spoke French as a little one."

We continued. An impressive glass-domed building with rock walls, open windows, and long porches came into view. "The library." Ravi used his cane as a pointer. "Tenzin's in charge."

The valley became clearer. The library's dome lit the surroundings. The Sutlej River met the mystical Saraswati River, then meandered around a neighborhood of yurts that circled the library. "The Saraswati River is not underground here?" I asked.

"She converges with the Sutlej before making a tunnel inside the cave," Papa said.

"I've never seen such a beautiful river," I said.

Between the library and yurts was a green with walkways and garden tables that extended around the building. A woman in a yellow sari left the library. A man sat at a table facing west—I supposed, watching the sunset. I didn't catch any more of them but color and shadow.

"You have electricity here?" I asked as we passed over the last step and onto the green.

"Oh, yes, certainly," Papa said. "Solar and wind energy."

A small woman clapped her hands and then widened her arms in an air embrace. She wore a sand-colored bib apron over a mid-calf skirt and a violet-colored blouse. Her white hair floated in curls that touched her shoulders. I knew her because Deva Tara resembled her sister, Yeshe Maya. "Our child has returned." Deva came up to my chin, and I barely topped five feet. Even in the dark, her eyes shone.

My father repeated, "*J'ai attendu ce jour.*"

"First thing, Tenzin," Deva said. "We must let our travelers rest. Reunions are for sunlight." She turned her attention to Ravi. "You and Maya will be in the garden cottage—it is large and comfortable."

Ravi nodded.

My father grasped my hands into his large ones and said, "*Je dois prier.*" Then in English, "I am so exuberant I forget to speak in English. It is time for prayers. Thank you for coming home, Maya." He nodded as if he wanted to say more. He kissed me once more on either cheek. "Good night, my daughter." He hugged Ravi, whispered something that made Ravi smile, and then left on a path that bridged the river.

"I put a kettle of soup in your cottage, and we will see you in the morning," Deva said. She grasped my head with her capable hands, bringing my forehead to hers, then took my hands into hers. Her presence reminded me of Yeshe Maya; I recognized Deva's powerful energy. "Go on now. The soup will be cold." Before leaving, she kissed Ravi on the cheek.

I leaned on Ravi's walking stick. "Wow," I said.

"You remembered him?" We watched my father cross the bridge.

"It all came back. I was screaming when we left—I'd never been separated from Papa before—we all slept together. I was so young—before I was three."

"You OK?"

"I am physically and emotionally exhausted." I felt compelled to tell him how I felt about him and this journey. "I don't know if this is the right thing to say or if I should say anything other than thank you. I can't believe what you undertook to get me here—but the thing is—I mean—I had more fun—even when my knees were rubbery—"

Ravi put his index finger across my lips; he shook his head. "No thank you is necessary. The yurt is not far, and Deva makes excellent soup."

"All right."

Our yurt was at the northeast corner of the library square. The heavy door, painted red and decorated with undulating curls of color, creaked when Ravi opened it. A pole centered the structure, and cotton rugs lay on the floor. We collapsed onto a large bed built into the front wall. Ravi's backpack and my bag fell to the floor. Another bed of equal dimension was on the other side of the entry. A three-panel-rice-paper room divider lent privacy to the sleeping quarters. Red and white striped quilts were on both beds.

Ravi rolled towards me. "The toilet and bath are outside the kitchen back door, where the light is flickering. You will see the little toilet house just off the porch. The bath is private—it's a natural hot spring and where we bathe."

"Is this where you usually stay?" I rested my chin on my elbow and contemplated the perfect symmetry of his eyes and mouth.

"Yeah. Jack and Natalie stay here, too, when they're about." Ravi stretched, then wielded himself into a standing position. "You want to use the bathroom first?"

"A real toilet? Sangam has plumbing?" I asked.

"It's a composting toilet—fertilizer for the gardens."

I took Ravi up on the offer. A solar light glowed at the entrance to the toilet house. A mirror over the sink showed a weary woman who was extremely dirty. I wondered how clean my clothes were in my watermelon bag. The toilet operated about the same as a regular one. I wasn't sure where the shit went and didn't think too long about that. My toothbrush—I wanted to brush my teeth—but the toothbrush and everything else I brought was in my watermelon bag, and all that was in the main room.

Ravi knocked on the door. "Hey," he said, "why don't you get into the pool while I check in with Deva—I need to update her about Taylor and the bowl."

I poked my head out of the door. "Yeah, that sounds perfect."

White, flat stone surrounded the small hot spring inside a wall that was my height. I stripped off my filthy clothes and put them into a pile, carefully placing the pouch containing the sunstone on top like a crown.

Ravi had hung two large towels over the privacy wall. I was cold from toes to ears but hesitated to get into the pool because I didn't know how deep it was and didn't see a way out. The cold necessitated action, and as I dangled my feet in the pool, the warm water beckoned me despite the slight sulfur smell. I eased over the edge. I extended my cramped legs outwards and giggled at the bubbles. I tried to catch them and clapped my hands to pop them. The whirring water and soothing motion relaxed me. The water cleaned as if I had lathered my body with soap. I put my head back, floated without pain, cupped my hand, and reached to the heavens as if I could scoop stars. My eyes closed, and I drowsed off, and I did not know for how long, but my fingers were wrinkled from the heat when I woke up. My first thought was to get out of the bath and into my towel.

The problem came when I tried to get out. I didn't have the strength to hike myself over the edge. I pressed my hands against the lip of the hot springs, but my hands slipped time and time again. I tried walking up the pool's side with the idea of heaving my body over the edge. My feet slipped on the slick sides, and I slid back into the water. I ended up floating on my back, giggling at my dilemma.

"Everything OK?" Ravi was in clean shorts and a t-shirt, evident to me that he had bathed somewhere else.

"I can't get out." Embarrassed at my nakedness, I turned over, grasped the pool's side, and plunged below the water. I bobbed up and down to keep everything below my shoulders covered.

"Let me help you," Ravi said.

"But I'm naked," I said.

"I can see that." Ravi laughed.

"You can help me, but don't look." I allowed Ravi to lift me over the ledge and bring me upright. He wrapped the towel around me.

"I bet soup sounds pretty good right now," he said. "Let's get inside."

"Yeah, I'd like soup," I said. "But I need to brush my hair and get dressed—nothing is clean."

Ravi peered at me. "Did you check your drawer? Sometimes Deva leaves clean clothes."

"You didn't tell me I had a drawer to check," I said.

"I forgot. Drawers are under the bed. Mine's to the right." Ravi left me to investigate while he ladled soup into bowls.

I found a white cotton sleeveless t-shirt that hung below my knees. Folded next to the t-shirt was a wool shawl that I wrapped around myself. I had my toothbrush and toothpaste in my watermelon bag and brought them out along with my journal. I dried my hair with the towel and then brushed it out.

Over potato chowder, I asked, "Where'd you bathe?"

"At Deva's. She has a pool, as well. She thought you might want some time alone, and, I admit, I ate some soup at her cottage."

"Where does she live?" The soothing wholesome soup warmed me, and the bread's soft interior and crunchy crust were divine. "Hmm," I said, this is good." I devoured it.

"On the far side of the library," Ravi said, "I'll show you tomorrow." He stared at me. "How are you doing? Amazing what you pulled off."

"I'm officially beyond words." I took a breath. "What a day or week or month or however long it has been since we began this day." The bath had more than revived me. Honestly, it made me happy. I stared into space, unable to connect with the reunion I had with a father I thought I never knew. Was any of this real? Should I dance or cry for joy? I studied the glimmering candle on the table and watched the flame disappear into smoke.

Ravi tapped my hand. "Have you seen the cat?"

"What cat?" I jolted out of my meditation.

"The library's cat, Atlas. He usually comes around when I am here."

"Well, I fell asleep in the pool, so he could've come through without me knowing. I look forward to meeting him—all great libraries have cats, you know."

We piled dishes in the sink and got ready for bed.

"You want to sleep together?" Ravi said when I returned from outside. "No pressure either way."

"I would like that."

"What side do you want?" Ravi plumped the pillows and drew back the covers.

"Outer one, OK?" I said. "Sometimes, I have to pee in the middle of the night."

"You and everyone over sixty," Ravi took my shawl and folded it, placing it on a chair. We crawled under two hand-quilted blankets. "Are you comfortable?" he asked.

"Yeah, very comfortable," I nestled under Ravi's arm. I felt safe having him so close. "I can't believe I met my father or I am here."

"An adventure," Ravi whispered.

"I want to thank you for everything you've done. I am grateful."

Ravi snored quietly in response.

I remembered that moment in Nepal after the bus ride when I thought I was as happy as I ever could hope for—I thanked the gods for another such moment and fell asleep.

Chapter 24 Meeting the Neighbors

Atlas, the library cat, swiped his paw across my face as I opened my eyes. I remembered Ravi asking about the cat, but I was confused because I thought I was in my bed at home. Then a deadening thud in my center coincided with a strategic jump by the cat: this was not La Conner. I opened my eyes and squinted at clothes laid out on a chair, clothes I did not own. I guessed Sangam was expecting me.

This moment of privacy gave me time to dress. *Aw, nice.* Loose white drawstring pants with banded cuffs and a cranberry red tunic with matching frog closures fit beautifully—*pretty*. I rubbed the frayed hem of the tunic between my fingers and wondered whose clothes these used to be.

Light from the backyard made rainbow halos as they pierced the deep shadows inside. Wonderland. My father. Without knowing the hour, I figured it must be late morning and that I was late for something—but for what? Breakfast? I was hungry. As much as I had slept, I was still tired.

"Atlas, I'm Maya. Have you seen Ravi?" I petted the large brown, short-haired cat. His gold eyes surveyed me carefully, and then he hopped off the bed and led me outside.

Murmuring river sounds met sunshine that embraced me. Flowers predominated the garden. Primula banked the far end in a tall hedge—the red, five-petaled flower had a yellow center, and because it grew in clumps and fluttered in the breeze, I thought of butterflies, fluttering butterflies. On the porch, two high-backed, wooden chairs sat side-by-side. Faded golden knobs on either corner of the pagoda-style chair-backs gave them a royal feel. Someone had recently rewoven the seats with green bamboo. On a small table, an empty teacup hinted that Ravi had been here earlier. I walked back to investigate the primula, and by the pool wall, I saw Fragaria bearing tiny green strawberries, its white flowers vanishing. But the scent of wild rose made me hunt for where it hid amidst the showy primula. I strolled back to the chairs, and that's when the hummingbirds began to dart and play amidst the mass of primula and rose. The pool bubbled, and the river burbled. Butterflies flitted. I closed my eyes. *So, this is paradise.*

Ravi patted my shoulder.

I jumped at his touch. "I didn't hear you," I said. "This is just a gorgeous garden, and it's so warm out!"

"Yes, and yes." He was in jeans and a blue shirt. "Aha! My teacup. Would you like tea—I'm steeping a pot."

"Gosh, I must have dozed off out here. Yes, tea is fine," I said. "Or coffee, whatever you have going."

Atlas brushed between Ravi's legs and repeated the action. Ravi picked the cat up, and Atlas jumped on his shoulders and sat around his neck like a shawl.

"Atlas woke me up!" I said. "I think he likes you best. How are you today? Did you sleep OK?"

"I slept well enough—I'm usually wakeful at night, and so it was last night," Ravi said. "You slept very still. I envied your dreams—you had a contented look on your face."

"And drool on my chin. Did I snore?"

"Yes," Ravi said. He kissed his index and middle fingers and touched my forehead. "You looked beautiful to me." Ravi picked up his teacup. "Tea is ready. I made it Indian style," and he left to retrieve it.

An assertive little hummingbird caught my attention. I watched it do aerial pirouettes, pausing mid-air, then jetting to the top of the tallest, reddest primula—a tiny angel on the Christmas tree.

Atlas sashayed through the open doorway. He popped himself into Ravi's chair and delicately cleaned his paws. When Ravi delivered the tea, Atlas stared at him and continued to tend his toes. "May I sit down?" Ravi asked the cat, who ignored him. Ravi picked Atlas up and set him on the ground. With a swish of an annoyed tail, he went exploring in the garden, then did an about-face and jumped into my lap.

"I think I have met with approval." Worn outlines of golden elephants paraded around the porcelain tea mugs. I took a sip. "Oh, this is perfect."

"Spicy with milk and sugar," Ravi said. "I'm glad you like it."

"Truly speaking," I said, "you make me very happy." I drank more tea. "What were you humming in the kitchen? You sang it in the car."

"A song called 'Saiyyan.'" Ravi sang a few bars.

"What do the words mean?" I asked.

"The title means 'beloved.'" Ravi folded his hands in his lap and raised his eyebrows as he looked straight at me. "It has awesome lyrics written, over the top, by a man in love. 'I want to be a garland of love and fall upon your body/I want to get lost in your name/My days are full of dance and my nights of song/' . . . And so on."

To hear Ravi say those words made me blush. "Well, it's a pretty song. Maybe I shouldn't have asked what it meant."

"Maybe I shouldn't have told," Ravi answered.

"I'm glad you did." An awkward silence ensued. I was in love with Ravi, but I felt unsure what to say or how much to say. I was leaving, wasn't I? He might be merely translating lyrics, or did he think of me when he sang the song? We had only arrived, and I fell in love with everything that morning. I motioned to the hummingbird. "You see?" I asked. "At the tip-top of the primula? The bird stayed there for the last ten minutes or so."

"What a cool little man!" Ravi said.

"It's a lady bird," I said.

"How do you know?" Ravi said.

I shrugged. "I don't."

"The hummingbird has started her day, and we must begin ours," Ravi said. "Before you meet with Tenzin, I want to tell you a little more about Sangam." A woman in a yellow sari interrupted Ravi. She came up behind us and tapped us both on the shoulders.

"Your door was open, and I heard chatting out here," she said. "I left naan and jam in the kitchen."

"Thank you!" Ravi stood to allow the young woman a place to sit. I had seen her briefly the night before.

"And you are Maya?" The woman stared directly at me. "Oh, yes, the resemblance is in the eyes." The young woman with bountiful curves and onyx eyes appraised me from head to foot. Her name was Claire. And she informed us that she was on the way to the caves for prayer. We chatted about the journey into Sangam and the lovely morning when a man, who appeared to be in his fifties, joined us with an empty teacup. He filled it from our teapot. The opened front door welcomed visitors. As I shook his outstretched hand, I thought he was Hemingway's doppelganger. He must be Jethro Zane.

Claire bowed her head towards our new visitor and squeezed my right hand. It crumpled in her firm grip. "May you be happy," were her parting words.

Mr. Hemingway sat on his haunches and sipped tea. He wore a skullcap over his curly gray hair. Barefooted, he wore jeans and a gold t-shirt. No one wore shoes indoors. I had noticed a bin of flip-flops on the front porch coming in. Shoes must be communal, I figured.

Ravi introduced him as Jethro Zane.

"You know, I heard about you; you have a striking resemblance to Ernest Hemingway. It is so good to meet you!"

"I have heard that before," he said. "A beautiful moment meeting Tenzin's daughter. I am charmed."

Like Ravi and Jack, Jethro traveled back and forth between Sangam and the outside. He, too, had eyes on Motu. When Jethro mentioned the guru, I honestly had to think about who he was—so much had happened in the last forty-eight hours, my brain was over-stimulated. I recalled the showy diamond watch the man wore in the Delhi bar and the threat he posed to Sangam.

Dial, that irascible magpie, landed on Jethro's head. "*Bonjour, bonjour,*" Dial said. Hemingway with a multilingual bird on his head? No, Dorothy, you are not in Kansas anymore. Atlas jumped from my lap and waltzed into the house. "Kitty, kitty, bye-bye," Dial said.

"Are you going to Mahamaya today? Shall I wait for you?" Jethro asked Ravi. I couldn't place the accent.

"Yes, after I take this lady to Tenzin," Ravi said. "Meet you back here, an hour or so?"

"Right-o," Jethro said. He nodded at me and left.

I turned to see if we had any other visitors when Jethro returned with the bread and jam Claire had left. With a lathered-in-jam naan in hand, he retreated for a second time.

"Where is Mahamaya?" I asked, stunned that Ravi was about to leave me for wherever it was. I helped myself to the jam and naan.

"Not far, a two-hour walk." He pointed in the direction he would take. "It's a lively community of farms that produce most of our food. It lies on Sangam's Chinese side, and the folks there keep track of border patrol activity."

We munched on the warm bread as Ravi told me about the Mahamaya Valley.

Ravi had supplied them with a satellite phone, which was in the care of Jampa's father. Jampa was Sangam's cook, and her father was a farmer. Daily, he tracked Chinese patrols along the southeastern entrances to the Saraswati cave system. Ravi likened the network of passages to a rabbit warren. Ravi said the people at Mahamaya had to remain vigilant. "The Chinese are always dangerous and never something to take for granted."

"Mahamaya is remote but accessible like Tashigang?" I said.

Ravi offered me the last of the tea, and I took it. "Yes." Ravi raised his scarred eyebrow. The cat chased a butterfly at my feet. "Picture a vase with a narrow opening at the top and a hole at the bottom," Ravi said. He told me that the vase opening, high in the Himalayas, was off the Tea Horse

Road, a trading route linking China and India used in the seventh century. Climbing down the three-hundred-meter neck of the vase "is notoriously dangerous," Ravi said. Below lay a labyrinth of stone passageways going deeper into the valley, opening to the indigenous Mahamayan people's farms and villages. As remote as it was, the Mahamayans traded in a limited way with the outside world.

Atlas jumped into my lap and kneaded my legs, and Ravi continued his description of the Mahamayans.

"Some people have blue eyes." Ravi went on to say that centuries before, it had not been uncommon for Western traders to marry valley women, so the gene pool was what he called "unique." The villages were tucked into the rocky cliff-sides while the farms existed below. The "hole" in the bottom of the vase was a hidden cave entrance wound deep then veering upwards into Sangam—the cave route Jethro and Ravi would take today. Ravi said stories about how these families came to be in Mahamaya began in antiquity. However, centuries before, Guru Rinpoche became aware of Sangam by going through Tashigang then finding his way out through Mahamaya.

"Is there a force field or something here? You said Mt. Kailash broadcasts a field of some kind. I've read about that."

"Yes. Mt. Kailash is the locus, and you have seen the effects of the sunstones; they act like magnets.

"What does Kailash mean?" I asked.

"Crystal—pure peace that resides inside a yogi."

"Like my father has?"

Ravi smiled in reply.

"Jack told me Sangam means confluence, where the Sutlej and Sarawati rivers meet, but what does Mahamaya mean?"

"In Sanskrit, it means 'piercing the veil,'" Ravi said. "Guru Rinpoche's experience upon entering Sangam. According to an old story, the monks of Tashigang allowed Guru Rinpoche entry with promises to protect it and to ensure its holiness."

"What does Maya mean?"

"It means 'illusion'—or 'veil.'" Ravi had a little jam on his chin.

I wiped the jam off and rubbed my fingers together. "So together, the words mean piercing the veil to inner peace, clear as crystal. The names tell the location of Sangam, don't they—like this is the way to inner peace?"

"You have an intuitive understanding of Sangam," Ravi said.

"OK," I said, "what does Ravi mean—your name in Sanskrit?" One piece of naan remained. I offered it to Ravi. "It's yours."

He declined. "Sun, like the star—the meaning of my name."

"Oh, on so many levels, that makes sense."

My thoughts turned to the day ahead. Ravi was the only one I knew here. I wished he were going to stay. This trip would soon be over, and I'd be back in La Conner and never see him again. A flower blossom landed on my shoulder. I shook it off. "I need to thank Deva for the clothes and the beaded pouch." I stood and stacked our empty cups.

"She is a remarkable woman. Deva is like you; she always thinks ahead," Ravi said. "We have a tradition of leaving something we have worn behind when we return to the outside world. We pass some of the clothes along to others in the valley. Some stay here. So, there are always extras." He picked up the cups and teapot to return them to the kitchen. He eyed me thoughtfully. "I must say red is your color!"

"Well, thank you."

"Let's get on with the day." Ravi held the door open for me to pass through.

"This was a great start," I said.

I found a pair of flip-flops on the porch, then Ravi took my hand, and we stepped over Atlas as we left the yurt.

I was nervous about being alone with my father. He seemed like a wizard from a fairy tale my mother made up. Perhaps, I spun him from fantasy. Maybe I was in a psych ward in Seattle or locked in my La Conner house, totally delusional.

"You're quiet," Ravi said.

"You help the farmers in the valley?" I asked rather than go into my weird mindset.

"Yes, Jethro is going to help with machinery, and I have a ewe who is about to deliver and human medical needs to tend to." His eyes twinkled. "You have nothing to fear here. Kindness is a practice, and there will always be a hand to help you."

"I know," I said, "but it won't be your hand."

He wrapped his arm around me and held me close. "I will be back for supper, and you will have amazing stories to tell me—then a late swim in the pool. Meteor showers tonight."

"That'll be lovely," I said. "I can't place Jethro from his accent—where's he from?"

"Israel." Ravi took my hand, and we continued our walk to the library.

"Oh." The beanie was a yarmulke.

"He's a rabbi in Levis," Ravi said. "Yes. Most of his family died in Mauthausen, a death camp in Austria. His mother was liberated in 1945, migrated to Israel, and married. Jethro was born in the sixties."

"How'd he get to Sangam?"

"Like everyone else, you will meet— through the Saraswati Cave— connected by a calling.

I stopped as Ravi took a step forward. "Wait a minute. I thought everyone was a Buddhist—or became one—here."

"Oh, no, honey. Not at all. Remember, Buddhism is not a religion but a path. It guides us, but our current residents come from Islam, Hinduism, Judaism, and Catholicism. Your father is a Buddhist."

"I love that. So Jesus, Buddha, Mohammed, and Moses sit at the same table here?"

"Exactly."

Chapter 25 The Librarian

"My mind—nothing is as it first appears." I pointed to the immense field surrounding the library. "Oh my gosh, last night, I thought this was just grass. The more I look, the more I see." The green came alive with hollyhocks, lavender, columbines, and red flowers that I thought might be zinnias. Near the ground, dandelions hummed with honeybees, and double-winged red dragonflies maneuvered in the sky along with hummingbirds who directed their attention to primula. A takin munched on grass. "What's that little building over there?" A conical stone structure with a birdhouse on its thatched roof and an engraved door partially hidden by bamboo caught my attention. Pots of pink and blue asters with purple flowers I could not identify headed the graveled way.

"The library toilet-house and laundry," Ravi said.

"So, a combination?" I said. "What kind of flowers are with the asters in the pots? So pretty."

"Called a wishbone," Ravi said.

"I bet the bees like it," I mused. "So magical. All of it."

"Morning is the busiest time on the green," Ravi said lightly. "Our path goes straight through. Be careful of the ladybugs. And the cats."

"I'm not talking about cats and ladybugs." I squinted as I looked around. I was ready for a fox or a white leopard to take a bow.

"You'll get used to it." Ravi kissed me on my crooked lips. "Let's go see your father." We removed our flip-flops and put them into a receptacle. A large gilded bronze prayer wheel supported by a wooden axis and embossed with *Om mani padme hum* on its large drum stood at the entrance; we took turns spinning it. I imagined prayers floating on the breeze like musical notes. Inside the doors were small bins of apricots and pears. Ravi took some of each and motioned for me to do the same.

The library's spacious entry felt grand with its smooth, cool tiled floors. Peering up into the high dome, I saw a pulsating crystal globe, and below in the lobby was a gold statue of Guru Rinpoche. The upper tiers had open hallways with a balustrade surrounding each floor. Doors led off here and there. We stopped in front of the statue, and Ravi bowed, then placed the fruit offerings at its foot. I copied his obeisance. "Thank you," I whispered to Guru as we left the lobby.

"He was the first librarian," Ravi said in a hushed tone.

Had I heard Ravi, right? My father had the same job as Guru Rinpoche? I said nothing, but the image of Moses came back to me.

One of the doors opened onto a stairway, and two halls led in different directions around the building. By the stairs, we paused in reverence at a golden likeness of Yeshe Tsogyal. It is said that Yeshe Tsogyal transcribed Guru Rinpoche's teachings in a secret language only a devotee might understand. She hid these treasured texts throughout Tibet. As we paid homage to the ancient Buddhist teacher, Yeshe Maya came to my mind, and I thanked her for the request to see me on Chamberlain Island. Ravi and I placed offerings and bowed before Tsogyal's likeness. Odd how spiritual connectivity was natural here. We simply stopped, acknowledged, made offerings, and said prayers. It was automatic, like praying the Rosary. After the homage, Ravi took the lead, and I followed him on the tiled steps just as we had done so many times before.

On the second-floor landing, an arch opened into a spacious room to my right. Another stairway angled left and went to the third floor, where, Ravi explained, residents met for meditation and gatherings. I stopped to look at the statue of Guru Rinpoche below and then to the dome with the pulsating globe above us. Sunlight flickered through the dome windows and spread out in feathery directions. Awestruck, I whispered. "It's so beautiful, like nothing I've ever seen."

"My first and lasting impression, too," Ravi said. He pointed to a door slightly open ahead of us. "Tenzin's waiting."

Papa sat at a green-painted table with white wooden chairs around it. His attention was on photographs of what appeared to be cave walls. As we entered the room he motioned for us to sit with him. I noticed an illustrated map on the table as well.

"Good morning," I offered.

"Hello, Maya, I hope you slept well." He raised his head from the documents.

"Yes, I was awakened by a cat," I said.

"Atlas, I presume," Papa answered.

"I'm out of favor," Ravi said. "Maya has won Atlas's heart." He paused before continuing. "You see what Jack's latest photos of the Saraswati Cave reveal?"

"I'm grateful you brought them to Deva last evening," Papa said. "I have compared the old map with the latest photos." The map illustrated passages through the cave in gold ink. Papa turned the scroll around to share what he had discovered. "Amul is trying to break his way through the cave to get to us, and the cave is slowly collapsing." He pointed to lines on the illustrated map. "This passage is gone altogether." Papa tapped a line that stopped at a marker in the form of a green-plumed parrot. "This passage linked the other three entries to the cave. Gone with the cave-in." He picked up one of Jack's photo's and put it down. "You can see the damage." Papa sighed audibly. "How many more from Amul's groups will come with chisels and hammers?" He left the question in the air.

"The bowl we found and Taylor's position confirmed Motu was a step ahead of us again, as we figured he might be. Taylor waited for us and followed us back," Ravi explained to me.

"Wait a minute," I said. "You wanted us followed?"

"Yes," Papa said. "We led him here."

"Why?" I asked.

"Amul's ambitious," my father said. "We needed to know how much he knows about us."

"He's been knocking at our door for quite a long time," Ravi said. "And now we have to answer."

"He'd have people meditating in the caves and charging them a hundred grand," I remarked, recalling the video of followers who paid over sixty thousand to see Kailash from Nepal.

"Exactly." Papa folded his hands over the map. "After Amul confirmed the Saraswati River ran through the cave, he knew that the other stories about Sangam might be discoverable, too. He is a dog with a bone." Papa patted the folded map, and his face fell solemn. "Yes, the cave may die."

"Is there a way you could talk to him about how fragile the Saraswati Cave is without bringing Sangam into the conversation?" I asked.

Papa shrugged. "A magician might outwit Amul because greed is his folly." He gazed at me. "But who is to know?"

Ravi's chair scraped across the stone floor. "I promised to meet Jethro." He patted my hand and turned to Papa. "Anything you need from the valley?"

"Give my regards to Jampa's father and tell him Maya is home." Papa stood while I looked on as Ravi nodded his reply to the old monk and left us for the day.

All my father needed in his attire was a wizard's hat, I thought. The green suspenders and brown trousers were the same as he wore the day before and appeared ordinary enough. When I had direct eye contact, I felt mesmerized; he saw things beyond imagination: a humble figure with incalculable powers.

Somehow, I had to connect him to the world I'd shared with my mother. As he rolled the map neatly and tied it with the gold thread, I asked, "Did you miss my mother? She wanted you to know how much she always loved you."

His face paled when he turned toward me, but he said nothing.

"Did you blame me?" I asked. "For her leaving, for taking me?" Still no reaction. "Have you been happy?"

Without a word, Papa took the scroll and photographs and motioned for me to follow him to a floor-to-ceiling, worn but waxed and buffed wooden bookcase on the other side of the doorway. Finally, he spoke, but only to ask me to hold the documents while he positioned a library ladder under the middle section, and then he agilely climbed to the near-top rung. I handed him the photos and then the map, which he placed on the high shelf in a glass box. When we finished the task, he asked me to come with him to a closed door across from us.

"*Voilà, mon cellule.*" Papa opened the door to his small living space. Positioned straight across from us was a single, iron-frame bed. A lit candle in a glass bowl illuminated a shrine to the side of us.

I turned to face the altar and gasped. "Sweet God." I stared into my mother's eyes from a mural Papa had painted upon the wall. Her hair haloed over exposed shoulders, a mix of reds and gold, long strands caught in the flickering candlelight. She held an infant close to her, their cheeks nearly meeting. My God, that was me!

On the highest shelf under the mural were statues of Guru Rinpoche and Yeshe Tsogyal. On the second level, artifacts abounded: a pearl embossed barrette that had belonged to my mother, pencil drawings of the three of us, a baby's moccasin, and a faded photo of his mother and grandmother were among the artifacts. A piece of red silk draped on the lowest shelf.

My father's eyes studied my reaction.

"*Je suis là,*" I said in French that I thought I had forgotten, and I was with him, right there.

Papa held me at arm's length. He nodded towards the mural. "You have grown," he said with a laugh.

"I didn't think I was strong enough to make this trip—and I would've been able to without Jack and Ravi—and—"

Papa held up his hand. "I knew you were strong." He touched the middle point of my forehead with his tapered index finger. "When you are awake, you can do anything. Your mother was fearful but raised a strong child with strong insight. Always follow it." He pivoted to the door. "There are other rooms in the library; let me show you."

I followed Papa down the narrow staircase to the bottom floor. I wondered how I could have missed the display cases abutting the circular walls when Ravi and I came into the library that morning. Taken by the presence of the golden visage of Guru Rinpoche and the glowing orb high up in the dome of the building, I failed to see the exhibit of ancient text, bits of broken statuary, and a stone cup in one case. Between the displays were statues of what appeared to be angels or saints. One looked like Jesus. I recognized the crown of thorns.

"That cup?" I asked. "That couldn't be like the Holy Grail? Could it?"

"No," My father shrugged his Gallic shoulders. *"Mais Jésus e visité ici."* Papa spoke in a firm, quiet voice.

"Was the cup his?"

"A long time ago."

My mouth dropped in a wordless response. What would someone like Amul do with artifacts like this? The thought had a chilling effect. We moved around the room to see other displays. One held precious stones: sapphires, diamonds, and pearls that sparkled under a candlelit sconce. I noticed more cases, but today our tour was brief.

Next, Papa took me down a hall by the stairs to a book-lined room with four tables. Residents came into this room to study, to write, and "to drink tea," he said.

Papa poured tea into two porcelain mugs with copper glazes. The buffet had a bowl of apricots, as well. "Fill the basket with the fruit," Papa said. "We'll sit outside." He led us through an outer door from the tearoom onto the green, where we sat at a picnic table.

"Who makes the tea?" The world about us was a flurry with bees amid flowers and dragonflies. This time I noticed tiger lilies and a frog that teased one of the sleek brown cats. I heard the river burble in the background, and the smell of earth and lavender permeated the air.

"Masa, the tea maker and linguist and *pandit*, he makes the tea," Papa said. "An ancient man.

"What's a pandit?" I asked.

"A highly knowledgeable teacher of Vedic scriptures and Hindu philosophy," Papa answered.

"And he makes the tea?"

"He was once the librarian and asked that I assume the role. You will like Masa very much."

"I look forward to meeting him."

Dial flew from a tall cairn, mid-field, and landed on my father's shoulder. He offered the magpie bits of his apricot, which the bird ate from his hand.

"Fruit des dieux." Dial hopped onto the table, then back onto Papa's arm.

Did that bird just say, 'fruit of the gods?'" I asked.

"That he did," Papa said.

We both laughed at the magpie's insistence on more apricots. I fed him a piece as well. He bowed and hopped, performed a little dance, bolted upwards, and landed on my head. Papa burst into laughter at the shocked expression on my face. The magpie leaned over my brow and said, "Pretty Dial. Pretty Dial." He flew off and disappeared into the canopy provided by a large oak nearby.

Dial's antics broke apart any formality left between Papa and me. "What was that?" I said.

"Dial likes you," Papa said.

"I like him, too." The milky and sweetened tea had cooled; its nutty malt flavor mellowed as I sipped. Soon, my father and I shared stories as well as apricots.

He told me about the direction his life had taken. Papa had learned Tibetan from Masa. Papa took over the elder's position when one-hundred-five year old Masa's eyesight began to fail. Papa described a happy, simple life for which he had no regrets. He went on to tell me about the people who lived at Sangam. Six people claimed residency. Deva Tara managed Sangam, and Claire, the woman in the yellow sari, helped her. She was Pakistani. Jampa, from the Mahamaya Valley, was the cook and Claire's best friend. The sixth resident was Father Emilio, a Catholic priest from Togo, an apprentice librarian, a master of languages, and an accomplished yogi.

Dial returned for more handouts and flapped his wings in delight when he received them.

I recounted the trip to Chamberlain Island and my growing wanderlust guided by Yeshe Tsogyal. "This is as far from home as I could ever imagine." A scarlet and violet-striped butterfly landed on my hand.

Papa smiled. "And this is your true home."

"Home to me was a red house on a bluff with a little dog who acted like a warrior guide." I sighed and drank the last of my tea.

"Tell me more about your dog," Papa said softly.

"She had all the insistence that Dial has, but Penni-P's main job in life was to make sure that I was OK. She weighed eight pounds, and when I picked her up, she still growled at the mailman." A vision of Penni-P made me smile. "I miss her."

"As you do your mother," Papa said.

"Yes, I miss her so much, especially today," I said. "Mother was beautiful until the day she died."

"*Mon belle ange,*" Papa said.

I told him how she, like he, had created murals. My favorite one featured a magical garden with queens and kings riding on clouds while children played with unicorns and a small girl peeked from under a periwinkle shell. One room in my bedroom was polka-dotted with round golden balls.

Papa smiled at this. "She was a gifted artist."

"And a good mother," I added. "And as beautiful and passionate as she was, she never expressed romantic interest in a man."

"I was an art student in those days." Papa folded his hands in front of him on the table. "After your mother left, I became a monk." His eyes twinkled, and he stared at his fingers. His cheeks bore a pinkish glow. He was as handsome as she had been beautiful.

"A love story," I said. "Yes?"

"*Oui,*" he said, "*histoire d'amour, oui.*"

"*Oh làlà,*" I said.

High clouds played above us. Papa talked about his childhood in Paris and his mother. "You are strong, like she was, an adventuress, with deep spirit and an easy laugh. She learned Tibetan and chatted with the Dalai Lama. Like a magnet, your grandmother was drawn to Tibet, to the stories about Yeshe Tsogyal, then to Mt. Kailash, to Lhasa and Sangam. I, too, was born here."

"Tell me more about her." I offered Papa the last apricot in the basket; he shook his head and urged me to me to take it. "I look forward to reading her books." I popped the apricot into my mouth and listened to my father describe my grandmother.

"She disguised herself as a hillman. She crossed into territory forbidden to her as a Westerner and a woman. She ate yak and drank butter tea—she a socialite from Europe." Papa laughed. "She loved your mother."

Atlas walked stealthily through the grass. "I've wondered why Mother was so protective of me when she was such a free spirit."

"She listened to her fear guides instead of spirit guides." He shrugged. "I think she tried to recreate Sangam in that red house on the bluff—for you and possibly, for herself."

I said, "I think you're right. Exactly right."

Deva Tara stood on the library stairs and directed her voice towards us. "Our midday meal is ready. Must I always search for you, Tenzin?"

The gentleness in her tone showed no rebuke. Deva Tara moved with the lightness of a gazelle. She, too, wore the same clothes as she had the day before, the apron crisp.

A bell tolled as soon as Papa and I entered the dining room. We were the last to arrive, and lunch waited on us. An open kitchen in the back, tables set, and all residents seated, created a homey scene. French windows banked across the exterior wall. Outside, a kitchen garden thrived. A yellow rose tree caught my attention—blooms as wide as double my hand. Two parrots ate at a feeder, built high on a perch, filled with fruity tidbits from luncheon preparation. Two or three garden cats prowled below.

Father Emilio stood, acknowledged Papa and me, then led a chant that I supposed were grace words. Afterward, Papa explained that the Tibetan grace acknowledged the work that brought the rice from seed to harvest. The prayer thanked what Tibetans call the three jewels: the Buddha, the Dharma, and the Sangha.

Papa held my bowl when I filled it with corn chowder at the buffet table on the counter, separating the dining from the preparation area. The vegetable soup looked good, too. A basket of warm *balep*, Tibetan-style flatbread that Jampa continued to fry, sat next to a platter of *sha phalay*, Tibetan seasoned beef and cabbage pies. A bowl of apricots and pears was stationed by a two-burner gas-fueled hotplate, with kettles of water bubbling for tea. Residents shared teapots.

Father Emilio joined us. I was curious about his cleric's collar and his recitation of a Buddhist prayer in perfect Tibetan. After introductions, my curiosity overcame my manners, and I said, "I know that Buddhism is a practice and that Catholicism is a religion, but do you believe in God?"

The middle-aged African man with deep black skin and bright brown eyes replied by asking, "What do you think God is?"

"That's a good question," Papa said.

Both men waited for me to respond. "I used to think God looked like Jesus, except older. Now, here in Sangam, and getting to Sangam, all that I once accepted seems naive. I feel the spirit world here; for me Yeshe Tsogyal has guided me. There is so much to learn. How did you get to Sangam?" I asked Emilio.

"I was a priest from Togo with a gift for languages, so I was sent to Rome to translate Pope John Paul's talks into the Niger-Congo language groups and Éwé languages." He paused to eat some soup. Emilio looked over at Jampa and threw her a kiss. "She is such a fine cook," he said to me, wagging his spoon in the air for emphasis. "Pope John Paul chose me to be his African delegate to a peace conference at Assisi in the late nineties." Emilo smiled at the memory. "I met the Dalai Lama, and was impressed by his calm endurance and quiet humor in the wake of the Chinese insurgency—I asked him what gave him inner peace? The Dalai Lama laughed and told me, 'Buddhism, naturally.' His words. That was the start." Emilio pointed his index finger at me. "I wanted to know more about Eastern spirituality and its role in genuine human liberation. I took a sabbatical soon after, and studied in Dharamsala."

Papa waved a piece of balep for emphasis. "For many years, I meditated in the Saraswati Cave, and in that time, I met many travelers." He tore off a piece of bread and ate it.

"Papa," I asked, "Is this where you met Father Emilio?"

"Yes."

"How did you know he belonged here?"

A smile was his reply.

"What do you make of your experience?" I asked Emilio.

He looked down at his soup bowl and made circles with his spoon in the hearty broth. "St. Paul said, 'For now we see through a glass, darkly; but then face to face: now I know in part; but then shall I know even as also I am known.' Shaded truths dissolve in light at Sangam and make breathing easier." Emilio looked up from his soup. "Do you follow me?"

"I think so."

"Souls transform. The gifts given here can only be shared with humankind by prayer. We pray for all life, all paths that lead to what Buddha calls liberation, and to what the Pope calls faith." He drank some tea and raised his fork to make a point. He turned a questioning eye at me. "You know my references, don't you?"

"Yes," I said. "What you quoted is from Corinthians, right?"

"Yes: Corinthians 13:12."

"So, St. Paul tells us about the problem, and the Dharma as it's practiced here, helps clean things up?"

"It's more than meditation or homilies," Father Emilio said. "This physical place on Planet Earth can transform souls. All who enter Sangam are emissaries through prayer to the wider world."

"We need to pray harder these days," I said. "There is so much darkness."

"We pray," Papa said.

I began to understand that Sangam was more than a child's mural or a shrine in my father's cell. Simple food fueled happy people who prayed to enlighten the world and, from what I could infer, keep the world on its axis.

"Did you like the meat pie?" Jampa sat down next to Father Emilio. Her voice lilted. She wore a short black skirt over loose black pants and a deep blue embossed top like mine. She braided her long hair with silk ties. She was youthful, the same age as Claire, I figured.

"Delicious," I said.

"The beef is from my family's farm in Mahamaya," she said. "Tenzin, you are enjoying your daughter's visit?"

"Yes!" The grin opened on Papa's face.

Residents and a few farmers from the valley began to leave the dining room. Papa told me that some would attend afternoon meditation while others worked on projects, and the farmers who had delivered goods returned to the valley.

Papa and I walked to the garden doors. He asked if I might want to rest this afternoon. He said he was going to the sundial for prayers.

"The sundial?" I asked. "Where is that?"

"A half hour's walk," he said. "If you wish to accompany me?"

"The wonderful food has made me sleepy," I said. "I would like to go another time, though." I paused. "Father Emilio deeply impressed me."

"We are grateful for his instruction," Papa said.

"Was Sangam always like this?" I asked.

"Like everything, it changes," my father answered. "Spirit is steady."

"How could Mother leave? How could she leave here? Leave you?"

"At the end of her life, I think your mother prayed very hard and wrote her letter. The other world responded. We are corrected, and you have returned."

"I loved Olivia Moore, my dear mother, so much," I said.

"Your laugh reminds me of her," Papa said. "You have found your way home."

"With a lot of help," I answered.

"With a lot of help."

Our assessment was the same.

"Until we meet again, my daughter," Papa said. "Be happy." He turned his attention to the narrow, uneven stairs, and I started back to the yurt.

Atlas ran inside as soon as I opened the front door. He cuddled next to me under the quilt. I hadn't realized how tired I was until my head touched the pillow. I fell into a deep sleep.

I woke up to a day fading into night. Deep shadows fell across the room. When I opened the back door to go to the toilet house, Atlas jumped outside and stretched on the porch.

On my return, Deva Tara met me, carrying laundry.

"Clean clothes! What a wonderful surprise. Thank you," I said. "Thank you so much."

Deva handed me the sun-dried laundry, and the cotton sheets crackled at my touch. We walked into the house, where I put them away.

"Would you like to go on a short walk—we can watch the sunset."

I grabbed my flip-flops, and we went over the wide-planked river bridge, then down a path of soft red earth. A frog croaked from a leafy plant hanging lazily overhead. His red and gold eyes glowed, and then he projected his scarlet tongue, and a bitty fly disappeared. "He's such a cute little critter," I said to Deva.

"He is a funny one." Deva took my arm. "You like Sangam?"

"Oh, my goodness. I am surprised every minute here. But meeting my father?" I burst into unexpected tears. I wiped my hand over my eyes and tried to walk on as if my heart had not opened wide.

"Stop, stop, child," Deva said. "Allow yourself to absorb this reunion." She peered heavenward. "It is nearly sunset. Follow me."

In the late afternoon, the mountains glowed in multicolored light. A stand of birch trees appeared on the right, and I glimpsed a lake tucked inside. Deva turned off the main path, and we ambled onto a trail worn with foot treads that wound its way to the lake. The air felt holy; birds took to the breeze that carried the scent of wild roses and lavender that grew profusely among bunches of daisies. Birch leaves vibrated in answer to the wind, and whispered stories of the day to the waning sun. Families of swans swam—the black, sleek birds glided, making "s" patterns in the emerald water.

We sat quietly on rocks. An egret landed on a red rowboat pulled high onshore. The world, with its layered colors, shimmered. We did not talk; I allowed the moment to be the metaphor for how quickly the fine line between night and day changes the landscape. I thought about my father. He was not the sun at high noon. No, he was the sun as it fell into gold light and then into sleep. "How glorious the passing moment is," I said as the lake fell into shadow and the egret flew.

Deva patted my hand. "Tenzin is so pleased you are here. I am, too," she said.

"I am so happy to meet you! Thank you for taking me on this walk," I said.

"I hoped you would like it." Her soft white hair glowed.

On the way back, the mountain valley air began to cool. Deva and I hurried along to help Jampa lay out leftovers from the midday meal, the mainstay of the day.

"Deva! You walk too fast!" Jethro's voice hailed from behind us, and he and Ravi joined us.

Ravi wrapped an arm around me and gave me a side hug. "How was your day?"

"Incredible!" I squeezed him tightly.

"Did Tenzin show you around?" Ravi asked.

"Oh, yes." I shook my head in wonder. "The library is about the most amazing place I've ever seen. And him? I don't have great enough words to describe him. He made the whole day so easy. I talked his head off!"

"What did I tell you?" Ravi took my hand and tucked it inside his arm. Deva linked arms with Jethro, and we walked back in the twilight.

Ravi was hungry, and I joined Jethro and him in the dining room. The ewe had delivered, and the tractor repaired. I asked Jethro, who noticed first his resemblance to Hemingway.

"My mother told me that first. She said it explained my love of cats."

We talked about Paris in the 1920s when Hemingway wrote on the Left Bank, and Jethro told me about opera in Vienna in the same era.

"I am so sorry for what your family endured," I said.

"What a kind heart you have," Jethro said. "We will be good friends."

When Ravi and I strolled back to the yurt, I said, "I am blown away by today. No one could explain Sangam, you know?"

"Why we work to protect it," Ravi said.

"I missed you today." I sat next to Ravi on the bed by the door.

"I missed you, too." He kissed my nose. "I love your face; have I told you that?"

"Is that a come-on?"

"Only if it works," he said.

Little kisses on the cheek led to passionate kisses as we rolled around the bed like teenagers.

"I think it's working."

"Then, I am pleased."

"It's like the day holds two suns," I whispered. "One sun is for me and one for everything else."

Whatever clothes we still had on fell off, and it was just us. After the laughing and moaning and crying and the making love was over, we rolled from one another's arms and went out to the pool.

Ravi jumped in first, and then I slid in over the edge, and somehow the kisses began again, and it was as if we were having a reunion of the soul. My back was against the side of the pool, and Ravi and I made love again. His mouth on me in places I once held secret opened a world of passionate responses I did not know I had inside of me. Water curled around us as the stars played on in the sky.

Chapter 26 Well, Oddly Maybe

Over morning tea overlooking the garden Ravi and I watched the sun peel away clouds. He was quiet while I basked in the sunrise. My head back, I studied the sky and how the sun bent rays of brilliant light in a rainbow that bounced off the sides of the high canyon surrounding Sangam.

"Doesn't that look like Shiva—in the cloud?" I touched Ravi's arm. "Magical." Sunlight broke through. "A light show shooting from his head."

Ravi did not reply.

I repeated, "Did you see it—oh, it's gone now."

Another lengthy pause happened before he spoke. "Maya," he said, "I need to talk to you." Ravi's serious tone caught my attention.

"OK," I said. I felt that he was about to dial back some of the bliss.

"Until recently." Ravi stared at his hands. "Very recently," he continued, "a friend of mine occasionally visited. Allie, Allie Rogers is her name. She comes to Sangla on holiday—how we met. She lived in Auroville in India, off and on in the eighties and nineties." He paused. "Jack may have mentioned her to you?"

"No." I sat straight up; shock registered in my eyes, resting on Ravi. "Jack never mentioned her to me."

"OK, let's see." Ravi tapped his fingers on his thigh. "She lives in Hawaii now. I should have told you about her, and I apologize for not explaining. Because of the distance between us, our relationship has never been monogamous."

"Well, she's not here now, and I won't be soon," my voice cracked at the admittance.

"She is here, at the hotel," Ravi said. "I'm changing the hotel into a meditation and conference center; you knew that?"

I nodded, still wrestling with what Ravi had said.

"She wants to be part of the change and wants me to create space for a yoga retreat—go in business with me—"

"And you've decided to do this?"

"I haven't given her an answer."

"While I was in Nepal when you returned to the hotel, you were sleeping with her?" I asked, my heart beating louder than my voice.

The look on Ravi's face told me the answer. Of course, they slept together. I stared at the little hummingbird perched again on the primula. The little bird helicoptered in the air for a moment and disappeared into the flower hedge. Vanished. "Are you telling me that Allie is moving to Sangla to live with you?" My muscles tensed, and my toes constricted. "Full stop?"

"Yes, to answer your question." He lifted his teacup and put it down without drinking. "But this was not my idea." Ravi shook his head. "Gobsmacked, I was." Sweat appeared on Ravi's brow. "I put her in a bungalow at the hotel, but I did not commit to her business proposition or to living with her."

"You should have said before, at least before last night," I said.

Ravi stared straight ahead. "I was caught in a dilemma."

"Really, a dilemma? I'm a fucking dilemma." My nostrils flared. "Well, it's really pretty simple. In two or three days, I'll be leaving, and you can go to Allie and commit yourself or not to a relationship with her."

"I don't want to live with Allie or go into business with her, and I think she knows that, but I haven't found the opportunity to let her know my decision." Ravi raised his head to assess how I was taking this news. It wasn't well.

"Why didn't you tell me about her before getting here—I mean, the bed, last night, and the night before?" My insecurities bled out from my wounded heart. "Why didn't you tell me before last night?" I repeated. He had said he loved me. Hadn't he said the same thing to this woman I didn't know existed ten minutes before? "You had plenty of time."

"I should have," Ravi said. "But there it is."

"Oh my God," I said. Too angry to cry, I stood quickly. "I'm going to get dressed," I said. "You can have your t-shirt back." I pulled at the hem to make sure it covered my bare bottom and left him outside.

I got into my khakis and blue batik turtle print tunic—clothes I wore on the Nepal bus ride. Jack had said Ravi liked me. *Really Jack? You might have told me about her. Men!* I pulled the wadded sheets into a bundle. And threw them onto the floor and sat on the edge of the bed feeling defeated, all the oxygen sucked out.

I heard Ravi come in. I braided my hands together as he approached.

"Knock knock?" he said.

I glared up at him.

"May I join you?" he asked.

"Suit yourself," I said.

"Has anything like what happened between us last night happened to you before?" Ravi asked me.

"Of course not," I said. "That's why I'm sitting here staring at my heart where you left it on the floor. Did you sing that fucking song to her, too?"

He ignored my last question. "Never before last night has anything like that happened to me. Like stars colliding—spiritual—" He edged closer to me, and I moved an equal distance away.

"Please cut the pretty words." I wiped my nose on the back of my hand. "What confuses me is this: if besides that other stuff hadn't happened—including the pool part, which I don't have words for—would I have just been someone you met and easily forgot?" I shut my eyes and moved a little further away from him. "No need to tell me about Allie? At all?"

"No, no, no," Ravi said. "Would you get over here?" He patted the place next to him. "I was going to tell you a dozen times. When I told you about Brenna. And, yes, when you told me about chair yoga, but I didn't. When we sat outside yesterday morning, Claire came along. The whole thing with Allie was so settled with me, and I didn't think it was necessary. I was just hedging while I figured out a less confrontational way of dealing with her. She's headstrong."

"I don't care if she is headstrong, or beautiful, or a yogi who can stand on her head." I began to cry. "I never would get involved with someone in a relationship."

"I'm not, though. Buddhists practice clear communication, which is where I failed; I didn't tell you about Allie. I am not involved with her; I have not agreed to any terms."

"Well, buddy, she moved to Sangla to live with you—and she thinks that will happen. That defines involvement!" Atlas surveyed us from a few feet away and left the room. "You fooled me last night, damn it. Damn you. How could I be so stupid?"

Ravi stared at his folded hands. "You left the States less than two weeks ago," he said. "Please keep in mind how fast time has gone." He took a deep breath. "As you know, Jack and I made a plan to get you here, and that was the commitment. Jack will be here in a few days."

A commitment to a friend? So that's what I am? I thought. I opened my mouth to speak, but Ravi raised his index finger.

"Wait," he said, "let me finish. Nothing prepared me for someone who embraced an adventure like you, and the more I was around you, the more I wanted to be around you. You are brave and funny and kind and unafraid to be vulnerable. I started falling for you when I saw you sitting next to the Tibetan woman on the Nepali bus. You had such a wonderful smile, and you didn't know where the hell you were going, but you were present. Jack had told me what a cool woman you were, but he also said you were returning to La Conner. I decided to enjoy all the time that I had to spend with you—I was going to break it off with Allie long before we met, but I haven't and frankly—until last night—when I knew I wanted to marry you—Allie—that conversation—wasn't important."

Marry me? Had Ravi just asked me to marry him? "Is that like a proposal?" Was this ridiculous, or what?

"Oddly, yes," Ravi answered.

"Well, oddly, maybe," I shouted. "I meant, no, maybe?" My voice softened. I looked into his deep brown eyes. "Are you serious? I've only known you for eleven days."

"You ever had a night like we had?" Ravi reached over to me and took my hand. "I am seventy—and in all this planetary time?" He shook his head. "You know, I never noticed the hummingbirds in the primula until you showed me—or Shiva in the cloud. I'm sorry I missed it—I was so preoccupied—I—"

"Oh, stop, please, don't apologize." I reached for his hand. "This is crazy. A month ago, I didn't know you, and," I said, "yes, and I can't believe I'm saying this, but, yes, I will marry you and live with you here or in a tree house, or at the inn wherever you are—but I'm going to sage it first. And I'm getting a dog."

He pulled me to him and kissed me. "I will buy the sage."

I backed out of his arms. "You promise to tell Allie. First thing."

"Of course, yes," he said.

Our lips were about to meet again when Deva Tara poked her head in the front door. "Are you ready to go to morning meditation?"

Ravi and I still sat on our mattress that had such a working out the night before. The sheets lay in a heap on the floor. I turned towards him; our noses nearly met. "I didn't tell you, but I'm going to the caves with Deva this morning—she invited me."

"You are going through the catacombs?" Ravi asked Deva.

"Yes," Deva smiled. "I haven't taken the ladder for fifteen years."

"What are the catacombs?" I asked.

"In ancient times, a burial place—" Deva straightened her shawl and tucked a wisp of white hair beneath a blue crocheted headscarf. "A stairway goes up to the caves—many steps, but it is not bad and has a railing."

"Is Guru Rinpoche buried there?" I stared at Deva and then at Ravi. Both faces remained blank. "In the catacombs?" I was curious. "Yeshe Tsogyal? Is she buried with him? Or by herself?"

"Not buried—they dissolved into space." She shrugged. "No one knows. But others are buried in the catacombs. I will show you," Deva said. "Yeshe, you know, she is sometimes believed to be the manifestation of Saraswati, the goddess, and some say, Tara, too."

"Saraswati?" Like the river goddess?" I stood up.

"The same." Ravi bundled the sheets into a neat pile. "Goddess of art and eloquence—"

I tossed Ravi's t-shirt to him to add to the laundry. "It's the most beautiful river I've ever seen."

Deva motioned to my boots, sitting on the front porch. "You will need those today," she said.

"Then I will wash the bed linens and towels," Ravi answered. A smile blossomed on his face. "Shall we tell her?"

"OK," I said.

"Maya has agreed to marry me," Ravi said.

"Aha!" Deva clapped her hands. "Let's go tell Tenzin!" She hugged us both. "We thought something was astir between you two." She blushed and said, "And then we go to prayers and give thanks."

We found Papa at his green table studying maps once again. He stood. "Hello, *bonjour bonjour*," he said. His furrowed brow showed concern—the Saraswati Cave kept him up at night.

Ravi blurted our news—

Papa's demeanor changed; sweet awe lit his face. His blue eyes shone brightly. "It would be my honor to bless your marriage." He peered into our faces. "You will need correct paperwork, however, in India. And you will stay near me."

"Yes. Yes, of course! Jack has to be here," I said and hugged my father.

Papa touched our foreheads. "May you be blessed with loving kindness, generosity, and clear communication. Your union is blessed."

"Did Jack miss the wedding?" I asked.

Ravi squeezed my hand. "We will tell him all about it."

"Yes," I laughed, "yes, we will." Deva Tara and Papa smiled at us then the thought occurred. "What about Amul?"

"He is a problem if you are here, in Sangla or La Conner; we will have to work on that."

Chapter 27 Learning to Pray

On the way to prayers, Dial landed on Deva's shoulder. "The caves, the caves," the bird repeated.

The sky was a circus of circling cumulus clouds—a fully bright sun suddenly caught a shadow, and the day darkened, and as quickly, brightened. Our path diverted from the birch woods to a large terraced garden where fairy-wrens and oriental turtle doves sang from hidden places in rockeries above us. Deva said nothing, and we continued under Dial's watchful eye. I struggled to stay centered. My father had just married me to Ravi, absent the paperwork. I was not going back to La Conner. It was over my life there. Focus. Carol was not going to believe this. Was this real? I pinched myself. I had left the fear guides behind.

Dun-colored walls of the barrel-shaped Sangam appeared; I craned my neck for a panoramic look at the enclosure of this sacred valley. Like a medieval walled city, I thought. Gold and silver ribbons of minerals striated the stone, like I had witnessed in the Saraswati Cave. Sunstones, like mine, lay amidst pebbles lining the path, the more I looked; the more I saw.

"We are here," Deva said. "Well, nearly." Her smile beamed confidence that I did not feel.

"Where?"

"Here." She pointed to what I thought were rock indentations, but on closer inspection, I saw that it was a stone door cut into the canyon wall, as I had seen in photos of medieval castles. Deva pressed against it, and it opened with a groan.

"Noisy door. Noisy door." Dial flew in with us.

"Oh, my." We were inside one of the mountains surrounding Sangam. A golden sphere, embossed with tiny symbols, blinked on and off at the center of the arena-like room. Was it communicating with something beyond us? Deva studied the globe with a questioning face.

"Does it usually pulsate like that?" I asked.

"Yes, but the rhythm is different. Could be a storm on Kailash."

I was mesmerized by its rhythm: two beats on, and a pause, then one beat and another pause.

"I will ask Tenzin the meaning of this change. Follow me."

We circled the cave's piazza to a stairway lit by candles in wall sconces. Deva brought her hands together at her heart center. "Our ancestors," she said, as we took to stairs going downward, "are buried here."

"Who keeps the candles lit?" I asked.

"Masa does this task every day," Deva said. "When we enter the catacombs, we do not speak."

As my eyes focused, I saw that stone and human bone divided the gravesites. Some sites had flowers, remnants of silk, or photographs. Cairns were a common feature, as were skulls.

Down a separate passage was a stairway like the one in the library with a narrow railing. "We climb now," Deva said. "The way I go—steep but easy—OK?"

"Yes, this will be fine," I said.

She led the way. "Be careful; nothing is even."

Covered in red dust, my hands faded as we rose higher and higher until darkness engulfed us. I could feel the sharp edges of the treads through my boots, and on occasion, I felt a break on the railing. A piece of the step broke loose, and I listened to it echo as it tumbled down the stairs. My concentration broke. I gripped the railing tighter and stared into the dark. The moment lightened when I heard Dial's throaty voice: "This way, this way." That crazy bird had followed us.

I took it a step at a time and prayed the railing would hold. On and on we went. The stairs flattened into a tunnel, and I lost sight of Deva in a mass of bright light. The next I saw her, she sat on a bench dusting off her workaday hands.

With a heaving sigh, I sat next to her and rubbed my hands against my khakis. As I adjusted to the bright light, I saw a narrow pathway with rows of cave entries peppering the mountain. My heart landed in my belly when I saw how high we were. Clouds teased the view of Sangam below as they swirled through the heavens. I touched the warm, rough cliff-side.

"You should have a cane," Deva said. "Don't look down."

"Easy promise," I said.

Prayer wheels built into the stone appeared around every curve. Masa stopped to say hello as he came from prayers. Deva introduced us. He reminded me of Gandhi. It may have been the wireless glasses he wore or the peace that emanated from his being.

Around the next turn, Dial perched briefly on my head, and his antics made me laugh. He felt weightless; and, in his raspy voice, said, "Count with me: one, two, three." He hopped over to Deva's outstretched hand, which he climbed to the shoulder.

"Dial plays," she said. Then she traced the cave entrances with her finger and leaned slightly to the left. "Mine is this way."

Deva's cave was festooned with flags and feathers floating in the breeze like the rest. I leaned over to enter the cave, and again my eyes needed time to adjust.

A low square table on a plain red rug centered the small space. A mural of Yeshe Tsogyal took up the side of the cave. I noticed a framed photo of Deva's sister, Yeshe Maya, on the altar, the same portrait I had seen at the Matipokhara hospital. Deva pulled some bananas and a handful of rhododendrons from her bag and replaced the old offerings with the new ones.

I noticed a small blue box at the place set for me at the table. Deva said, "A gift for you from Tenzin. Open, open."

The lid came off easily, and prayer beads lay inside a piece of yellow silk. The red rosewood beads shone and smelled like juniper. A large bodhi seed marked the end and the beginning of the strand of one-hundred-eight beads. "Oh, they are beautiful." I held them to my nose to take in the lovely scent, then wrapped them around my right hand and lifted them high to admire.

"For you," Deva's eyes sparkled. "I will teach you to pray."

While we talked, Deva had brewed tea on a small gas burner centered on the low table. She turned off the stove and let the tea steep. We chatted about the crumbling stairway and the people who once lived in the caves. Then Deva poured tea.

With the beads still wrapped around my weak hand, I took a sip.

"Do you like the tea?" Deva lifted her cup in both hands and made a slight bow.

"The rose hips are so fragrant," I said.

"You thank Jack for that. He brought rose hips from Chamberlain Island when you visited," she said. "A gift for me." Her eyes brightened. "My sister wanted to meet you. To tell you things. But Death has its own time. Its own reason."

"I'm sorry I could not talk to your sister—that I could not thank her for bringing me into the world."

"Jack said you felt her presence when she died."

"Oh, my goodness, she is the reason I am here. I felt her leave her body."

"And she felt you were coming back into this world," Deva said

"Was your sister a manifestation of Yeshe Tsogyal?" I asked.

Deva smiled and drank her tea. "Yeshe Tsogyal is a lot like you. You both faced many obstacles. Many have told you what you cannot do. You show what you can do. She did the same, like your grandmother, too. You listen to Yeshe Tsogyal, and she wisely instructs."

"Back at home," I raised my cup to my lips and sipped, "so many times I felt moved along by Yeshe Tsogyal. From the moment I met your sister, I felt Tsogyal's presence. She wants me here. I think your sister tried to tell me that." I smiled at Deva. "You and Yeshe Maya came here. When?" I asked.

"From the valley." She held the round teacup in both hands and drank. "The tea is good. I am glad you like it."

I nodded. Deva had answered the last of my questions. The sunstone in the pouch around my neck started vibrating and warmed against my chest.

"We will meditate now," Deva said. "This is how. You hold the bodhi seed in your hand and pray a prayer of reverence for all sentient beings: For our teachers, Guru Rinpoche, who guides us, and Yeshe Tsogyal, who is kind enough to guide us, too. For those beings whose deaths clothe and feed us. For those in peril and for each who suffers. Then you hold the first bead, and you say, *'Gate gate paragate parasamgate Bodhi svaha.'*"

"The Heart Sūtra mantra?" Words were barely out of my mouth when the earth replied with a warning rumble. Then, BOOM! The table shook, and tea spilled. "Did you hear that?" I asked. "What happened?" A high-pitched sound came after, almost human, like a keening. My sunstone was hot.

Deva rose from her floor pillow. "Follow me."

Another boom followed, and the ground jolted. Prayer flags shook in the air—I trailed Deva. Bells rang cacophonously. Deva raised her hand—her head forward as if she were listening to something I could not hear. "The explosion likely came from the catacombs—we will take the ladder on the outside if it looks OK."

And what if the ladder didn't look OK? I simply nodded. I promised myself a full-out panic attack when we were on solid ground—right then—I had to get there. The valley lay hundreds of feet below. My guide, close to ninety, hadn't been on the ladder for years. Single file, our bodies brushing the cavern side; we proceeded. I watched Deva pivot around a boulder that had fallen from somewhere above us. The outside of the stone lay close to the edge of the path. I faced the rock, and with my back to the drop-off, I maneuvered around the stone, cupping it between my legs.

I stood for a moment to breathe, but Deva pulled my sleeve—she sensed danger. Our path spiraled higher. More caves appeared, but we stood alone at the topmost row of caves. At the end of the narrow walkway, a tunnel angled downwards,

"I will go first," Deva said, "It may be blocked." She grasped my weak hand and squeezed it hard. "No talking in the tunnel; we must not disturb the stone." Her grip remained firm. "After I leave, take two deep breaths, and say The Heart Sūtra —if all is well, I will be on the other side." She raised an index finger. "Enter the tunnel backward. There are notches in the stone to rest feet."

I took two breaths and prayed, then backed into the dark, feeling with my strong left foot for the first foothold. I held onto the rough edge of the tunnel and took the next step down. Secured. My prayer beads remained strung around my right hand; for now, they had to stay put as I grasped the rung above me with my strong left hand. My feet together. The sunstone glowed through the pouch and was the only spark of light save a circle of sunlight haloed above. I stared upward and tried to move my weak foot down a rung, but my body froze with fear. My foot didn't seem to know where it was supposed to go, and I forgot to breathe. Sweat chilled the back of my neck. I paused for seconds, then tested the handholds along the narrow walls, and they were firm, and I whispered to my feet, "Please behave." I willed my way onwards.

The light blinded whatever was on the other side of the tunnel exit. From below, I heard Deva say. "Close your eyes while going through the doorway. Too bright at first. Don't talk. The walls may fracture."

I did as she instructed.

The light warmed me, and the world behind my eyelids turned red. I felt Deva's firm grip as she led me to a stone bench on the wall side of the path. "Keep your beads around your hand," she said.

I clutched the beads tighter. "I thought the tunnel started the ladder down." We faced a biting wind, and clouds obscured part of the path.

Deva shook her head. "The next part is trickier." She raised a warning finger again.

"You're going to make it just fine," I said. "We both will." I wrapped my right arm around her, and the beads glimmered in the sunshine. The pouch was hot to touch, and the sunstone continued to vibrate. I figured our odds were more like a negative seventy to thirty. "Let's do it," I said, "before I vomit on my shoes."

With worried eyes, she surveyed my face.

"That was a joke," I said. "Kind of." And I laughed. I stood on unwilling knees and said, "After me." The pathway continued at a steep downhill slant. My legs and knees shook, but I kept taking small steps until I found myself facing the stone wall and grasping handholds, with one way down to the valley eight hundred feet below. *Holy shit.* For Deva's sake, I faked bravery. "Not as bad as I imagined," I said to her. *Far worse.*

A slight rumble from the earth caused gravel to spin down from above. "I will die here," Deva said. "You go. I don't know that the ladder will hold both of us."

"No," I said. "We both go. Me, first, as we planned." I felt the texture of the stone under my fingers. The prayer beads pressed into the palm of my weak hand. I thanked the ladder for helping me and thought of the hundreds of steps others had taken descending, and then I edged over, put my strong foot on the first wrung, sucked in a breath, and wheeled my right leg over. I stood belly flat against the wall, hands clinging to the holds impressed in the stone, and scared as hell to move, my nose touched the cliff.

Again, I willed my feet to make a tentative step down. With my weak foot anchored, I used my strong left foot to find the next step, slowly drew my weak leg down, and repeated the action several times. "I start now," I heard Deva call from above. I did not look up but kept focusing on my hands, finding the insets, as my feet did their business. Sun warmed my back as I continued downward. My hands and legs coordinated in rhythm, naturally compensating for the weakness on one side with the strength from the other with surprising agility—the sunstone beat in rhythm with my heart. I repeated The Heart Sūtra mantra and the mantra my mother taught me: *Om mani padme hum.* When the ladder wobbled, I feared that Deva had fallen and might fall on me. "Be strong." Words whispered in my brain. The prayer beads dug deeper into my right palm as I grasped rung after rung of the ladder, continuing to give thanks to the ladder and to whoever built it. I repeated the prayers over and over.

Deva's voice interrupted my stone meditation. "Hop off," she said.

"What?" I answered. I kept my eyes shut as I spoke. I took another step down, and the earthen floor of Sangam greeted me. Wiggling my toes, I opened my eyes and peered over my shoulder.

"We're here?" I breathed a deep sigh and gazed upward as Deva took the final rungs down. "That was amazing." I turned again to the cliff and touched my forehead to the rough stony side. "Thank you," I said.

With her hands folded, Deva observed me with calm, bright eyes. "And, now, you have learned to pray."

Chapter 28 I Failed You

"THAT WAS QUITE A LESSON." I kissed the beads, still wrapped around my hand.

As fast as either of us could, we hurried back to the others with trepidation about what we might find. The animals, whose music usually filled the air, were eerily silent. My sunstone remained hot, but my thoughts went to Ravi and Papa. I prayed they were OK. Dial flew above and in front of us, stroking the air like a swimmer pacing his teammates.

Jampa met us on the green. "You are here!" Her eyes grew wide. "You took the ladder?" She said something to Deva in Tibetan and then to me. "We have gathered at the sundial. We must go."

"Wait, wait," I said. "Is everyone OK?"

Jampa nodded and cast a glance at Deva.

Deva held her hand up. "We need to have water," she said.

"Can we take five minutes?" I cast a glance toward the library's toilet house.

Deva and I took quick turns in the toilet house, and Jampa greeted us with cups of water. We drank, stacked the cups on the library steps, and were on our way. I noticed that the yurts and the library were untouched. Whatever had caused the noise had not affected them.

The women explained the power fields in Sangam and Sangam's relationship to Mt. Kailash as we hurried to the sundial where the others waited. "Five elements: air, earth, water, wind, and fire, make Mt. Kailash," Deva said. "Picture clotheslines strung from the top of Mt. Kailash to the library, catacombs, and the Saraswati Cave," she continued. "Mt Kailash creates a field. Mt. Kailash may have spoken."

Jampa and Deva affirmed legends that I had read about Mt. Kailash. According to these old stories, the center of the world, the *axis mundi*, was the pyramid-shaped Mt. Kailash. The four sides of Kailash represented the cardinal directions and emitted sacred energy creating a vortex that sometimes confounded compasses. "You said the catacomb orb was out of sync with the others?" I patted the pouch around my neck. "Like my sunstone?"

"Yes," Deva said.

"Why are we meeting at the sundial? I asked.

"It comes from ancient days," Deva continued. "It tells time with the spirit world. Only masters can use it."

"In English it's called a scaphe," Jampa added.

As we neared the sundial, ti plants bordered the path. Variegated red and green blooms opened skyward. Then, I saw Papa standing on a stone altar with a the oval-shaped sundial at its center. A small gold ball spun from the tip of the vertical gnomon that centered the base of the bowl. Papa motioned us to join the others in a semicircle below the altar. "We are glad to see you," he said.

Jampa had said everyone was OK, but where was Ravi? I turned to Deva, who held an index finger up to keep me from speaking. The three of us took our places. I rechecked the group to see if I had missed Ravi, but he wasn't among us. As hard as it was for me to do, I remained quiet. Time would sort this out soon enough.

Papa peered into the overcast heavens. A breeze blew. He reached with hands high over his head and lowered himself to the ground until his head touched the altar. My father then stood. A hole opened in the clouds, and the sun haloed him. He faced the direction towards Mt. Kailash, two-hundred miles away, and turned toward us. Father Emilio brought a red pillow to the altar where Papa sat. The cleric returned to the circle, and with a nod from Papa, everyone began to meditate. I tried to digest what I had just observed. Had my father caused the cloud to part or direct the sun to shine on him?

What had I witnessed? And now a meditation, but for what purpose were we praying? I held onto the pouch as if it were a guide. My hand heated up. What had caused such a disturbance in the caves: an earthquake? Was this the beginning or the ending of the trouble? Was Amul close? It appeared we were praying to Mt. Kailash. My prayer beads were still around my weak right hand. I let go of the pouch, shut my eyes, fingered each bead, and said, thank you for our safety. I prayed to Kailash, thinking about its meaning: crystal—clear—a yogi's clear warning. This Buddha world was spirit rich with pathways, and something threatened this one.

Sharp pain followed momentary inner peace—an ice cream headache that caused me to open my eyes. Papa watched me, nodded in my direction, shut his eyes, and returned to his meditation. The golden orb pulsated as it had in the catacombs. I had questions, but this was not the moment to ask. I had faith that Ravi was OK. But where was he? And why the throbbing-sharp headache?

Before I returned to prayer, I looked around. Father Emilio said the Rosary on worn beads with the practice of a saint. Claire raised her head and hands, palms up, eyes closed. Back straight. Lovely Jampa prayed side-by-side with Claire. Prayer sisters. A slight man in white kurta pajamas, Masa sang words I did not know, his head high, eyes closed.

A blister on my left hand began to swell. I licked my lips and tasted dust; dirt patches covered my linen shirt. Tired and hungry, I shifted my position and wondered how long we would stay here. Ponds of lotus flowers in full bloom that I had somehow missed seeing coming into this group drew my attention. I hoped Ravi would be at the library or sitting on the yurt steps petting Atlas when we returned. My thoughts turned to the pool and the night before.

Deva nudged me with an elbow, her way to call me out.

I shut my eyes and worked to clear my mind, then began to chant The Heart Sūtra mantra, barely above a whisper. I pictured the conical Mt Kailash dripping in gold. A yogi in prayer—like Masa—the image morphed—Shiva maybe. Kailash made human. Shiva became the mountain itself. Blue-skinned Shiva, his soft black hair moving in a slight breeze, eyes on me. The image softened into crystal orbs that floated, and I dissolved deeper. I asked my third eye to open, or someone asked me to open my third eye. A spiral in light appeared, and I spun inside it. Piercing light filled the ring. I sat in the presence of third-eye light, fingering the beads swept away. My heart sped up, and I spun around and around and around. I heard someone speak, and some words I felt instead of heard; all the while, my father's visage emerged clear. A voice said, "He knows."

Deva tapped the beads on my wrist. "Slowly," she said. "Come back slowly. Breathe."

I opened my eyes and tried to focus. Papa and Deva sat on either side of me; I licked my lips. "What happened?" I asked.

"I was going to ask you the same thing," my father said.

"I was told—" my head screamed in pain, and I shut my eyes and caught my breath. "A voice told me why I'm here, but I lost it." Papa and Deva remained quiet. "Oh, God, I am so sorry." I unwound the prayer beads on my right hand, and the impressions on my palm were so deep I wondered if the indentation was permanent. Darkness, sunset—the sky told me that hours had passed. I searched Deva's face and then my father's, waiting for them to speak. "I failed you."

"You will remember," Papa's touch on my right hand sent an electrical current through me, and I saw Yeshe Maya in my brain the day she asked to hold my weak hand. I experienced the same jolt of insight from my father's touch. "Go, father," she whispered in her final breath. I thought it was for a reunion, but I was wrong.

Chapter 29 A Multitude of Rainbows

Deva stood, using my shoulder to help herself up, then offered me her hand. "You need to stand to walk."

I shook my head and didn't move, wanting to retrieve the words from my meditation.

"Time to go," my father said.

"Oh, God, where is Ravi?" Panic rushed through me.

Papa took a slow, deep breath. "Ravi and Jethro went to the Mahamaya Valley so that they could speak to Jack—to tell him about the tremor." My father spoke slowly, choosing his words carefully. "They can use phones there. They left after Masa returned. Ravi knew you were all right because Masa used the stairs, and the noise did not come from the prayer caves."

"It sounded like it. Was there an earthquake in Sangla? Is that what we heard?" I searched my father's face.

"We don't know. Ravi has not returned."

"Jack could be in trouble or dead?" I paused as my body calmed. "No," I closed my eyes, "no, he is OK. Both Jack and Ravi, but something is very wrong." I shoved off the blanket covering the ground with my steady hand. Standing, I took a breath and stretched my stiff neck, raising my shoulders to my ears and releasing. "Amul is behind this. That's the only thing I know."

We began the walk back to the library. In my mind, I kept returning to that headache, the pain, the sudden pain. I had experienced it before when Yeshe Maya died. Was it a warning that something cataclysmic had happened or was about to happen? Or did someone want my attention?

We were by the curve of the river where it stretched across the library green. Water spouted, it may have been a fish jumping to the surface, but the trail of drops sparked multiple rainbows spiraling and falling into the river. In that mega-moment, I understood my headache, where my meditation took me, and what I needed to do now.

I touched Papa and Deva. "Stop," I said. "Motu is waiting for me. I have to get him out of the cave before the cave implodes. He's not alone."

Papa nodded. "We will wait for Ravi and Jethro—"

"I can't wait for long."

"I will call the Sangha," Papa sounded relieved that I understood what he had known all along.

"I better eat something," I said to Atlas who led me from the garden to the kitchen. Everything inside the yurt was as we left it that morning. The laundry was gone, and the bed lay bare. I was aware of my heart beating in a weird rhythm as if it were harmonizing with the sunstone, and I wondered if it was in sync with the holy mountain. Leftover naan bread and jam was the quickest thing to eat. I gulped a cup of water; all the while, my headache grew stronger.

The headache came with a recurring image of Motu Amul, the ambitious yogi. I foresaw groups of tourists circling the cave entrance while he spun stories of secret villages and supposed Shangri-Las, making thousands off of each head. I saw the cave implode, walls collapsing as the river struck back in a fateful blow, killing the cave and causing landslides pouring storms of rocks into Sangam. Whatever force delivered the messages was not giving up on me. The image of Yeshe Tsogyal reoccurred. She was a manifestation of the river goddess, Saraswati, and she was shouting.

My temples pulsated, and my hands trembled as I opened my clothing drawer. I found black drawstring pants with banded cuffs and the red tunic I had worn the first night I was here: new clothes, a new adventure. I packed my passport and a change of underwear in my watermelon bag. I am an adventuress; I shrugged at the irony of that thought, and maybe, a married adventuress. I had to go up that stairway into clouds alone or die within this world.

I slung my bag over my shoulder crosswise and studied the visible impression left in my right hand from the prayer beads. I immediately wrapped the beads back around my right hand again. Powerful—a talisman. *Now, if I can keep from falling flat on my face*, I thought and slugged the air for encouragement. I was still the woman from La Conner edging up the attic stairs, but I'd managed, and somehow I would manage now.

"The Sangha has met. Father Emilio offered to go instead of you." Papa's voice startled me. "How long have you been here?"

"Just now," he answered. "Emilio offered," Papa repeated.

I shook my head. "You know as well as I—"

"Yes—the spirit world gave me the same instruction." This simple man in green suspenders spoke amiably about communicating with mysterious forces.

"When you were on the dais, you looked at me during the meditation. Yeshe Maya sent me, didn't she? That was the meaning of 'go, father.' Not for a reunion but to help Sangam. Did my grandmother's book expose Sangam to danger?"

"Amul uses Mother's books as his guide. Yeshe Maya thought you would draw him out," Papa said.

"When Motu interrupted that meeting with Ravi and Jack, exposing the sunstone, books, and photos of me—Ravi staged it, didn't he?"

"According to my instruction."

"What am I supposed to say to Amul? And where do we talk?"

"It is time to talk—talk at the hotel." He tucked his hand under my chin. "Let him talk, not you. Encourage him to tell his truth. You must tell only the truth." He took a deep breath and slowly exhaled. "You saw a temple burned out by Red Guard revolutionaries on the way to the waterfall?"

"I called it the beehive temple. Yes, Ravi explained that Yeshe nuns once lived there."

"He believes an entry into Sangam exists there. He'll want you to go the temple."

"Through the Saraswati Cave? How will I know what path to take?"

"Let him guide. Ravi will tell you more tomorrow."

"But the tremors and screeching, the river will not want us there. Especially him. Neither will the goddess."

Papa nodded. "You will be protected." He handed me a tiny copper coin imprinted with a tiger. "A story: Monks in Bhutan called on Guru Rinpoche to subdue demons in the Paro Valley. He rode upon a tigress to caves high above the valley and meditated for three years, three months, and three days, triumphing over the demons. The tigress was said to be Yeshe Tsogyal," Papa paused. "Let her carry you, now."

I loosened my pouch, and inserted the tigress token with the sunstone. My head screamed, and I needed to get underway. "One last thing, Papa. Did your blessing on Ravi and me make us married?" I shook my head. "I know it's a dumb question, but—"

"Yes, you are married. You will need a civil ceremony, but in the eyes of our world, you and Ravi are married."

Someone rapped on the open door, then Deva let herself in.

I watched as she joined us. "I don't want to say goodbye so soon to my father." Papa held me close and let me go. "You know, I plan to come back!" I tried on bravery like a new suit. "When things are OK."

"And it will be 'OK,' as you say," Deva said, "I am certain."

The moon rose as the three of us climbed the bridge that arched over the valley below—moonlit silhouette—I made out the library, and the river sparkled. My throat was dry, and the steps were wet and slippery. I held hands with Deva. Papa was a step ahead of us. Dial, that crazy talking magpie, dipped and dove, guiding us onward.

On the platform where I had reconciled with my father, I had to say goodbye to him again. We touched foreheads, and he traced his index finger over the midpoint between my eyes. "Stay awake," he said. "Remember your grandmother."

Deva unknotted the pouch around my neck and withdrew the stone. "Keep this in your hand; you must have it to pass through." She laughed. "Like a garage opener?"

I nodded and kissed her goodbye.

"I will see you soon, Papa—"

He hugged me close and kissed me on the top of my head.

They turned; I watched them leave, and then I was alone. I returned the sunstone to the pouch, and without looking left nor right, I used the walking stick to aid my balance. My head throbbed as I reached the top platform. I faced the plateau where I knew Mt. Kailash to be. "Here we go," I said, half aloud. I took the sunstone from the pouch, raised my arms to the heavens, and the sunstone reacted to embedded stones in the cave wall opening the circular door.

CHAPTER 30 FOG AND MAYHEM

As THE ENTRANCE CLOSED behind me, the world fell into a loud, disquieting wail. My head pulsated in sharp pain each time the cave screamed for help; at least, it seemed as if it was sentient and crying out. Instinctively, I leaned against the wall, but the wall trembled, and I fell to the ground. I watched the stone slip through my fingers and tumble to the cave floor for one awful moment. *Oh God, oh God,* and I watched as it flipped several feet from me to my right. It was close to the edge, the river way below. The stone shone like a tiny beacon that lit up the narrow pathway as it veered downward. Flashing lights and muffled voices from below me provided enough information: I was not alone; Motu was closing in.

I stared at my stone, so close to the ledge, and knew that getting it into my possession had to be my immediate goal. I crawled on hands and knees over to the stone, still shining, and it began to pulsate. The ice cream headache returned. I grabbed the sunstone and put it inside my pouch. I saw boots, not one pair, but at least two pairs coming towards me from below. They weren't aware of me because the curve in the path hid me. I got myself upright.

Suddenly, three people confronted me; each wore a helmet outfitted with a headlamp. Their light fell sharply in my eyes.

"Hi." I squinted at Amul, "we need to get out of the cave." A sudden wail from the river and a burst of wind threw me off balance. Motu Amul caught me. "Thank you," I whispered. "Let's go now." I recognized Taylor and Rachel standing behind him. The cave shook, and fog and mist rose from the Saraswati below. Darkness stuck like ink. "We'll talk outside; it is best to stay silent."

Motu's flashlight lit the path where the fog swirled, creating an illusion of movement.

Amul motioned to Taylor and Rachel to turn around and said, "Yes. Taylor, please help Maya; I will lead."

The river goddess, Saraswati, screamed in my head. No one spoke as we left. I whispered, "I hear you, and we are leaving."

The river twisted and disappeared, and I recognized where Ravi and I had entered the cave by the distant roar of the waterfall; tonight, we went north instead of south. The nearby Sutlej River was quiet, and the night eerily still as we crawled over boulders at the entrance to the cave on the Indian side; we followed a forest path that widened to a rutted trail and the motorbikes not far from the highway. Taylor held me fast, and I was grateful for his help. Rachel handed me a water bottle, and the three of us stood on the narrow dark road of the Shipka Pass, famous for its hairpin curves.

"We are returning to the hotel. We will take you, OK?" Motu said.

"On a bike?" The four of us stood by the motorbikes tucked behind a boulder with a tarp over the vehicles.

"Have you ridden one?" Amul asked.

"With Ravi," I answered.

"How long have you known Ravi?"Motu asked.

"Long enough to be married," I grinned.

"Congratulations." Motu smiled at me.

Taylor and Rachel hauled both bikes up to the empty piece of road. "You'll ride with me," Amul said. He took my watermelon bag and put it in the motorcycle side case. I folded my walking stick and handed it to the guru. "Are those prayer beads on your hand?" he asked.

"Yes," I answered.

"And the pouch around your neck?"

"A gift from my mother."

"I've been waiting for you," Amul said.

Rachel boosted me into the passenger seat. Rachel and Taylor rode on a similar machine. Off we went into the deepening night.

The headlights showed how narrow the road was, rough in most places. Florescent yellow paint on rails around steep curves marked the edges. We were high in the mountains and coming down into the Sangla Valley—a few lights glowed from there. Amul drove slowly. One time a truck approached us head-on, lights on bright, spreading gravel debris across the road. I wondered what light below might be La Maison. I could not see vehicles coming toward us until they were upon us. Bad visibility did not slow the drivers. Amul chose the road's center and weaved around trucks and small cars. White water spewed over the rocky wall abutting the treacherous roadway; waterfall spray soaked my clothing.

Lights twinkled from La Maison Fortune as Motu and Taylor rolled in the drive. A rose arbor led to the inn's front doors. My body continued to vibrate when Amul shut the Kawasaki off.

Fairy lights from a walled back garden twinkled. Bungalows lined it. The main building was two stories, with the hotel sign perched above the double door. Jack was passing through the lobby when he saw me.

"Maya?" His surprise appeared genuine. He took my hands, then hugged me. "How are you doing, Sunshine?"

"You happen to have a room?" I smiled at my lifelong friend. Exhausted, I trembled in wet clothes. "I need to get out of this wet stuff and into something warm."

"We didn't know where you were," Jack said. He turned to Motu. "And, where were you?" he asked the guru. "You left quite early." Jack looked at Motu, then the others, and focused on me.

"Maya's needs come before any conversation with us." Amul squeezed my hand. "We will talk tomorrow; you promised," he said.

"In the morning, we will arrange something," I said.

"Until then," the guru said, "be well." With a flourish, he turned, flanked by Taylor and Rachel leaving Jack and me.

Jack wrapped his arm around me. "Honey," he said, "let's get you in the apartment."

"In a minute," I answered. "I want to take this in."

I stared at the intricately engraved mahogany reception desk to our left. Vaulted ceilings with massive timbered beams and chandeliers made the reception airy. Tall windows banked the outer wall. And then, I saw the mural of Yeshe Tsogyal on the wall behind the reception. The black-haired beauty, crowned in flowers, sat lotus-style in front of a lake in motion; she was bare-footed, her wild hair wind-blown. In the back of the teacher, Mt. Kalish, drawn in brown and black, drifted into perpetuity; rivers ran from the host of mountains to Yeshe. She held a skullcap filled with nectar, jewels, and a long-life vase in her left hand. Her hand was outward, an offering to the observer.

"Wow, she's stunning," I said. "I saw her in a dream. She's been looking out for me all day." I bowed my head in thanks as Jack pulled me toward Ravi's apartment.

"I'll give you a tour later." Jack had his phone to his ear when we went into Ravi's apartment through bleached white wood doors inset with engraved thick glass.

As soon as the doors shut and Jack locked them, he turned to me. "Sunshine, so Motu was in the Saraswati Cave? His presence caused the disturbance? And you got him out?"

I hugged him for a long time. "Oh my God, it's been such a day."

"Can I get in on that hug, too?" Natalie said. "I've been watching the car park from the back garden. Thank God you are safe."

I hugged Natalie.

"You knew about me leaving?" I asked Jack.

"I was talking to Ravi on the phone just now; he filled me in. He's with Jethro."

"Where are they?" I asked.

"They're about twenty minutes behind you—Ravi and Jethro got back to Sangam within a half-hour of you leaving. Tenzin told him what happened," Jack said.

"How are they getting here?" I asked.

"We keep motorbikes stashed off the main road about a mile from where Motu parked his." Jack said. "They can make pretty good time at night."

"Have you eaten anything?" Natalie asked.

"My head hurt so badly I couldn't eat," I said. "I'm in desperate need of a shower." Then I took a breath and looked around the room. Floor-to-ceiling windows faced the large area with a sectional, curved couch welcoming me. Each of the eight sections had tufted backs. One cushion featured large white lotus blossoms on a deep green field, while another bore a field of pink flowers. Plain persimmon and lemon-colored cushions interrupted the brightly designed ones; I was taken by the beauty of the stone floors and plush white floor rug, too.

"Let me lead you to the loo," Jack said. "We'll see what we can find in the kitchen."

The bathroom had red walls with wood filigree around a stained-glass window. A footed tub with a shower installation jutted away from the window. Heater towel racks held large white towels. A bathrobe hung on the back of the door; Jack told me it was mine. Before washing up, I unlaced the prayer beads from my hand. Two of my fingers were sound asleep.

Who was this in the mirror? Dirty hair and smudges marked my face. Were my eyes bigger? Brighter? I ran the shower over my aching body.

"Do you have like a bottle of bubbly, Jack?" I asked as I joined Natalie and him in the lounge.

"If you want a drink, I—"

"No, I'd like to raise a glass when Ravi gets here."

"Well, fine," Jack looked curiously at me. "I think Ravi has one in the fridge." He raised his index finger toward me. "Are you announcing something?"

"Could be." I shrugged.

"Meantime, we're making toasted cheese sandwiches for you guys and sliced apples."

"Jack, could you help me?" Natalie called from the kitchen. As he turned to leave, we heard noises outside the doors.

"I bet that's Ravi. I'll get it," I said.

Jethro high-fived me when I opened the door. "Where's Ravi?" I asked.

"He stopped to say hello to the night clerk. He'll be a minute."

I waited at the door for Ravi to arrive, and when he did, I pressed my hands against the sides of his face. "What a day," was all I could think to say.

He kissed me. "You know," he said, "we followed you. I'm so proud of you." Ravi held me by the shoulders. We kissed again, and he touched his index finger to my nose. "Did you vomit?"

We laughed. "No! But I thought I might. You're soaking wet," I said. "You, too, Jethro. And I bet you're both hungry."

The men cleaned up and dried off; we ate picnic-style perched on pillows around the curved couch. They told us about getting to Mahamaya, checking in with Jack then returning to the Sangha. They stayed together until Papa sensed the danger was over.

"It was the river talking to the mountain, then to Tenzin, and lastly, to you," Jethro said.

"What exactly did you do?" Natalie asked.

"It was mostly my father's doing," I said. "When Deva, Papa, and I returned from the sundial, my head was on fire with pain. I kept thinking there were words behind the screaming. I heard the river goddess, or what I believe to be Saraswati say, just under the wailing, 'Get him out of my home'—I knew I had to leave Sangam to convince Amul to get out of the cave. This is the reason I was at Sangam at all. Everything else followed."

Ravi stretched his arm around me. "Tenzin told me that you are the chosen ambassador between worlds. And he's outlined a plan, but that can wait until tomorrow."

"That's what Papa said, and to do more listening than talking."

"So, what did you say to Motu when you saw him in the cave?" Natalie asked.

"The first words I spoke to him were, 'we have to get out of the cave.' Dense fog and a sudden burst of wind threw me off balance, I fell, and Amul caught me, or I'd fallen over the ledge. He wasted no time and directed all of us to leave. I told him we'd talk at the hotel. That's tomorrow, guys."

"Saraswati was at work," Jethro said. He was anxious to get some rest. While in Sangla, he boarded at the inn. Jack and Natalie invited all of us over for breakfast at the tree house. We gathered in a circle as Jethro prepared to leave. Ravi asked, "Have you told them?"

Jethro kissed me on the cheek and winked. "Congratulations. Are we raising a glass?"

"Hey, you two," Jack said, "what are we talking about here?"

"We're married." Ravi and I said it together.

"What? How did that happen? You guys, I mean, I love you both, but you've known each other for approximately ten minutes."

"Eleven days and thirteen minutes," I said. "Best eleven days and thirteen minutes I've spent on the planet. And," I added, "in dog years, that's about three months."

"I gather Tenzin blessed your marriage?" Natalie asked.

Jack appeared baffled like he'd lost his best friend. I knew how he felt. "I wanted you with me, Jack, you know that. Please be happy for me. Give me a hug."

"Aw, Sunshine. I love you, little sister." He hugged me, then kissed me on the cheek. Tears filled his eyes. "I'm happy for you both, and I'll get the bubbly."

We clinked our glasses and shared a glass of champagne.

Natalie paused after her first sip. "Does Maya know about Allie?" She laid concerned eyes on Ravi and then on me.

"Ravi told me," I said, "it feels like about ten years ago."

"It'll be fine," Ravi affirmed. "She's all about her business venture."

"I don't know," Natalie said with a shrug. "She seems ready to hang curtains." She took another sip. "And, does Amul know you are married?"

"I told him," I said.

CHAPTER 31 PLAN NO PLAN

OUR FRIENDS LEFT with plans to meet in the morning in place. Before arriving at La Maison, Jack set me up in the suite he had reserved for his mother. My clothes were cleaned and hung in the closet, and he charged my cell phone, iPad, and Kindle. Ravi suggested we stay in the guest suite since it was already for me. Jack and Natalie now lived at the tree house, and Ravi was in mid-move to the hotel. I peeked into his bedroom and saw folded clothes lying neatly on an unmade bed. A few wooden crates held other possessions.

"Ask the night clerk for the passkey." Ravi kissed me. "His name's Jalal. I won't be long."

I still wore the white terrycloth bathrobe when I crossed the lobby. In a pink sports shirt and denim jeans, Jalal talked to a willowy, slim woman in a floral skirt and sleeveless ruffled yellow blouse. She had a plumeria tucked behind one ear, and big gold hoops hung from her earlobes. It was apparent the woman knew Jalal well from the easy chat.

"Yes, I saw him!" Jalal said. "He is at his apartment."

"And when did he arrive?" the woman asked.

"Maybe an hour? His friends left a few minutes ago." He winked at her and nodded in my direction. "I'll be right with you."

"Thanks," I said.

The woman with the red flower in her hair stared at me with a half-smile greeting, and left for Ravi's. Well, that'll be interesting, I thought. She left a scent trail of ylang-ylang.

"Ms. Maya—Jack said for me to take care of you. You have a lovely room. Come with me this way."

"Who was that nice lady you were talking to?" I asked. "She looks like a celebrity."

Jalal inserted the passkey into the door slot. "She is a frequent guest. Allie Rogers." He nodded.

"Oh," I said and thanked Jalal. *Oh, indeed.*

My room's window faced the little garden on the side of the inn. Clothes I had stuffed in my red train case were washed, folded, or hung, in the closet to the left of the small entrance hallway. My phone and iPad waited for me on a nightstand by one of two queen beds with white duvets and feather pillows. Jack taped a note to a mini-fridge. Help Yourself!

She's beautiful. I wondered what the reunion was like between Ravi and Allie. I peered at my exhausted self in front of a full-length mirror. "Well, at least I'm clean." I tried my best not to think of Allie Rogers as competition, but I did. She was beautiful, but that ylang-ylang was a tad overkill. *Oh, shut up*—my thoughts kept coming.

I took my phone, and it felt foreign in my hands. I checked my i-Messages, and I had a ton of them from Carol, who was going apoplectic in La Conner because she had not heard from me. I quickly texted.

> (ME) At Jack's—have been in paradise with the love of my life. Late here. Details in the morning, my time.
>
> (CAROL) With Jack?? Wow.
>
> (ME) No! His name's Ravi. More later. Never been better. Internet bad.

I rummaged through the minibar, found a bag of generic M&M's, and opened my Kindle to an Agatha Christie mystery I'd started on my flight from SeaTac. I felt as if I'd begun the novel on another planet. My cell rang, and it was Ravi. He asked me to get dressed and come to the apartment, and I agreed with no questions asked.

I wore my drop waist elephant print, mid-length sundress fresh from the inn's laundry service. *Thank you, Jack.* The courtesy hairdryer fluffed my drying hair, and I looked presentable with a little lip gloss.

Ravi's door was propped open. I stuck my head in, "Hello!"

Allie sat straight-backed at the center of the couch on a violet and azure striped cushion. She assessed me as if I were packaged lettuce at the market. "I asked to meet you." She peered up at Ravi, who stood between us. "So, it is true you are married?"

Ravi walked toward me. "Yes, I am proud to present my wife, Maya Moore."

"And you recently met? Jack's friend, right?" Allie sounded more curious than hostile.

"It felt like we knew each other through lifetimes," I said, frozen in place.

"Have you done the paperwork yet?" Allie asked. She played with the gold fringe on a sage-colored sofa pillow.

"Not yet," Ravi said.

"Then officially, you're not married according to India?"

"According to the Buddhist monk who blessed us, we are married," I said.

"Ravi," Allie tossed the pillow aside, stood, and stretched her long arms palms out to the universe. "You've been taken up by one 'hobby' or another in the past and then grown weary of them. I'm not seeing your fascination here, but I won't be surprised if it also passes."

"Time will tell that story," I said.

Allie swooped passed me and left the apartment.

"You'll have to tell me about some of your hobbies, honey," I said while ylang-ylang still hung in the air.

Ravi kissed me. "Let's go to your place." He shut the lights out, and we walked back to my suite. We stopped at the reception desk, and Ravi introduced me to Jalal as his wife. Being the charming hotelier that Jalal was, he extended his hand to me to shake and wished us a happy life. I doubted Jalal would send Allie to the apartment again.

"God, it feels so natural sleeping with you," I said as we dozed off. We spooned in a big white bed, lights twinkling through the drawn shade.

"Yes, my love," Ravi said, "like the world is right."

The next morning, I awoke to my cell phone ringing. I reached for my phone; Ravi sat up. "It'll be Amul," he said.

"Good morning," I said to the caller on the phone.

It wasn't the guru but Taylor, his aide. "Hi-o," Taylor answered. "I hope we're not too early." He had us on speaker phone.

"Well, gosh, it's right at 7:30," I said. "I think I read that Amul is an early riser."

"Indeed, he is. He'd like to know what time you are free this morning?"

"What time does Amul want to meet?" I repeated the question to let Ravi in on the conversation. He mouthed twelve, noon. "How about at Ravi's apartment at noon?"

After a pause, Taylor responded positively, adding, "He requests you meet alone."

"Of course," I said.

Taylor hung up.

"Papa said he talked to you about a plan involving the beehive temple." I rubbed my foot against Ravi's. "Or are you going to make me wait to tell me?"

"I'd rather wait until we meet the others for breakfast, OK?"

"You look so serious, but OK," I said and nestled back into Ravi's embrace. "I'm not worried."

We rode out to the tree house on motorcycles. Jethro led. Buses and trucks took turns honking and passing one another. A cow sometimes showed up; goats grazed alongside grassy areas. Strings of small open-air markets appeared in the more populated areas. Shopkeepers and customers haggled over prices of oranges and baskets of pears. On occasion, Ravi and Jethro passed one another and honked, and we waved back and forth. I was happy not to talk but to feel the steady motor vibration as I hugged close to my husband.

We came to a gated drive that angled upwards from the narrow road. Ravi parked the bike and opened the fence gate, allowing us through. The house peeked out from the center of a golden oak tree. We walked along a gravel path, then upstairs to the front door, and passed through a vertically planked, pale oak foyer. Two low futon couches covered in muted red and yellow lotus-patterned fabric brightened orange pillows and beckoned conversation in the main living space. On a small marble platform, a gold statue of Guru Rinpoche was tucked in a corner between the couches. A rattan swing chair completed the conversation area. The ceiling fans hummed rhythmically while Jack and Natalie greeted us.

Jethro claimed the swing chair, and I assisted Natalie in making tea. As we chatted, I recounted last night's visit with Allie. "You were right," I said. "She was ready to hang curtains—like she'd given Ravi an ultimatum or was about to."

"She's been here most of the time you've been in India, but Ravi's been away helping you, and when he was here, he avoided her. Put her in a cottage," Natalie said. "She's asked after him daily. So, last night—"

"She was ready to pounce," I finished Natalie's sentence. "She's a beautiful woman; she'll recover," I added.

Tea water and milk bubbled in a large cooking pot. Natalie added Kanga tea leaves to the mix, then strained it into a large metal cup. She poured the tea back and forth between the pan and the oversized mug. Natalie told me where to find the large brownstone teapot in the cupboard to the side of the stove. I brought the cups and Natalie the tea and sugar, which we set on the small table in the conversation area.

Over tea, we began our discussion about my meeting with Amul.

"I want to know, straight up, Ravi, what is Papa's plan?" We all turned our attention to Ravi, who quietly sipped his tea.

"We're attempting to trick a master trickster," Ravi said. "Your father wants you to convince Motu that there is nothing to the rumors about Sangam. The Yeshe temple above the Sutlej River waterfall interests Amul, too. Many stories circulate about nuns disappearing inside that temple; Amul believes that the temple may have a hidden tunnel where nuns escaped to Sangam during the Chinese Cultural Revolution. And he's right about that. You may need to take him inside to show him the temple is in ruins. The door will be open, and I'll come down from where we found the silver bowl if I see you go inside. But Tenzin emphasized to only go inside the temple if you cannot talk Motu out of his interest in Sangam. I'll not be far away."

"What?" I turned to look each of my friends in the face. "Should I sing him a song, or what in the world am I supposed to say? He's brilliant."

"Your strength is words," Jack said. "You might have to stretch a point for dramatic effect."

"You think?" I laughed.

"I'm leaving now," Ravi said. "Eyes on you the entire time."

Chapter 32 Branded

That's all I remembered from our planning session at the tree house. As I awaited Motu, I tapped my toe impatiently on the plush white carpet. Jack was behind the reception desk, Natalie stayed home, and Ravi was at the temple. I wound my prayer beads around my weak right wrist. With the sunstone and Yeshe Tsogyal's tigress token tucked inside, my pouch hung from a beaded strand beneath my high-necked linen blouse.

At noon, straight up, the knock on the door, and I answered. Motu Amul appeared bigger to me; his full white beard brushed atop his broad shoulders. Diamonds surrounding the watch face of his Rolex gleamed like miniature beacons when he placed his hands in prayer position, lowered his head, and said, "Namaste."

I lowered my head and uttered, "Namaste." The sunstone heated up against my skin.

Motu wore loose white pajama-style pants. He had a gold scarf tucked under his beard that fell above the hemline of his white open-necked, kurta-styled shirt—a diamond stud in one ear. I offered him tea which he declined. "Shall we sit at the table?" I motioned to the red mahogany table in the room behind us, allowing Motu to lead. He sat at the head of the table, and I sat at his left. "I know you have questions," I said. "Please ask."

"How did you know I was in the cave?"

"I sensed your presence," I answered. Motu's giant head reflected in the shining surface of the table.

"Look at me," Motu said. "Lift your head and look at me, and answer my question."

"I answered your question." My eyes bore holes into his. "You are a powerful man, one of great means; what is your interest in the cave or the community it protects?"

Motu laughed softly. "So. Quiet Maya has a backbone."

"Please, kindly answer my question," I said with firmness matching his.

"I want answers," Motu said. "Sangam is the community you protect—powerful sages and teachers traveled there: Guru Rinpoche and Yeshe Tsogyal; an old hermit fellow told me Jesus meditated in a cave above it. Mt Kailash centers the earth's axis; it created Sangam's special atmosphere. The mythical Saraswati River runs under it. We both know the stories. I want to speak to its leader."

I shrugged. "Did Buddha burst from his mother's side? Did Yeshe Tsogyal transform into a tigress? Was Jesus born of a Virgin? I think we can agree all sorts of stories exist. Is Mt. Kailash an alien-built pyramid? Everyone hears stories."

"The Saraswati River exists, and Sangam exists. You have been there. I see it in your eyes. Take me to Sangam and your father, its leader."

"And what would you say to such a leader?"

"That's between him and me."

"Would you ask such a leader for a tourist visa?" I laughed. "Maybe construct an ashram? How do you plan to profit, Motu?" My sunstone beat in time with my heart; I felt the tigress token and prayed quietly to Yeshe Tsogyal. Words fell from my mouth without my request. I remembered the same experience telling Jack I, too, was selling my house at Haliday's when such an idea seemed spontaneous. Had Yeshe visited me that December night last year?

"I am intuitive beyond your imagination." Motu closed his eyes and took a deep breath, and slowly exhaled. "Can you take me as far as the Yeshe temple where you met Taylor?" He shrugged and appeared innocent to me, as if he had lost the argument but wanted one concession.

I sighed, opened my hands, stared at the palms, then met Motu's eyes. "Yes. To go there, we must cross through the Saraswati Cave. The temple is in the disputed border area between China and India, probably, China-controlled. Nothing is there. It's a bombed-out structure." I returned the slight shoulder-shrug and raised my eyebrow. "But, I am willing to take you to examine the temple yourself. And one more thing. One story is true. The cave is sentient. Your intentions are notable, and you must be of pure heart if you wish safe passage."

Jack caught up with me as I passed through the lobby. "You OK?" he said. We walked together outside

"I better be. On the no-plan, plan," I said. "We're off to the temple." I patted my pouch "I'm not alone; Ravi will be close by." Motu and Taylor stood outside the entrance to the motor house where the hotel kept its vehicles.

Motu wore the same garb with a large hat and sunglasses. I noticed his pajama pants hit the top edge of his brown boots, which were dusty and well-used. With my helmet on, Jack helped me mount the large, shiny motorcycle behind Motu.

"Hang on," he said. And to Motu, "Take good care of my girl."

The guru nodded. The engine purred loudly, my sunstone grew uncomfortably warm, and off we zoomed back to the Indian-Sutlej River entrance, where we exited the night before. He took an auxiliary road off the highway, no more than a goat path, and parked the bike in the same place he had the night before. We averted a bright green snake with red eyes and reached the river's edge. A skinny footbridge partially submerged led to the cave. I offered my earnest, silent prayers as we stood side by side at the cave's entrance. I asked for help to protect Sangam and that I was there in good faith. A noise from above us brought me out of prayer. A minor rockfall from the cliff tumbled onto the small bridge we had just crossed. The Sutlej River flowed with greater urgency. Motu bent his agile body low as we entered quietly.

Papa had figured Amul would insist on leading, which was good because I had no idea where to go once inside the cave. Indeed he knew his way and insisted on taking charge.

My headache began as we entered. The mist was thick inside, and the passageways were slick. Every little while, we stopped so that Motu could scrutinize the map Taylor had made for him. I leaned on my walking stick until he was ready to go again. The air felt hot. I wondered how the white fish swimming among the koi could survive in the heat under the yellowish cloud that cloaked the cave's interior. The high-pitched sound Papa described grew louder the deeper we went into the cave.

An echoing boom shook me. I peered over my shoulder as our path crumbled behind us. The sound of rock falling into the river below reverberated in the inky dark as we traipsed upwards. The cave was alive and unhappy. The next we stopped, I prayed to Yeshe Tsogyal, who brought me to this moment. I felt her in my footstep and saw her in the contents of my mother's old Samsonite suitcase. With these visions, I let go of any hindering thoughts. In my mind, I repeated, "Know my heart," which became my mantra as I traced my fingers over the prayer beads. "I am the tigress," I said, unaware I spoke aloud.

"Are you praying, Maya?"

Motu shone the flashlight my way. The sunstone throbbed like it was heartbroken. Was our so-called plan to end Motu's interest in Sangam meeting utter failure? Had the goddess and the cave decided the best way to deal with Amul and me? I nodded without speaking.

"I am, too. We're at the place we found you last night. Do you recognize it?"

"No, I don't," I answered. Though it was my voice coming from my body, it felt foreign.

"Can we get to Sangam from here?" Motu asked. "The sunstone you wear under your jacket, is it causing you pain?" He shone the flashlight in my eyes.

I pointed with my walking stick. "The cave is unhappy—let's go on."

"In a moment. Is your sunstone like this one?" He pulled from his pocket a stone like mine. "The old man who told me the story of the cave gave me this as a souvenir. Mine is hot to touch."

I shook my head. "You are foolish, Motu, and I am surprised at your gullibility. Based on an old man's story, do you think a stone can move a cave wall? It's like asking the winds to brew a hurricane." A sudden blast of air sprayed gravel across the path. I averted my head. "Then again," I said, "maybe the old man had something there."

A sudden yelp—Motu held his trembling hand out. The stone had seared his flesh, and he flung the glowing rock into the Saraswati River far below us. His eyes widened in pain.

"You will not forget this day," I said. "Let's go on."

It took a quarter of an hour to reach the waterfall. Motu walked hunched over, grunting now and then in pain. As we crossed the Sutlej River, the world calmed down. Amul finally spoke. "The stone you carry did not burn you. Why?" My hand—I am wounded." His voice quivered.

"No, you are branded," I answered. "Ravi is waiting at the temple. I'm sorry for your injury." We followed the trail above the river and down into the shallow valley of the temple.

"How did you know I would need a doctor?" Motu asked.

"I didn't, but we figured you might want to see the temple. You might have believed the old stories about how the nuns escaped the Red Guard. We never trusted your motives, and Ravi thought I might need help." As we drew closer, I saw Ravi, binoculars to his eyes. I raised my arm and waved. "One more thing, Motu, I am the ambassador between our worlds. Pray for us as we pray for you and never try such foolishness again."

He nodded in assent.

Ravi never went anywhere without his medical bag; he treated Motu's wounded hand. The sunstone was perfectly etched onto Amul's palm, a forever reminder of a story he might share as an old man, but not at present. He remained stoic and silent. His hand wrapped, Motu reluctantly agreed to follow Ravi and me through the cave. The cave moaned; stone steps gave way, and fine gravel frequently showered us, but my headache vanished. A boulder fell as we passed through the cave and crossed the river on what remained of the footbridge. Ravi called Jack, and he brought Taylor out in the hotel's car. Ravi and Amul returned by the car and Taylor took me back on the motorcycle.

Motu Amul and his entourage returned to his ashram the following day, as they had arrived, by helicopter. He thanked Ravi, but ignored me for which I was relieved.

The cave needed recovery time. When we return to Sangam, we will go through the Mahamaya Valley; meanwhile, Ravi and I did our paperwork and made our marriage official.

Next, I'm getting a dog.

ABOUT THE AUTHOR

Mary Elizabeth Gillilan is the former editor-in-chief of a celebrated arts magazine, *Clover, A Literary Rag*, and author of *Tibet, A Writer's Journal*. Her lifelong interests in Tibetan Buddhism, and the *axis mundi*, Mt Kailash, bring her back to this sacred region. The story was influenced by Alexandra David Neel, who ventured to Lhasa, Tibet, in 1924. Mary creates a daunting set of factors for her protagonist to master. She hopes you enjoy *Confluence* and invites you to follow her at maryegillilan.com.

CPSIA information can be obtained
at www.ICGtesting.com
Printed in the USA
JSHW042048090223
37472JS00007B/216

9 781734 187847